Murder Next Door

A Charlie Kingsley Mystery

Books by Michele Pariza Wacek
MPWnovels.com/books

Secrets of Redemption series:
It Began With a Lie (Book 1)
This Happened to Jessica (Book 2)
The Evil That Was Done (Book 3)
The Summoning (Book 4)
The Reckoning (Book 5)
The Girl Who Wasn't There (Book 6)
The Room at the Top of the Stairs (Book 7)
The Search (Book 8)
The Secret Diary of Helen Blackstone (free novella)

Charlie Kingsley Mystery series:
A Grave Error (free prequel novella)
The Murder Before Christmas (Book 1)
Ice Cold Murder (Book 2)
Murder Next Door (Book 3)
Murder Among Friends (Book 4)
The Murder of Sleepy Hollow (Book 5)
Red Hot Murder (Book 6)
A Cornucopia of Murder (Book 7)
A Wedding to Murder For (novella)
Loch Ness Murder (novella)

Stand-a-lone books:
Today I'll See Her (novella)
The Taking
The Third Nanny
Mirror Image
The Stolen Twin

Murder Next Door

A Charlie Kingsley Mystery

by Michele Pariza Wacek

ISBN 978-1-945363-36-8

Library of Congress Control number: 2022935290

For my family, for always believing in me.

Chapter 1

"Charlie!" Mildred, my tea customer, opened her door and ushered me inside, straight into a cloud of floral perfume so strong, I could feel my eyes watering. Her blue pantsuit was clean and pressed, and her grey, permed hair looked freshly styled, like she had just returned from the hairdresser. "Oh, you didn't have to make a special trip for me. But since you're here, come in, come in."

"It's no trouble," I said, trying to unobtrusively dab the tears from my eyes still stinging from the overbearing fragrance. Hopefully, they would quickly adjust. "I was running errands anyway, and your house was on my way."

"Oh, you could probably use a break then. I'll make you a nice cup of tea, and you can have a seat and just relax."

Before I could answer, she was already bustling off toward the kitchen. I wiped my eyes for the second time and hung up my spring jacket. Then, I tucked my brownish-blondish-reddish hair (which was particularly wild and curly that day) behind my ears and made my way after her.

To be fair, I had expected this. Mildred was a sweet, albeit slightly overbearing, elderly woman. A retired school teacher who had never married and had no kids of her own, she had devoted her life to keeping a very close eye on all the happenings in her neighborhood, and then making sure whoever would listen was kept up to date.

I knew far more than was healthy about the marital life of the Thompsons ("He drinks too much, but I don't know if I can blame him, as she's always coming home late from work … I can't remember the last time she cooked a nice dinner for him"), the family life of the Swanns ("Jamie is running for student council president, and little Teddy was on the JV basketball team … can you believe it?"), and Mrs. Miller's pregnancy ("She is so huge … I'm sure she's having twins").

Yes, Mildred was a bit of a busybody, but she was harmless and lonely, so I didn't mind spending a little time with her when I dropped off her orders.

I ran a tea and tincture business out of my home, so I was typically out and about delivering orders at least a couple of times a week. I had a handful of clients who always asked me to stay and visit, so I made a point of spreading their deliveries out over different days, allowing me the time and space to chat with them. This was Mildred's day.

"Oh my goodness, I have so much to tell you," she said excitedly as she placed a pot of tea and platter of shortbread cookies in the middle of the table. The teapot and matching cups were made of a delicate white china and sported a pink rosebud pattern. Rimmed with gold, they were quite lovely. "You would not believe what just happened with the Thompsons."

I listened to her prattle as I nibbled on the cookies and sipped my special blend of chamomile and rose petal tea that she always saved for my visits. As always, her kitchen was bright and cheery as the sunlight slanted through the sparkling windows. The scent of lemon and bleach was barely detectable under her perfume. Even her orange tabby sleeping in his basket in the sun matched the yellow and white decor.

"But that's not even the most important news," Mildred continued after recounting her very pregnant neighbor's emergency hospital trip. Apparently, Terri had thought she was in labor, and Mildred kindly offered to drive her to the hospital, but it ended up being a false alarm. Mildred took a deep breath and a quick sip of tea, making a slight face in reaction to it having grown cold. "Jonas seems to have hired a housesitter."

"Really?" Jonas lived in the house right next door to Mildred. He was a middle-aged single man who worked in the Redemption post office. I rarely heard about him, as it seemed all he did was go to work, come home, heat up a microwave dinner, and eat it in front of the television while enjoying a couple of beers before going to bed and repeating it all the next day. Needless to say, Jonas didn't garner Mildred's attention the way the rest of her far more interesting neighbors did.

Mildred bobbed her head up and down as she reached for the teapot to top off her cup. "I know. I can hardly believe it myself. I was sure he would have mentioned something if he was planning a trip, but he didn't breathe a word to anyone. I can't even remember the last time he took a vacation."

"Maybe he was saving up his vacation days," I suggested.

Mildred frowned. "Well, that still doesn't explain why he didn't tell anyone. I mean, I have no idea when he left or when he's coming home! It's very upsetting."

"If you didn't see him leave, how do you know he's gone?" I asked.

"His car is gone," Mildred said.

"He parks his car outside?"

"No, in the garage. It's not in there."

I tried hard to keep my expression neutral. "You … looked in his garage?"

"Of course! I hadn't seen him leave for work or come home for a few days, which made me worry he was sick or hurt and needed help. So, I went over to check, but no one answered the door. Well, I was beside myself. Did he have a heart attack? Stroke? Or maybe he slipped in the shower and was lying there in the tub, wet and cold and starving for days on end! I mean, how could I do nothing, knowing he might be suffering? I debated calling the police, and I would have, but I also didn't want to bother them with such a matter when I was sure they had better things to do. I certainly didn't want to waste taxpayers' money, especially when there was an easier solution."

"Of course," I murmured, hiding my smile against the cup.

"So, before I called anyone, I decided to check the doors, on the off chance one was unlocked. I started with the garage. It was locked, of course, but when I peered into the glass, I saw his car was gone, and there was a different one in its place."

"Maybe he got a new car?"

Mildred pursed her lips. "That thought crossed my mind, too, but the one in there now is old. Much older than Jonas's.

I can't imagine why he would trade his in for that. Remember, Jonas bought his car just a few years ago, so it's still nearly brand new. Plus, it has an Illinois license plate, and that doesn't seem right at all."

"You were able to see the license plate from outside?"

"Oh, heaven's no. It was way too dark for that."

I blinked. "I thought you said the garage door was locked."

"I meant the door to the house," Mildred said. "That was locked."

She stared at me, sipping her tea, an innocent expression on her face. Briefly, I wondered if the side door that led to the garage was unlocked, as she seemed to be implying, or if her busybody skills included lockpicking.

I decided I didn't really want to know.

"So, is that when you realized Jonas was gone?"

"Well, that's what I thought, but I decided I'd better call his employer just to make sure everything was on the up and up."

"Very smart," I said.

"They said Jonas was on vacation for a month. A month! Can you believe it?" She shook her head. "He hasn't had a vacation in years, and now he decides to leave for a month? And not tell anyone?"

"Well, clearly, it was overdue," I said.

"I suppose. But he still should have let the neighborhood know. I could have kept an eye on his house for him, instead of him inviting a weird housesitter to stay."

"You met his housesitter?"

She shook her head. "Not yet. I've gone over there twice to introduce myself, but there was no answer when I knocked. And I know he was there, because his car was in the garage. Talk about not being very neighborly."

"No, that doesn't sound very neighborly," I said. *Of course, Mildred skulking around in the garage wouldn't have anything to do with him not answering the door*, I thought, but refrained from verbalizing it.

"But I did see him," Mildred continued. "Once. He was walking around the yard in the middle of the night. I couldn't imagine what he was doing out there. How could he see anything?"

"Maybe he heard something in the yard, like an animal or something."

"I didn't hear anything," Mildred said. "I'm sure there was nothing there. But that's not even the strangest thing about him. Come." She heaved herself out of the chair and beckoned me to follow her to the window.

"See that?" She pointed to the nondescript ranch house next door. As far as I could tell, it looked as it always did.

"See what?"

She sighed. "The windows! See how the shades are pulled down?"

Indeed, all the shades were tightly closed.

"Why would he pull all the shades on such a nice day?" she asked.

Maybe to keep out noisy neighbors who had no qualms poking around in other people's garages, I thought. Instead, I said, "Maybe he works nights and sleeps during the day."

"But I don't see him leave," she countered. "I don't see him at all, except when he's walking around the backyard in the middle of the night."

I had to admit, it was a little peculiar. "Maybe he's an artist or writer and has strange hours."

"Maybe. But still, it's not normal." She put her hands on her hips as she shook her head. "I just don't know what this neighborhood is coming to."

"I haven't a clue, Mildred."

Chapter 2

"Did you see Redemption's new psychic yet?" Pat asked, helping herself to a brownie. We were in my sunny, warm kitchen enjoying a cup of tea and afternoon snack. Midnight, my black cat, had joined us, and was curled up in one of the chairs closest to the window, which overlooked my very-brown-and-dead garden. Spring had barely sprung, and it was still freezing at night, so it was a little too early to get to planting all the flowers and herbs I customarily used in my teas. But soon, that would change.

"You mean it isn't a joke?" I asked. I had heard the talk about a psychic setting up shop on Main street, just in time for the summer tourist season, but I thought it was just that … talk.

"Well if it is, it appears they've taken it so far as to pay rent," Pat said. She was a good decade or so older than me, and the best way to describe her was "round." She was plump, with a round face, round black-rimmed glasses, and short, no-nonsense brown hair that was turning grey. She was one of my first tea customers and had since become a good friend. "'Psychic Readings by Madame Rowena.' At least, that's what the sign says."

I raised an eyebrow. "Rowena? Seriously?"

"Her full name is Rowena Tanveer."

"Like that isn't a totally made-up name."

Pat shook her head. "You mock at your own peril."

"I'll take my chances." Considering I not only lived in a "haunted house," but that half the town thought I was some sort of witch who was actually selling potions under the guise of "herbal teas and tinctures," I thought I had some expertise on subjects like spells and psychics. "Is she actually open for business?"

"Not yet. She's supposed to have some sort of grand opening next week."

"A grand opening for a psychic. That should be interesting."

"We should go," Pat said as she picked up her mug. "Maybe you can talk to her about reselling your teas in her store."

"Oh, that sounds like a great idea," I said drily. "With my luck, she'll rename my lavender rose tea 'Cupid's Arrow by Rowena,' or some nonsense, and then I'll have even more people asking me to make them love potions."

"'Cupid's Arrow' … that's actually kind of catchy," Pat mused with a grin.

"Well, psychics and love potions aside, any new gossip? Or," she waggled her eyebrows. "Any new cases you're busy solving?"

Despite my best efforts, I was starting to develop a reputation for being an amateur sleuth. It wasn't something I had sought out. I was very content keeping a low profile and not calling too much attention to myself as I baked, made teas, and gardened. But over the past few months, I had discovered two things that had changed all of that. One, I had a knack for solving crimes. Two, my customers had a knack for attracting the kind of trouble that required assistance from someone with my particular knack.

"I'm still between cases," I said as Pat's face fell. Unlike myself, she had no mixed feelings around amateur sleuthing. "Unless you count the case of the missing neighbor," I added. Sure enough, her face lit up.

"Missing neighbor? That sounds promising. Do tell."

"There's not much to tell, as I think the case was pretty much solved by the time I was brought into it," I said. "It's one of Mildred's neighbors."

"Oh, well, of course she would know if one of her neighbors went missing. But I don't understand. Is the neighbor actually missing? Or not?"

"Well, I guess he's sort of 'missing.' It's Jonas, the one who works at the post office. Apparently, he's on a month-long vacation, and Mildred is miffed because he didn't bother to share his plans with her. She's even more miffed at his apparent housesitter."

Pat gave me a surprised look. "A housesitter? Jonas doesn't strike me as someone who would need a housesitter, even if he is gone for a month. Especially with Mildred next door. She would have been happy to do whatever was needed while he's away, I'm sure."

"Mildred would definitely have been thrilled with the job," I agreed. "Although maybe he didn't want the neighborhood's number-one gossip going through his medicine cabinet and underwear drawer. Anyway, she apparently didn't see Jonas leave or the new housesitter move in, which is bothering her."

Pat pursed her lips. "Well, actually, I would find that odd, as well. Not to mention a little creepy. I mean, you know how Mildred watches the neighborhood like a hawk. For her to miss something like that, they would practically have had to plan it at a time when they knew she wouldn't be watching. And why would they go through all that trouble? What are they hiding?"

"You've got a point," I said. "Although I would assume Jonas just wanted his privacy. Same for the housesitter."

"But why would Jonas care about his 'privacy' when leaving on vacation?"

"Well, I suppose it's possible he thought Mildred might not notice anything at all, if he snuck out," I said.

Pat snorted. "Fat chance. What's worse is, if he WAS looking for privacy, he just guaranteed getting an earful when he returns."

"Yeah, I wouldn't want to be in his shoes."

Pat finished her brownie and wiped her hands with a napkin. "Now, this housesitter … I guess I can see why he would want his privacy. I'm assuming it's a 'he'?"

"Mildred saw him, so yes. And I agree—he definitely seems to want his privacy." I then filled her in about the shades being drawn and only coming out at night.

"That's weird," Pat said.

"Yeah, it is, but as I told Mildred, maybe he works at night."

"Even so, most people who work that kind of schedule are still seen in daylight," Pat said.

"Maybe he's some sort of artist and only likes the dark."

Pat widened her eyes dramatically. "Or, maybe he's a vampire."

I rolled my eyes. "That's probably it."

Pat slapped the table. "I'm serious. If he were, it would make so much sense. Keeping the shades pulled, only going outside in the dark …"

"With a flashlight," I interrupted. "Wouldn't a vampire be able to see in the dark?"

Pat waved her hand airily. "I'm sure he had a good reason for the flashlight."

"Yeah, because he's NOT a vampire and can't see in the dark."

"Or, he was trying to scare some animal away without drawing attention to himself," Pat said. "But forget about the flashlight. If he's a vampire, it also explains why he wouldn't want to draw attention to himself. The last thing he would want is to have someone like Mildred checking in on him. So, he tried to be sneaky, not realizing that doing so is probably the one thing that would draw Mildred's attention to him like bees to honey."

"When you say it like that, you're absolutely right," I said matter-of-factly. "Jonas's housesitter is a vampire. I don't know why I didn't think of that sooner. Case solved."

Pat preened. "Not everyone is blessed with my special combination of smarts *and* good looks."

"No question there," I said. "And of course boring, stable Jonas, whose most exciting activity appears to be mowing the lawn on the weekend, would not only seek out, but know where to find, a vampire."

"Maybe the vampire found him," Pat said, wagging her eyebrows again. "Maybe the vampire put him under a spell and told him to take a month-long vacation, so he could housesit."

"Because Jonas's house is the perfect lair for a vampire?"

"Maybe. How do you know what a vampire likes or doesn't like?"

"Fair point. I've never met one."

"That you know of," Pat said mischievously. "But we are talking about Redemption, after all. Is it so surprising to think we might have a vampire or two roaming around?"

Redemption, Wisconsin, had quite a history. In 1888, all the adults suddenly disappeared during a terrible blizzard, leaving only the children. They swore they had no idea what happened to their parents, and the mystery of what happened to them continues to this day.

But that was only the beginning of all the strange events that plagued Redemption. It has had more than its fair share of disappearances, murder, and madness, not to mention ghosts and hauntings. Take my house, for example. Back in the early 1900s, Martha Blackwell, the lady of the house, killed her maid Nellie and then herself. The locals are sure Martha continues to haunt my house to this day, although I have my doubts. However, I can't say I haven't experienced some ... well, *odd* occurrences.

"A few ghosts floating around isn't the same as vampires," I said.

"No, but if there was going to be a vampire anywhere, Redemption would be the place."

"That is true," I agreed. "If vampires exist, you'd likely find them here."

"We really should investigate," Pat said. "Maybe we can visit Mildred ..."

I was already shaking my head. "We are absolutely NOT telling Mildred about this. The last thing we need to do is give her more ideas about her neighbor's housesitter."

Pat pouted. "You're no fun." She leaned back in her chair, considering. "Maybe we should ask Madame Rowena about the vampire. Maybe she's seen something ... you know, like in her crystal ball, or whatever."

"Yes, that sounds like a plan. We can ask a make-believe psychic about a make-believe vampire."

"You don't know if either are make-believe. At least not until we've actually investigated."

I rolled my eyes. "Fine. We'll ask Madame for her take on the situation. But unfortunately, we'll have to wait until next week's grand opening."

"Actually, we could go tomorrow," Pat said. "She IS open … it's just low-key until the grand opening."

"WE have a party to go to tomorrow, remember?" I asked.

Pat hit her forehead. "Of course. How could I forget?"

Claire, my first friend in Redemption, was having a party for her two-year-old daughter Daphne in the back room at Aunt May's Diner, which is where I met Claire. She was a waitress, and I had stopped by for a bite to eat while I figured out where I'd gone wrong with my driving. I had always been directionally challenged. One thing led to another, and I ended up staying in Redemption.

"So, I guess Madame Rowena will have to wait for another time," I said.

"I suppose," Pat sighed. "Hopefully, the vampire won't need a a snack, or worse yet, a meal, before then."

Chapter 3

"Thank goodness you're here," Claire said, greeting me with a warm hug. She looked more frazzled than normal, her strawberry-blonde hair pulled back in a messy ponytail, and her hazel eyes exhausted and stressed. "I don't think a party was such a good idea," she confided in my ear.

Eying the chaos of screaming, crying toddlers and mothers as frazzled as Claire, I thought that was an understatement. "Think of it as socializing," I said. "You know how important that is for children to grow into decent adults."

Claire gave me a wan smile as she released me. "I'll try."

Claire and I were the same age, but unfortunately, the stress of raising a child was taking its toll on her, and she was starting to look far older. That, or something else was going on with her health. She hadn't been well since the pregnancy.

"You're a good mother," Pat said, giving her a one-armed hug as she held a gaily wrapped gift in the other. We had gone in on a Cabbage Patch doll. I'd wanted to get an American Girl doll, but Pat talked me out of it, saying it was too much for a toddler. So, Cabbage Patch it was.

"I don't know about that," Claire said with a sigh, glancing behind her as Daphne yanked a stuffed Snoopy out of another girl's hands, who promptly started to bawl.

"I better go," Claire said, hurrying over to try and smooth out the mess. Pat made her way over to the gift table while I surveyed the scene.

Aunt May's was designed to look like an old-fashioned diner, and the back room was no exception. White and black checkered vinyl floors, cozy red faux leather booths, and wood tables completed the look. The smell of cheeseburgers and fried onions wafted through the room, making me a little homesick.

Waitressing at Aunt May's was also my first job when I moved to Redemption, and although I didn't want to be waitressing anymore, I did sometimes miss seeing everyone.

"Charlie?"

I glanced over, sucking my breath in when I recognized the speaker. A blonde, blue-eyed ice queen glared at me. "What are you doing here?" she demanded.

"Same as you, I suspect. Claire invited me," I answered.

Louise narrowed her eyes as she strode over to me. Claire glanced up from her negotiations with Daphne and uttered a quick apology to the other girl's mother before hurrying over. "Don't start, Louise," she begged.

There was a time when Louise, Claire, and I were all friends—back when I first moved to town. Alas, everything shifted when Louise's brother, Jesse, disappeared. Louise was convinced I had something to do with it, and nothing I nor anyone else said could persuade her otherwise. Since then, she had made getting me to leave one of her top goals. Unfortunately for her, that wasn't going to happen.

Louise turned her fury on Claire. "But she doesn't even have a child," she snapped. "Why would you invite her?"

To be fair, Louise had also blamed Claire for Jesse's disappearance, but as both she and Claire had given birth around the same time, they had more or less called a surface truce. Dig a little deeper, though, and all the bitter animosity came pouring out.

"She's Daphne's godmother," Claire said quietly. "Of course she's invited."

Louise pressed her lips together in a tight, thin line. She was still an attractive woman, but grief and unhappiness had ravaged her face. Her brother Jesse was truly gorgeous, and by the looks of Louise's daughter, Jessica, she was destined to be equally beautiful.

"No one wants her here," Louise insisted.

"Louise, don't be like this," Claire said, her voice tired.

"I'm just stating the truth," Louise fired back, raising her voice. "No one wants her here. Not at this party, and not in Redemption. The sooner she goes back to New York, the better."

"Oh for goodness sake," Pat muttered, appearing at Louise's elbow, hands on her hips. "What would your mother say about you being so rude?"

Louise flushed an angry, unattractive red. "I'm just saying what everyone else is thinking," she said defensively. "It's not my fault if you don't like it."

"That isn't the truth, and you know it," Pat retorted in my defense.

"Never mind," I said, grabbing Pat by the arm and dragging her away before she could launch into full mother-lecture mode. "I'll see you later, Claire."

Claire bit her lip. "You don't have to leave."

"I think it's better if I do," I said.

Louise smiled triumphantly. "Yeah, do what you do best," she said. "Be a coward."

"Seriously, Louise," I said tiredly, wishing I didn't always have to get into it with her. Why couldn't she just take the win? Why did she always have to push? "You want me to leave, and even when you get what you want, you still insult me. Would you rather I stay after all?"

"I'd rather you never came at all," Louise said.

"Well, that wasn't really an option," I said. "Just like me leaving Redemption isn't an option. But unlike you, I don't want to cause a scene and ruin an innocent child's party, so I'll go." I shot her a look before turning on my heel and marching out of the room.

"You didn't have to leave," Pat said as we headed out together.

"Why make more trouble for Claire?" I asked. "She has enough on her plate as it is. I don't need to add to her issues."

Pat huffed a sigh. "Louise needs to get over herself," she said. "She doesn't get to decide who stays or goes in this town."

"Yeah, that's Redemption's job," I said with a smile, nudging Pat. As if the town didn't have enough strange events associated with it, the townspeople were convinced that Redemption itself decided who stays or goes. "But seriously, Louise has had a hard enough time, as well. She never wanted Jessica to begin with, as she already had her hands full with her eldest. And then her brother disappears after that horrible fight they had. It's clear she hasn't gotten over either of those events."

"It doesn't matter," Pat said. "We've all had our struggles in life. It doesn't give us the right to insist that other people do as we want. She's being a child, and she needs to grow up and get her act together."

"You'll get no argument from me about that," I agreed.

Pat huffed another angry sigh before giving herself a quick shake. "Okay, well, since our plans have changed and we've got some time on our hands, want to go meet Madame Rowena?"

I shook my head. "Seriously, Pat?"

"As a heart attack. Come on … it will be fun! And the best part is, it's within walking distance." She took my arm and propelled me down the street.

The last thing I wanted to do was meet the so-called "psychic," but I had a feeling Pat wouldn't rest until she shoved me through the door, so now was as good a time as any.

It was a perfect spring day for a stroll. The sun was out, the air was fresh and crisp, and the tulips and daffodils were just starting to peek their heads out of the dark earth. I breathed in deeply, thankful that I had survived another Wisconsin winter.

Madame Rowena's shop was the old Redemption Hardware store. Ted, the owner, had moved out the summer before and into a bigger building a few blocks away. Other than hanging a new sign, Madame Rowena had changed nothing. The windows were still full of dust, and it appeared to be closed.

"Are you sure it's open?" I asked Pat as we walked up to the metal door. The shade was pulled down, and the interior barely visible around the edges seemed dark and foreboding.

"That's what Nancy told me," Pat said, pushing open the door. "But let's see."

A cheery bell jangled as we entered, which seemed at odds with the gloomy atmosphere. The rows of shelves had of course been removed, and the built-in counters were now covered with a display of lit candles and burning incense, which somehow didn't mask the faint odor of sawdust and machine oil. I suspected Madame Rowena was going for a mysterious feel, with all the candlelight, but it wasn't working. The flickering glow seemed to highlight the shadows, giving the impression that the store was deserted.

"I don't know about this," I started to say, but I was interrupted by the movement of a curtain near the back of the shop. A shadowy figure emerged.

"Welcome," the figure said, stretching her arms out as she stepped into the light. "Please excuse the dust … we're still moving in."

Madame Rowena came into focus, so bright and sparkly, I fought the urge to shield my eyes. She was dripping in jewels, from her golden turban to a mass of necklaces and bracelets to her soft leather slippers. She was heavily made up, and combined with the poor lighting, it was difficult to discern how old she was. "I'm Madame Rowena, at your service. How can the spirits guide you today?" Her voice was a warm, rich baritone, reminding me of hot, buttery caramel.

"Err," I said, glancing at Pat, who also seemed flummoxed by Madame Rowena's appearance. "We, ah, thought you were open, but it looks like you're still in the process of getting ready. We can come back …"

Madame Rowena waved her hand in a brush-off motion. "Nonsense. The spirits' guidance can't be delayed. A little dust and sawdust isn't going to hurt anything. Now, how can I assist you? Do you have a question for the spirits? Or are you looking for something more general, such as a tarot reading? Or perhaps you're looking to connect with the spirit of someone who has passed over?"

I had absolutely no idea what we were looking for. This wasn't at all what I'd expected. I wanted to nudge Pat to say something, as the whole thing had been her idea, but I thought that might be too obvious.

Luckily, Pat finally found her tongue. "Actually," Pat said. "We were wondering if you could answer a question."

"Of course," Madame Rowena said. Her eyes were thickly lined with charcoal eyeliner, and her lips were coated with a dark-red lipstick. "That's what the spirits are here for. What kind of question? Is it about love? Or perhaps money, or your career … or maybe you're concerned about your health?"

Pat hesitated. "It doesn't really fit any of those categories," she said haltingly. "Maybe health."

"Great, whose health? Yours, or a loved one's?"

"Neither," Pat said. "More of …. the health of the greater good."

It was all I could do to not roll my eyes.

A faint crease appeared between Madame Rowena's eyes. "I'm not following."

"It's come to our attention that … well …" Pat dropped her voice. "That there might be some sort of danger here in Redemption."

Madame Rowena looked even more perplexed. "Danger? What sort of danger?"

"I … well, we can't really say," Pat said. "We don't know enough."

"I'm not sure what you're asking."

Pat glanced at me, a question in her eyes. I shrugged. *You started this, you can finish it.*

"Okay, so we have a friend who is convinced that … well, let's just say a not-very-nice person has moved to Redemption, if you know what I mean."

Madame Rowena raised a perfectly manicured eyebrow. "Have you called the police?"

"That's just it. This person hasn't done anything. It's just a feeling our friend has. So there's really nothing to tell the cops. But we were wondering if you could tell us if our friend has a valid reason for concern or not."

In the history of questions asked to psychics, that had to be the lamest ever. I was sure Madame Rowena would toss us out on our ears, convinced we were making fun of her. Which would be ironic, because it was actually a real question … minus the vampire angle, of course.

Madame Rowena didn't do that. Instead, she regarded us silently, head cocked to the side. "Twenty bucks," she said.

My eyes widened. Pat made a little choking noise in her throat.

Madame Rowena flashed us a sugary-sweet smile. "Normally, it's $35 for a thirty-minute session, but I don't think we'll need the full thirty minutes, do you?"

Pat shook her head. "No, no, I'm sure we won't." She fumbled in her purse. "I only have a ten," she hissed under her breath at me.

Great. Along with wasting time I was never going to get back, I was now paying ten dollars for the privilege. I dug out another ten and handed it to Pat.

Madame Rowena smiled brightly again as she took the money. "Right this way." She led us to a dimly lit corner of the shop that was tucked away behind a fabric room divider, complete with a round table and two chairs. She moved one of the chairs so it was next to the other and gestured for us to sit before disappearing for a moment. She returned with another chair, a lit white candle, and a worn tarot card deck.

"You're in luck," she said as she began to shuffling the cards. "The spirits are quite strong. And the fact that not many people have been in the shop means the energy is clear, so we should have no problem getting an answer."

It was all I could do to keep a neutral expression on my face. I had to hand it to her—she was really good at creating an otherworldly mood even while surrounded by the vestiges of a hardware store.

She offered the cards for us to cut. I declined, so Pat did the honors.

She flipped over a series of cards, laying them out in front of her. It was so poorly lit, I couldn't make out any specific images.

"Hmmm," Madame Rowena said as she studied the cards, tapping a French- manicured nail on the glass table. "Your friend is right to be concerned. See this? It means a great darkness has moved in, bringing a lot of danger with it." She went on to explain the different cards and their meanings, but it all boiled down to the same—Mildred was right to be concerned about her weird neighbor, although there was no mention of vampires.

"Do you have any more questions?" she asked when she had finished.

I shook my head. "No, this was very helpful, thank you." I quickly stood up before Pat thought of anything else to ask, especially since I might be the one paying for it.

"Yes, thank you," Pat said, getting to her feet as well.

Madame Rowena also rose. "I'm glad I could help," she said. Her expression turned serious. "Definitely tell your friend to be careful."

Something cold tingled at the back of my neck, and I turned my head quickly, sure I was being watched. I saw nothing but shadows and an empty counter behind me.

"We will," Pat was saying as I turned back around. Madame Rowena, however, wasn't paying attention to Pat. She was staring at me.

"You look familiar," she said. "Have we met?"

"I don't think so," I replied, suddenly wanting to get out of there. I was feeling more and more uncomfortable.

"This is Charlie, our resident tea expert," Pat said. "You may have heard of her. She makes teas and tinctures."

Something flickered in Madame Rowena's eyes. "Ah, of course," she said smoothly. "You're the one who lives in the haunted house?"

"That's her," Pat said cheerfully.

"That's got to be some dark energy," Madame Rowena mused.

"Oh, it's not too bad," I said. "For the most part, the ghosts are well-behaved."

Madame Rowena continued to stare at me.

"That was a joke," I said hastily.

"Yeah, the ghosts actually aren't well-behaved at all," Pat jumped in sarcastically.

I shot Pat a look. *You're not helping*. Madame Rowena didn't look amused.

"You two should really talk," Pat continued. "Maybe there's a way you could partner together."

I wanted to kick Pat just to get her to stop talking.

"We should," Madame Rowena said. "I of course have a tea supplier, but I'm always open to options."

"I'd love to, but unfortunately, we really need to be going," I said, giving Pat a not-so-gentle shove. "And I'm sure you must be swamped with everything you have to do before the grand opening."

"Yes, I am pretty busy," she agreed. "Maybe we can talk after that."

"Maybe," I said, herding Pat toward the door as Madame Rowena followed us.

"Thanks for the reading," Pat called out as we left the shop to the tune of the bright little bell.

"I can't believe we just paid her $20," I said as soon as we were on the sidewalk. "Whose bright idea was this again?"

"Hey, it's not my fault," Pat said. "No one told me it was going to be like that. I thought it was going to be like a store, where we could wander around and look at stuff, like candles and crystal balls or whatever. I figured Madame Rowena would be sitting behind the cash register, and we could have a nice chat while slipping in a question about whether she sensed any-thing about our new resident."

"Oh, so trick her into giving us a free reading," I said.

"Well, I didn't expect her to get the cards out," Pat said. "I would have been content with just her general feeling as to whether there's anything to worry about or not."

"Oh, that's much better."

"Hey, at least we learned something," Pat said defensively.

I raised an eyebrow. "Twenty dollars worth of 'something'?"

"You can't put a price on saving a life," Pat said.

"Whose life is in danger?"

"Well, Mildred's, of course," Pat said. "Now you can tell her that she's right—there *is* something off with her spooky neighbor, and she should stay far away."

"I'll let her know the new psychic said so," I said drily. "Even though you didn't actually name names, so you could have been talking about literally anyone."

"Oh, the spirits know," Pat said airily.

I grimaced. Pat had a point. "Based on that logic, I guess we can put aside the notion that there's a vampire living next door to Mildred, since the spirits didn't bring it up."

Pat sighed. "Yeah. That's a little disappointing. Having a vampire move in would have really spiced things up."

Chapter 4

"I figured it out." Mildred's voice was triumphant on the other end of the phone. "The housesitter is a vampire."

I blinked in surprise. "Have you been talking to Pat?"

"Pat?" Mildred's voice was puzzled. "Pat who? Pat Barron? Why, does she have a vampire living next door to her, too?"

I felt like we were getting off topic. "Never mind Pat," I said, tucking the receiver between my ear and shoulder as I continued my kitchen cleanup. "Why do you think the housesitter is a vampire?"

"Because it's the only explanation that makes any sense," she said, as though stating the obvious.

I closed my eyes. "Vampires aren't real, you know."

She sniffed. "Clearly, that's what they want us to think."

"I have no doubt if they *were* real, that's what they would want us to think, but that doesn't mean they *are* real."

Mildred's voice became very stern, as if she had slipped back into teacher mode and was letting me know in no uncertain terms how disappointed she was in me. "Charlie, I know you haven't lived here very long, but you must have heard at least some of the rumors and stories by now. There have been quite a number of strange and unexplained events that have happened here over the years. Why, the amount of disappearances alone is staggering. Quite honestly, having a vampire in our midst makes a lot more sense than some of the other explanations."

"So does his being a serial killer."

"Oh, Charlie, don't be absurd. He's not a serial killer." She huffed out a sigh. "You of all people should be open to the idea of vampires. You're the one living in a haunted house."

"Look, I agree with you that Redemption is … strange. But a vampire? That seems a step too far."

"You haven't seen the things I have." Her voice dropped. "Years ago, I still remember the story of … oh, what was her name again? I can picture her. Such an adorable thing. One day, she just disappeared. For days, no one could find her. We searched everywhere, but she was gone without a trace. Poof! She had vanished. But then one night, she just re-appeared, as mysteriously as she'd disappeared. As if by magic."

I was sucked into the story despite myself. "Was she okay?" Claire had told me a similar story when I'd first moved to town … was it possible it was the same one? I made a mental note to ask Pat how many missing children disappeared and then reappeared a few days later in Redemption.

"Physically, yes. But mentally …" Mildred clucked her tongue. "She had no memory of what had happened to her. None. It was like she had been hypnotized or something." Mildred lowered her voice again to a harsh whisper. "Just like vampires do. They can wipe memories, you know."

"Was there an investigation?" I asked, ignoring the vampire angle and hoping I could bring her back to the present.

"Of course! But nothing ever came of it."

I took a deep breath. Considering how an awful lot of crazy things happened in Redemption, the idea of vampires really wasn't as farfetched as it ought to be.

On the other hand, this was *vampires* we were talking about. Despite the unexplainable, it was still hard to fathom.

Plus, I was starting to wonder about Mildred's mental state. She usually seemed like she had it together, but there had been glimpses of forgetfulness—like when she was sure she had called me to bring over an order when she hadn't, or her forgetting she had ordered tea when I came by to drop it off.

At the time, I told myself it was probably nothing. These sorts of things happen when you reach a certain age. Heck, they even happened to me sometimes, and I was a lot younger.

But now, with the vampire talk, I was starting to wonder.

I decided to try a different tactic. "Why do you think the housesitter is a vampire?"

"Well, I only see him at night," she said. "And he still has the shades down. Even the window on the front door is blocked off."

"He could be a night owl," I said, deciding not to address the windows and how he perhaps just didn't want a noisy neighbor peeking inside.

"If he's a vampire, he's definitely a night owl," Mildred said.

"While it's true all vampires are night owls, not all night owls are vampires," I said. "Are there any other reasons you think he's a vampire?"

Mildred sucked in her breath. "Well, remember how I told you he only walks around the yard at night?"

"Yes. Is he still doing that?"

"Worse," she said, lowering her voice to a whisper. "He's digging holes."

Okay, that WAS weird. "Are you sure?"

"Positive," she said. "I just saw him doing it last night."

"Last night?"

"Yes. It was about one in the morning, and I was going down to the kitchen for a cup of tea. I just don't sleep through the night the way I used to. That's why I absolutely adore your lavender chamomile tea. That's the only thing that can put me right back to sleep."

I felt like we were getting off topic again. "I'm so pleased to hear that. Please go on … what about your neighbor digging holes?"

"So, when I was in the kitchen boiling the water, I thought I heard something. Like something was being dragged. Something big."

I seriously doubted Mildred heard any such thing. "You saw your neighbor dragging something across his yard?"

"Well, no," she said. "He must have already dragged it over to the hole by the time I looked."

"Ah, of course."

"I saw him digging a hole in Jonas's backyard."

"You could see that in the dark?"

"He had a flashlight propped up on the ground."

Again, with the flashlight. "But if he was a vampire, he wouldn't need a flashlight, would he?"

"How should I know?" Mildred was indignant. "And how would *you* know, either? Maybe vampires can't see well in the dark after all. Have you ever asked one?"

She had me there. "Okay, so he was digging a hole. Did you see what he did next?"

"He put a body in there."

"You *saw* him bury a body?"

"Well, not exactly." Mildred sniffed. "But today, when I looked at the backyard, the hole was gone. So clearly, he must have buried something."

I had to admit, it seemed peculiar. "Have you had a chance to meet him yet? You know, so you could maybe ask him what he was doing."

"Are you kidding? No! He is nowhere to be found during the day when the sun is out. Which is why I'm going over there now … to get to the bottom of this once and for all."

"*What?*" The picture of Mildred marching over to her neighbor's to accuse him of being a vampire threw me for such a loop, I knocked my mug over, spilling the dregs of leftover tea all over the counter. "You can't go over there."

"Why not? It's the middle of the day, which means he'll be at his weakest. Although," her voice sounded thoughtful. "I'm not sure he'll be able to hear me at the door."

I snagged one of my sponges and tried to mop up the mess without spreading it further. "Why wouldn't he be able to hear you?"

"Because he's probably sleeping in his coffin. I suppose if he doesn't answer the door, I can just let myself in …"

"*No!*" The word came out harsher than I intended, and I purposefully softened my voice. "Mildred, you can't break into someone's home."

"But someone has to stop him! We can't have a vampire running around the neighborhood and burying bodies. It's … unseemly."

I tossed the sponge into the sink. The counter wasn't perfect, but it was clean enough. "Don't do anything. I'll be right there."

"Oh, dear, you don't have to do that. I'm sure you've got a million other things to do."

"It's no problem at all," I said, forcing myself to sound cheerier than I felt. "In fact, I want to help. I would be worried sick if I don't come, wondering if something happened to you."

"Well … if you're sure." There was a note of relief in her voice, like she had been hoping I would volunteer to come help. "I must admit, I would feel better having someone with me. You never know what might happen in these situations."

"My thoughts exactly," I said as I dug my keys out of my purse. "I'm leaving right now. Remember, don't do anything until I get there."

"I wouldn't dream of it."

***

"I think you should let me do the talking," I said to Mildred as we headed up the driveway.

Mildred looked at me in surprise. "But why?"

I chewed on my lip, searching for an answer that would sound plausible. The truth was, I was fairly certain if I didn't do the talking, the housesitter would be on the phone with the police before we even left the porch.

Mildred had draped herself with both garlic and crucifixes, and she was carrying a small bag that she claimed was "full of supplies." I was afraid to ask what they might be. She had even made a garlic necklace for me, which only confirmed my suspicions that she had no intention of going to the house alone. I refused to wear it, much to her chagrin, but she had brought it with her anyway "in case I needed it." Needless to say, the smell of garlic mixed with her customarily overbearing perfume was giving me a headache.

"I just think you shouldn't be … uh … drawing attention to yourself," I said. "You're the one living next door to him, after all. If he's going to be suspicious of someone, it really should be me."

Mildred furrowed her brows. "I don't know, dear. I certainly don't want him going after you."

"I'll be fine," I said hastily. "It's unlikely he knows where I live, so it will be okay."

Her forehead smoothed out. "That's true. Well, if you're sure …"

"Very sure," I said firmly as we stepped onto the porch. I reached over to ring the doorbell. Mildred tried to put the garlic necklace around my neck again, but I not-so-gently pushed it away.

"I really wish you would wear it," she complained in a whisper.

"I told you, too much garlic gives me a rash." It didn't give me any such thing, but it was the only explanation she would accept.

"A rash is a small price to pay for keeping him from biting your neck," she fretted.

"It will be fine. As you pointed out, it's the middle of the day. Vampires don't eat during the day."

She grumbled something under her breath.

As we waited, I gazed around. Unlike the other houses in the neighborhood that were nicely landscaped with flower beds and stately, large trees, Jonas's house was neat but plain. A few bushes were planted next to house, and that was about it. The front porch was devoid of anything, even a doormat. As Mildred had said, all the windows were covered, and the house was utterly silent.

"I told you," Mildred hissed as I reached for the doorbell again. "He can't hear us. He's asleep in his coffin."

"We are NOT breaking in," I hissed back as I punched the doorbell a few more times. "If he's in there, he'll eventually come to the door."

"He won't if he can't hear us," Mildred started to say, but she paused as the sound of footsteps made its way toward us.

"Remember, let me do the talking," I muttered into her ear as we listened to the scratching of bolts drawing back and locks unlocking.

"I'm not deaf," Mildred complained. "Nor is there anything wrong with my brain."

Looking at her getup, I wasn't so sure.

The door opened a crack, and a sliver of a very pale face appeared. "Can I help you?"

I laid a hand on Mildred's arm as I offered my most welcoming smile. "I sure hope so. We're friends of Jonas's, and we wanted to check on him. We haven't seen him for a while, and we wanted to make sure everything was okay."

A very light-blue eye glanced between us. "Jonas isn't here."

"I know that," I said quickly before the door could shut. "We were wondering if you know where he is?"

The eye continued to regard us. "You mean he didn't tell you? I thought you're friends."

"We are. But you know Jonas …" I forced a laugh. "He can be so forgetful at times."

The eye didn't look convinced. "He's on vacation."

I nodded. "Ah. Yes. He had mentioned something about that. And you are …"

"None of your business." The door slammed shut.

"That went well," Mildred said behind me. "Glad you handled it."

I ignored her, instead reaching over to punch the doorbell again.

The door opened. "If you don't get off this property this minute, I'm going to call the cops."

"Go ahead," I said. "I think the cops will be very interested in discussing your nocturnal activities. Digging holes in a backyard is definitely an interesting choice of a hobby, especially in a house that doesn't belong to you."

There was a pause, and the door opened wider. "What do you want?"

The person standing in front of us was pale to the point of colorless. His hair was the color of faded straw, and he seemed to have no eyelashes or eyebrows. Next to me, I could hear Mildred suck in her breath. "I told you so," she whispered.

"Well, to start, maybe we could introduce ourselves. You know, get to know one another a little," I said. "I'm Charlie Kingsley, and this is Mildred Schmidt."

He stared at Mildred. "Is that … garlic?"

"Does the smell bother you?" she asked, narrowing her eyes.

He wrinkled his nose. "It's kind of … strong."

"So it DOES bother you!" She turned to me. "See? What did I tell you?"

"Doesn't it bother you?" he asked.

"It's for protection."

"Protection?"

"It's good for the immune system," I interrupted quickly. "Garlic can actually ward off a lot of diseases. In fact, during the Black Plague, a group of grave robbers used garlic along with other herbs to ward off the disease."

As I was talking, the man shifted his unsettling, intense gaze to me. "So you think I have the plague?"

Mildred was pawing through the bag she'd brought. "Of course not," I said hastily. "Garlic has lots of health benefits." I eyed Mildred, wondering what on Earth she had packed and really hoping she wasn't about to pull out a stake. "But enough about the garlic. We'd just like to get to know you a little better. As you're new here, you may not realize how much people look out for one another in this neighborhood."

"Where is it?" Mildred muttered to herself as she continued searching. "I know I packed it."

The man stared at me, and I could feel my stomach sink. He wasn't going to answer, especially with Mildred fumbling around looking for who knows what. But to my surprise, he finally relented.

"Drake. Drake Crimson."

Mildred's head snapped up. *Drake Crimson?*

Drake shifted back to her. "Do I know you?"

I placed my hand on Mildred's arm again. "It's nice to meet you, Drake. How do you know Jonas?"

Drake looked like he wanted nothing more than to slam the door in our faces again, and quite honestly, I couldn't blame him, with the way the conversation was going. The real question was why he hadn't yet. "His cousin introduced us," he said. "I was … between jobs, and Jonas was looking for someone who could keep an eye on the place and complete some projects for him while he's away."

"Like digging a grave in the middle of the night?" Mildred pointedly asked.

Drake blinked at her incredulously. "What? I wasn't digging a grave!"

"Then what were you doing in the backyard in the middle of the night?"

"I was digging a garden," Drake said. "Not that it's any of your business."

"A garden?" Mildred frowned. "Since when does Jonas garden?"

"How should I know?" Drake asked. "All I know is he asked me to create one, so that's what I'm doing."

"In the middle of the night?"

Drake shifted from one foot to the other, for the first time looking unsure. "I have a … condition," he said hesitantly. "It's kind of like an allergy to the sun."

Mildred's eyes grew very wide. "An 'allergy'? Is that what you're calling it?" I gave her a not-so-subtle shove, and she let out an "Ouch!"

"I said it's *like* an allergy," Drake said. "Which is why you'll probably see me outside a lot at night as I work on the house."

Mildred opened her mouth to answer, but I quickly jumped in. "Wow," I said, shooting Mildred a hard look. "That sucks, being allergic to the sun. Not to mention how difficult it must be to do outside work at night."

"It is, but I'm used to it," Drake said. "I've had this condition all my life, so I don't know another way to live. Now, if you'll excuse me …"

"I have a few more questions," Mildred started to say, but I interrupted firmly as I took a step back, tugging at her arm. "Of course. It was nice meeting you, Drake. Thanks for talking with us."

Drake didn't respond, as he had already shut the door. It wasn't exactly a slam, but pretty close.

"I can't believe you let him go," Mildred complained as I pulled her off the porch and down the driveway.

"'Let him go'? What are you talking about? He has every right to go back into the house he's housesitting."

"We only have his word that Jonas gave him permission," Mildred sniffed. "Jonas never mentioned any cousins to me."

I didn't point out to her that there were probably lots of things she didn't know about Jonas, as they rarely conversed. "Well, we know Jonas is on vacation. You confirmed that when you called the post office, right? And having a housesitter also do some work around the house seems pretty smart to me."

"Jonas doesn't even garden," Mildred said in exasperation. "Nor do I believe for a moment that he would ask a vampire to housesit for him."

"I don't think Drake is a vampire ..."

Mildred's eyes went wide. "What? Of course he is! Did you see how pale he is?"

"Well, he said he has a medical condition ..."

Mildred snorted. "Yeah. An 'allergy' to the sun! Have you ever even heard of such a thing?"

"Just because I haven't heard about it doesn't mean it's not real," I said. "He certainly seemed unnaturally white. Maybe he sunburns really easily."

"Oh, I bet he does," Mildred said darkly. "And then there's his name. Drake, which is obviously short for Dracula, and Crimson ... of course that refers to blood!"

Despite myself, I had to agree that his name was pretty strange.

"I will grant you that there's a lot of unusual things about Drake. But that still doesn't mean he's a vampire," I said.

Mildred gave me a disapproving look. "How can you say that? Look at all the proof!"

"He wasn't bothered by the garlic," I pointed out.

"He said he didn't like the smell."

"He said it was strong," I corrected. "And he was right. It IS strong."

Mildred huffed a sigh. "I can't believe I couldn't find my mirror."

A mirror? I could feel myself breathe a sigh of relief that she hadn't been searching for a stake after all. "So that's what you were looking for?"

"Yes," she grumbled as we mounted the steps to her front door. "We could have seen if he had a reflection or not. Then, even you would have been a believer. I was sure I packed it. Maybe we should find it and go back over there …"

"No," I said firmly as I opened her door and escorted her inside. "It's not safe." The last thing I wanted was for her to keep marching over there with various vampire-detecting tests.

"'Safe'?" She turned on her heel, giving me a confused look. "I thought you said you don't believe he's a vampire?"

"I don't know what he is," I said. While she was right that I didn't believe her theory, I also wasn't convinced he was completely safe, either. There was something about him that didn't feel right, and it was more than just digging holes in the middle of night in the backyard of a house he was only staying in temporarily. "Regardless, I think you should be careful. He is a stranger, after all. And until we know more, it's probably best to keep your distance."

Mildred gave me a shocked look. "But what if he's a danger to other people, and we don't do anything? Aren't we just as liable then, if something happens to someone?"

"We don't know that he's a danger to anyone," I said firmly. "All we know is he seems a little peculiar. That's it."

"But …" Mildred started to protest.

"Tell you what," I interrupted. "Why don't you keep an eye on him? Write down anything that seems weird …"

"What's weirder than digging holes in the middle of the night?" Mildred asked.

"Well, yes, that too," I said. "But keep a record of anything you see. And then, if it does look like we need to bring in the authorities, you'll have it to show them."

Mildred was quiet as she pondered my suggestion. I found myself holding my breath. The idea of her storming over there waving a mirror or bottle of holy water in Drake's face was giving me a headache. If she did, she'd be lucky if he only called the cops.

If she wasn't that lucky … I didn't want to even think about it. No, I didn't think he was a vampire, but he very well could hurt her, especially if he thought he was protecting himself.

"Okay, that makes sense," she said, and I let my breath out in relief. "It's always good to have a paper trail."

"Perfect," I said. "And you'll call me with updates."

"Of course," she sniffed. "Who else am I going to call?"

"And you won't go over there?"

She hesitated, looking like she might argue with me.

"Mildred," I said. "Promise me you won't go over there."

"But what if I see him … hurting someone?"

"Then you call the police," I said. "You don't go over there. Call me, too."

Mildred huffed a sigh. "Fine."

Chapter 5

"Any updates on the vampire?" Pat asked, stabbing at her chef salad. We were sitting at Aunt May's Diner for a late lunch, as I had just finished dropping off my morning tea orders.

"Other than the fact he's still digging holes in the backyard, no," I said taking a bite of my Cobb salad.

"Still in the middle of the night?"

"According to Mildred."

"That is just so weird," Pat said, shaking her head. "He's got to be hiding something."

"That's what Mildred thinks, but so far, it does appear like he's doing what he said—creating a garden."

"What does this garden look like?"

"It looks like it's going to border the back of Jonas's property," I said. "Although it's possible it's not a garden per se, but maybe a line of bushes or trees. Right now, no one has built behind Mildred's and Jonas's homes, but you know that's eventually coming, so it should definitely be a net positive for his house."

"The whole thing still seems bizzarre to me," Pat said, still stabbing at a particularly uncooperative piece of lettuce. "I mean, if Jonas wanted a housesitter who would do odd jobs for him, this vampire seems like a strange choice. Who ever heard of hiring a handyman who can't go out in the sun?" She put her fork down, briefly giving up the fight with the salad, and looked me in the eyes. "Do you believe him about his medical condition?"

"It's possible," I said. "It's true there are certain medical conditions that make you overly sensitive to light. They're rare, but they do exist."

"Know what else makes you sensitive to the sun? Being a vampire," Pat said, picking her fork back up.

"Now you sound like Mildred," I sighed.

Pat smirked. "Have you ever heard of the Vampire of Highgate Cemetery?"

Now it was my turn to drop my fork. "Are you kidding me? It's not bad enough that the Redemption cemetery is infested with gargoyles? Now you're telling me there's a second one complete with a vampire ..."

Pat laughed. "While I wouldn't put anything past Redemption, no, as far as I know, we only have a gargoyle issue in our cemetery. Highgate is in London. It's supposedly one of the most haunted cemeteries in the world."

"Well, of course it is, if a vampire lives in it."

"I have no idea if there is a vampire there or not, but what I WILL say is that in 1970, a lot of people were convinced there was."

I paused, giving her a hard look. "Wait. You're serious."

Pat nodded. "As a heart attack. Although if I have one, please don't bury me in Highgate."

I couldn't help but grin.

"So people really thought there was a vampire on the loose?"

"They did. Massive panic and hysteria. Apparently, some occult expert found evidence of a bunch of satanic rituals in the cemetery and convinced everyone that they had been done to bring a vampire to life."

I sat back in my chair. "Wow. I can't get over it. In this day and age, people actually thought a real-life vampire existed."

"My point is, there have been vampire scares for hundreds of years now," Pat said. "I'm not saying they exist or don't exist, but ..." she shrugged. "Mildred believing there's a vampire living next door to her isn't as ridiculous as you might think."

"People are plenty strange all by themselves," I said. "We certainly don't have to turn them into vampires in our minds."

Pat opened her mouth to answer, but there was a sudden flurry of noise and confusion near the counter.

"What's going on?" I asked, watching the commotion.

"I don't know," Pat answered.

I strained my ears, trying to hear what everyone was talking about, but all I got was the word "missing."

I could feel myself grow cold. Suddenly, Mildred's vampire talk didn't seem so silly.

"Are you hearing what I'm hearing?" I asked Pat, keeping my voice low. "Is someone missing?"

Pat nodded, her eyes round, like her thoughts were mirroring mine.

Before I could say anything more, Sue, our waitress, broke away from the knot of people and came toward us. "Do want a refill?" she asked, nodding toward my Coke. Her brown, curly hair was longer than she normally wore it, and it was starting to frizz at the ends.

"Sure," I said, not because I actually wanted more soda, but it gave me an excuse to talk to her. "What's going on?"

Her expression went grave. "Oh, you didn't hear? Polly Pembrook is missing."

Pat's mouth dropped open. "Polly? She's one of the youngest, right?"

"More in the middle," Sue corrected, blowing a piece of hair off her cheek. "She just turned seventeen."

"Oh, that's right," Pat said. "I keep forgetting about the one who just started high school. So, what happened with Polly? Did she just not come home last night, or what?"

"Did you say 'Polly'?" A tiny slip of a girl appeared at Sue's elbow. Her hair was limp and colorless, and she was wearing an unflattering brown dress.

"Oh, hey, Linda, I didn't see you come in," Sue said. "You're picking up, right?"

"Yes," Linda answered distractedly. "But did I hear you right? Are you talking about Polly Pembrook? Did something happen to her?"

"Nobody knows. She's missing."

Linda's eyes went wide. "Missing?"

"Yeah, I know. It's horrible."

Linda seemed to turn a shade paler. "What happened? How long has she been gone?"

"I'm not sure. I guess she didn't come home last night." Sue paused as a couple sitting at a nearby table began waving frantically at her. "Oh, I have to go. Let me go check on your order. I'll be back."

As Sue bustled away, I slid out of the booth and moved toward Linda with one of my friendliest smiles. "Hey. Want to sit with us while you wait for your food?" Linda didn't look well, and I was a little concerned she might collapse if she didn't sit down.

She blinked a couple of times, focusing on me. "I … I probably shouldn't. I need to get back to the office."

Now that I was closer to her, I realized she was older than I thought—more like in her mid-twenties than teens, as I had first assumed. I gently took her arm. "You'll need the order first, right? I don't think it will get here any faster if you're standing."

She still looked like she wanted to protest, but after a deep exhale, she let me lead her to our table. "I'm Charlie, by the way," I said. "And this is …"

"Pat," Linda said. "I didn't see you there."

"You know each other?" I asked, sliding into the booth.

Pat rolled her eyes. "Oh please. You haven't figured out by now that I know everyone? How's your mom doing, Linda?"

"She's fine," Linda replied, her voice as distracted as it had been when Sue asked her about her order. She perched on the booth next to me. "But, Polly … do you know what happened to her?"

"No, we just heard ourselves," Pat said.

"The family must be so upset," Linda empathized. "I should stop by, see if there's anything I can do."

"I'm just surprised it took so long for word to get out that she's missing," I said. "It's after lunchtime."

"I would assume it's pretty chaotic at the Pembrook household," Pat said. "There's what? Eight kids?"

"Eight?" I asked in disbelief.

"Actually, nine," Linda corrected.

"*Nine?*"

"As I said, it's probably nuts in the morning on a regular day," Pat said before giving Linda a considering look. "You were in school with the oldest, right?"

Linda's cheeks colored an unattractive shade of red. "Second oldest."

Pat nodded. "Was it Donny or Jillian?"

The color deepened. "Donny."

Pat nodded. "That's right."

"Well, with that many kids, I can see how they could lose track of one," I said.

"Yeah, I'm surprised it doesn't happen more regularly," Pat agreed.

"This is bad," Linda muttered, looking around. She had started worrying a corner of my napkin.

"I agree, but I'm going to keep hoping it's nothing," Pat said. "Maybe she had a little too much to drink and is sleeping it off somewhere."

"No, I mean, it's just … this whole day is bad," Linda said. "I was already having a bad day at work, and now Polly, and lunch is taking so long … oh, you must think horribly of me. Polly is missing, and I'm complaining about my trivial bad day."

"No, we don't think badly of you," I said as Pat shook her head in surprise. "Obviously, you knew Polly, so of course her being missing would affect your day. And if it was already bad to begin with, that just sucks."

"Yeah," Linda said, her fingers plucking even harder at my napkin, scattering little pieces of paper. "My boss hates it when I'm late with his lunch," she said in a rush. "I was already late leaving to get it today, and now, with what's going on with Polly …"

"Sorry about that," Sue said, appearing as if by magic and holding out a paper bag. "Did you need anything else?"

"No, I have to go," Linda said, quickly standing. "Thanks so much for letting me sit with you."

"Of course," I said, but Linda had already hurried away.

"Well, I hope her boss isn't too hard on her," I commented, turning back to Pat.

Sue rolled her eyes. "He's a jerk. Hopefully, once he hears about Polly, he'll go easy on Linda. Can I get you anything else?"

***

"Did you see today's newspaper?" Mildred yelled in my ear.

I winced as I tucked the receiver between my shoulder and ear, hoping she'd turn her own volume down. "I'm just looking at it now," I said as I started to unroll it. I had a bad feeling about what I was going to find.

"There's a girl missing," Mildred yelled again, and I winced again, shifting the phone further away. This wasn't good. I had been hoping Pat had been right, and Polly was just sleeping off a night of too much booze, not wanting to come home and face her parents. Clearly, it was more serious than that. "And you know what that means."

Inwardly, I sighed. I knew where she was going, but felt like I had no choice but to ask. "What?"

"The vampire!"

And there it was. "You don't really think …"

"You and I both know Drake Crimson is not planting a garden in Jonas's backyard," Mildred interrupted. "I suspect that's exactly where we'll find that poor girl."

Oh no. I could hear the alarm bells ringing in my head. "Please tell me you haven't been poking around in Jonas's yard."

"No," Mildred grumbled. "But Charlie, we have to do something! One girl has already disappeared. How long before he takes another one?"

I had to admit, there was something suspicious about a teenager disappearing just when someone new moved to town and happened to spend his nights digging holes in his backyard. "Give me a half hour. I'll come pick you up."

"Pick me up?" Mildred sounded surprised. "Don't you want to go back and confront Drake?"

"No," I said grimly. "It's time we talk to the police."

***

"Have a seat," Officer Brandon Wyle said, gesturing at the two chairs in front of his desk. He pawed through the piles looking for a pen. "You have some information on the Polly Pembrook case?"

"Yes," Mildred said eagerly, perching on the edge of her chair. It had taken some doing to convince her to talk to the cops. She was sure they wouldn't believe her, and even if they did, that they'd mess everything up anyway. Eventually, after I pointed out that the police were likely going to get involved one way or another, she reluctantly agreed. The truth was, the alternative to talking to them was digging up Jonas's backyard ourselves, in which case, Drake would call them himself.

"I suppose it makes sense to be the first to talk to the cops," she muttered, although it was clear she wasn't happy about it.

"Think about how happy the Pembrook family will be if we're the ones who help the police find their daughter," I offered, hoping to jostle Mildred out of her negative mood. It would likely not go well if Mildred started snapping at the officer while we gave our statement.

Apparently, Mildred decided she liked the idea of helping the cops find Polly. *Maybe a little too much*, I thought, worried she might be a little too exuberant in her efforts. We had discussed not bringing up the vampire angle, and she said she understood my reasoning, but she definitely looked a little disappointed.

I was also not at all pleased that the person interviewing us was Brandon Wyle. Of all the cops in Redemption, he was somehow always the one I ended up dealing with.

He didn't look any happier to see me than I was him. "Why am I not surprised?" he asked when he saw us standing by the front desk.

"Nice to see you, too," I countered.

Wyle shook his head as he beckoned us to follow him to his desk, which was located near the back. I hadn't seen him since we had both been trapped with Claire's family and a dead lawyer in a remote cabin during a terrible blizzard. Needless to say, it had been an exhausting weekend. Even though a couple of months had since passed, I thought he still looked exhausted. His dark hair was still on the long side, curling around his collar, and there was some puffiness around his dark eyes that seemed to indicate he wasn't sleeping well. I wondered if he was worried about Polly … or if maybe he was back with Lucy, Claire's cousin. She could surely be exhausting. The last I had heard, they had broken up, and while it really wasn't my business if they had gotten back together again, I still somehow found the idea bothersome.

He sat down in front of us, his uniform stretching across his broad chest.

"So, Polly," Wyle said, finally unearthing a pen and flipping over the cover of his notebook. All around us, the sounds of the clanking of typewriters, ringing of telephones, and dull roar of voices reverberated. The smell was the same as I remembered—a rancid combination of burnt coffee, sweat, and old socks. I tried to breathe through my mouth. "What's the information?"

"We know where she is," Mildred said.

"Not exactly," I interrupted as Wyle's eyebrows went up. "We have some information you might want to check out."

"And the sooner the better," Mildred chimed in. "It's possible he hasn't killed her yet."

"'Killed her'?" The front of Wyle's chair went down in a thump as he leaned forward. "You better start from the beginning."

"It's my neighbor," Mildred said before I could answer.

"Your *neighbor?*" Despite the fact that Wyle was wearing what I called his "cop face," meaning he kept his face expressionless, I could see the heightened interest in his eyes. "Why do you think it's your neighbor?"

"It's not exactly her neighbor," I interrupted. "She means her neighbor's housesitter."

"Where's your neighbor?"

"We presume on vacation," Mildred said.

Wyle looked perplexed. "You *presume* he's on vacation? You mean you don't know?"

"No!" Mildred leaned forward slightly. "Jonas didn't tell me he was going on vacation for a month. Don't you think that's odd? And he apparently hired a housesitter, who I've never met or seen before he moved in. I think this is very fishy."

Wyle took a breath, maybe to give himself a moment to process the barrage of words. "So, how did you find out about the housesitter if, is it Jonas, you said? If Jonas didn't tell you?"

"Well, we went over there, of course."

Wyle looked between us. "'We'?"

"Yes, I went with her," I answered.

It looked as though Wyle was starting to get a headache. "Was there a reason you went over to meet the new housesitter?"

"Because Charlie didn't think it was safe," Mildred said.

A muscle worked in Wyle's jaw. "What wasn't safe about it?"

Mildred started to answer, but I put a hand on her arm. "He had some ... peculiar habits. And we thought maybe it would be better to go introduce ourselves and give him a chance to explain."

Wyle made a face like he had just eaten a lemon. "And what were these 'peculiar habits'?"

"He only comes out at night," Mildred burst out. "Even to dig in the backyard."

"Dig in the backyard," Wyle repeated, but Mildred was on a roll.

"Not only that, he has all the windows covered. All of them. Clearly, he can't stand the sun. He even moved in in the middle of the night. And Jonas must have left in the middle of the night, too, if he left at all, because I never saw him go."

If he left at all ... I glanced quickly at Mildred, wondering where that newest hairbrained idea was coming from and hoping Wyle hadn't caught it, as well.

I should have known better. Of course he had.

"What do you mean, 'if he left at all'?"

Mildred straightened up. "I got to thinking that it's possible Polly wasn't Drake's first victim. That's the housesitter's name. I mean, there's been a pretty long stretch of time between people disappearing, but if he started with Jonas, that would make sense."

I closed my eyes. Oh no.

Wyle held up a hand. "Wait a minute. It sounds like you're not all that surprised that your neighbor's housesitter is, uh, making people disappear. Why?"

"Well, because he's a vampire," Mildred said with a totally straight face.

Wyle stared at Mildred. I don't think I had ever seen him at a loss for words before, but Mildred had managed it. "A vampire?" he finally repeated.

"We don't actually know that he's a vampire," I said quickly.

Mildred rolled her eyes. "Of course he's a vampire. What else would he be?"

Wyle pinched the bridge of his nose. "Why do you think he's a vampire?"

Mildred started to list off her reasons on her fingers. "Well, to start, his name. It's Drake Crimson. I mean, how much more vampirey could it be?"

"Totally," Wyle said faintly.

"And he only comes out at night, because the sun will kill him."

"That's not what he said," I said. "He said he has an allergy to the sun."

Mildred shook her head. "Yeah, he's got an allergy, alright."

Wyle glanced at me. "Are you serious with this?"

"Yes," Mildred insisted, but I put my hand on her arm.

"Okay, look, it's possible Drake Crimson does have an allergy to the sun," I said. "He's very pale, like albino pale, so it's possible. Rare, but possible."

"So, if he does have one of these allergies, would his behavior make sense?" Wyle asked.

"Yes. Depending on how bad it is, any exposure to the sun would be very painful. We're talking extreme sunburn, blisters, the whole bit. So, yes, if he was unlucky enough to have such a condition, he likely would avoid the sun at all costs."

"Okay, so what is this about him …" Wyle glanced at his notes. "Digging at night?"

"He says he's digging a garden for Jonas, but I have never seen Jonas garden," Mildred said.

"What exactly is he doing?"

"He's digging holes in Jonas's backyard," Mildred explained in exasperation. "Except I think they're actually graves."

"Graves for his … victims?"

Mildred nodded. "Exactly. Officer Wyle, we have to stop him. I mean, I know he needs to eat and all of that, but we can't have a vampire running around the neighborhood killing people."

"No, we can't have that at all," Wyle said with a sigh.

"So, you'll go check it out?" Mildred asked.

"Yes. But I have a couple more questions. Did you ever see this Drake Crimson with Polly?"

"No," Mildred said impatiently. "I told you, he only comes out at night."

"Yes, you mentioned that. And he's always alone?"

Mildred shifted uncomfortably. "Well, it's not like he would bury someone who was still alive, would he?"

"I couldn't say," Wyle said neutrally. "Have you seen any-thing else suspicious?"

"You mean more suspicious than everything we've already told you?"

"I was thinking something along the lines of maybe actually seeing him burying something," Wyle said.

Mildred brightened. "I did see him with a sack."

"A sack?"

"Yes. I couldn't see exactly what it was, but whatever it was, it was heavy, and he had to drag it out there."

Wyle's gaze sharpened as he made a note. "And when was this?"

Mildred screwed up her face. "A week ago or so. Maybe a little longer."

"So, before Polly went missing?"

"Yes," Mildred started to say, but then her eyes went wide. "It was Jonas," she gasped. "I must have seen Drake dragging

Jonas out to the backyard." She put a hand to her mouth. "Oh, poor Jonas."

Wyle glanced at me. "Anything else?"

Mildred shook her head. Her cheeks were pale, and her hand still covered her mouth.

"Do you need something? A glass of water or a cup of coffee?"

Mildred shook her head again, her eyes glassy. "No, it's just … I didn't realize. I didn't put it all together until now."

"We don't know it was Jonas," I said. "Remember, his boss told you he was on vacation, so Drake probably is a legit housesitter."

"Yes, but why didn't I see Jonas leave?" Mildred's voice was anguished.

Wyle signaled to a cop behind us. "Officer Smitty here will take you to get a cup of coffee."

Officer Smitty appeared at Mildred's elbow. He was middle-aged with a thick mustache and slight paunch. "Ma'am," he said, his voice respectful. "Let's go sit somewhere a little more comfortable."

"I don't know," Mildred said miserably. " Jonas probably isn't all that comfortable right now. I don't know why I should be."

Smitty glanced up and met Wyle's eyes. "Let's talk about it. It might make you feel better."

Mildred looked like she wanted to protest, but Smitty apparently wasn't taking "no" for an answer. He helped her up and led her away.

Once we were alone, or at least as alone as we could be in a busy police station, Wyle leaned his elbows on his desk and stared at me. "Charlie, what exactly is going on here?"

"I'm not sure, but I figured with a missing girl, you might want to check out the stranger who just moved in and has been digging holes in the backyard in the middle of the night."

Wyle pinched the bridge of his nose again. "That's not what I meant. What are you doing feeding into the delusional fantasies of an older woman?"

"Mildred isn't delusional," I said hotly.

"She thinks there is a vampire living next door to her," Wyle said. "You don't think that's delusional?"

"Well, it's not the first time there's been vampire hysteria," I said. "I mean, just twenty years ago in 1970, there was the Highgate vampire in London …"

"This isn't 1970 or London," Wyle interrupted.

"Yes, but some people could argue that Redemption is more twisted and haunted than London."

"I agree that Redemption has more than its fair share of strange occurrences, but a housesitting vampire seems too far even for it."

"Look," I said, leaning forward slightly. "I don't know what this guy's deal is. But it's weird that he's digging holes in the middle of the night, sun allergy or not. Especially in a house he doesn't own. Don't you agree?"

Wyle sighed. "Yes, I agree, but you still shouldn't have gone over there."

"Are you saying I should have let Mildred do it on her own? Because she was going to."

"No, I'm saying you should have called the cops."

I gave him an exasperated look. "Seriously?"

He narrowed his eyes. "You do understand what you did wasn't safe?"

I raised my eyebrows. "'Safe'? Wyle, this was a week ago. Polly hadn't disappeared yet. In fact, no one had disappeared other than Jonas, whose boss said he was on a month-long vacation. And we're calling the cops because the housesitter is digging holes in the backyard?"

"In the middle of the night," Wyle added.

"I know! That's why we went to check it out. But are you honestly trying to tell me you guys would have taken this seriously?" I held my hand like a phone, pretending to talk into it. "'Hello, officers? Yes my neighbor's housesitter never comes out during the day, only at night. In fact, he's digging holes in the backyard in the dark. We think he might be a vampire … could you come check it out?'"

Wyle gave me a look. "You could probably have skipped the vampire part."

"As if that would have made a difference."

Wyle threw up his hands in exasperation. "Maybe this guy is a serial killer. Have you thought about that?"

"Yes. I have. Which is why we came in today."

"You needed to come in before today," Wyle corrected. "Or, at the very least, not gone over there just the two of you. If some strange man was acting suspiciously, you really shouldn't have confronted him like that."

"We're just going to have to agree to disagree," I said, getting up. "Is there anything else?"

Wyle huffed a sigh. "Yes, don't go over there again. Leave it to us. We'll investigate. Alright?"

"Trust me, he's all yours," I said, turning on my heel and preparing to leave. I had no desire to talk to the very prickly Drake Crimson again. My only concern was making sure Mildred stayed away, too.

"What does that mean?" he asked.

I threw a quick glance behind me, flashing him a sideways smile. "You'll see soon enough."

Chapter 6

"Are you going to be okay?" I asked Mildred as we stepped outside the police department. The air was clean and crisp, with just a hint of the scent of geraniums, and I took a deep, cleansing breath. It smelled even better after the staleness inside the police station.

"I don't know," Mildred said as she let out a deep, shuddering sigh. "I keep thinking of Jonas and that poor girl. I knew there was something wrong. I should have done something sooner. Maybe one or both of them would be okay."

"We don't know that they're not," I said. "Wyle is looking into it. Why don't we wait for him to investigate before we jump to any conclusions?"

Mildred shook her head. "I don't know, Charlie. I just feel so awful."

I squeezed her arm. "Tell you what. It's close to lunchtime. Why don't we grab a bite to eat at Aunt May's. My treat?"

"Oh, I can't let you do that," Mildred protested, but I squeezed her arm again.

"Nonsense. It's the least I can do. We'll have a nice lunch, and who knows … maybe by the time we're done, Wyle will have already talked to Drake, and we might have some answers."

That perked Mildred up. I tucked her into the car and drove over to the diner.

I got lucky parking. Someone was pulling out as I pulled in, but the lack of open spots should have clued me in on how busy it was going to be.

"My word," Mildred said as we squeezed into Aunt May's. There were several people in line in front of us, and the tables were packed. "I had no idea it would be this busy."

"Lunch usually is," I said, but remembering my days working there, it seemed even busier than I remembered.

Sue waved at us as she hurried by, her cheeks bright red and her brown hair a mass of frizz. "It's about a ten-minute wait," she called out.

"That's fine," I said. The longer we were there, the more likely Wyle would find some answers for us.

Sue nodded as she grabbed the coffee pot, her eyes scanning the rest of the people in the line. "Oh, the kitchen is running a bit behind," she said to a customer. "We'll have your order out in a jiffy."

"Okay," came the answer, but the tone sounded anything but. I recognized it, and turned to see Linda standing at the back of the line.

"Linda," I said, waving. "How are you doing?"

Linda started, glancing suspiciously around before spotting me. "Oh, hi," she said. "Charlie, right?"

"That's right. Why don't you come stand with us while you wait for your food?"

Linda hesitated. Two middle-aged women were standing between us, and they gave us a wary look.

"She's just picking up a to-go order," I assured them. "Right, Linda?"

"Right," Linda confirmed.

One of them still didn't look convinced, but the other smiled and indicated Linda could step forward. I wondered if she really thought this was all a ruse to cut in line.

I introduced Linda to Mildred and asked her how it was going.

"Fine," she said, twisting her hair around her finger. Today, she had on a black blouse with a black-and-white skirt. She looked even more washed out than she had wearing beige. She really needed to update her wardrobe.

"Were you able to see Polly's family?"

She nodded. "I don't think it mattered, though. The house was full of people, and they were so upset … I'm not sure they even realized I was there." Her face was dejected, and I wondered if it had less to do with Polly's parents and more about the brother she clearly had been angling to see.

"It was good you stopped by regardless," I said. "And you can always try again. They're going to need a lot of support."

"Charlie!"

Uh oh. I recognized that voice, too, and it wasn't a good thing. I plastered a smile on my face and turned to meet a scowling Louise. She was at a table near the window. Little Jessica was in a high chair, her face smeared with what looked like macaroni and cheese, while Jillian, her older daughter, munched on a hamburger and fries.

"Hi Louise, nice to see you," I said, as Louise stood up from the table. She said something to Jillian, who seemed to shrink in her seat from acute embarrassment, before marching toward us.

"You have some nerve showing up here like this," Louise growled, her voice loud. Other patrons were starting to glance over at us.

"To have lunch at a diner? I thought that was the very point of a restaurant," I said.

Lousies's face darkened. "Don't play dumb. It doesn't suit you."

"What are you talking about now, Louise?"

"Wait, is that you, Lou?" Mildred suddenly jumped in.

Louise did a double take, staring at Mildred and clearly caught off guard. "Ms. Schmidt?"

"Yes, of course. Who else?" Mildred's eyes narrowed. "And what is the meaning of you causing a commotion like this?"

It was funny, watching Louise's face morph into the child Mildred had once taught in class. "But … but …" she stuttered.

"No 'buts,'" Mildred reproached her. "I taught you better than to make a scene. You even left your two little ones at the table. What has gotten into you?"

Louise swallowed and seemed to collect herself. "You don't understand. This is all Charlie's fault."

"What is Charlie's fault?" Mildred asked.

"Polly, of course."

Mildred looked mystified. "Polly? What does Charlie have to do with Polly?"

"It's Charlie's fault Polly is missing," Louise said pointedly.

I rolled my eyes. "Seriously, Louise? You're blaming me for this, too?"

Mildred looked even more perplexed. "Charlie didn't have anything to do with Polly disappearing."

Louise ignored Mildred, instead whirling toward me. "*Everyone* should be blaming you," she hissed. "Ever since you showed up here, bad things have happened."

"Oh, like nothing bad happened in Redemption before I arrived," I said.

"Look at all the people who have disappeared since you moved here! Jesse, Jonathan. Now Polly. It's all your fault! And still, you refuse to leave."

"Lou, listen to me," Mildred said, her voice urgent. "I don't know where you're getting your information, but Charlie had nothing to do with Polly's disappearance."

"Stay out of this, Ms. Schmidt," Louise said, her voice bitter and eyes like daggers as she glared at me. "You have no idea what Charlie is capable of."

"That's enough, Lou," Mildred said firmly. "You don't know what you're talking about."

"Oh, and you do?"

Mildred straightened up. "I do indeed," she said. "I know precisely what happened to Polly."

Oh no. Everyone in the restaurant was now staring at us.

"You know what happened to Polly?" Sue asked. She seemed frozen in place, a large tray of food propped on her shoulder.

"Actually, we don't," I started to say, but Mildred interrupted me.

"Yes, we DO know. And Officer Wyle is following up as we speak."

Sue looked completely stunned, and I was a little worried she might drop her tray. "It is true that Officer Wyle is following up, but it's not true that we know," I tried to clarify.

Louise looked completely flabbergasted. "You know what happened to Polly?"

"I do," Mildred answered.

"Well, what happened?" a man yelled from the back of the restaurant. He was a big, burly guy wearing a red plaid shirt and a Packer's baseball cap.

All I wanted to do was grab Mildred and drag her out of the restaurant, but I knew the crowd would never let us go. Barring that, maybe the Earth would open and swallow me up.

"My neighbor's housesitter took her," Mildred said matter-of-factly.

"*What?*" Sue's tray started tipping precariously, and I stepped forward to grab it, feeling compelled to help avert at least one inevitable disaster. "Your neighbor's housesitter took her?"

"Well, what are we waiting for?" The man yelled again from the back of the restaurant.

"Again, we don't know for sure," I yelled back as I continued helping balance the tray on Sue's shoulder. "That's why we told the police. They're investigating."

"But why? Why would your neighbor's housesitter take Polly?" Louise asked.

"Again, we're not sure if Drake took Polly," I said.

Louise blinked at me. "Who's Drake?"

"The housesitter."

Her eyes widened. "You know him?"

"I met him once," I said.

"See?" Louise said triumphantly. "It all leads back to you. It always does. You are the root of everything bad in this town."

"Oh for crying out loud," I said.

"Lou, you're talking nonsense again," Mildred said. "Charlie had nothing to do with it. Drake took Polly because he's a vampire."

Silence. I didn't think anyone even breathed. From the back of the restaurant, the man who had been yelling slowly sat back down.

All I could do was close my eyes.

"Did you say … 'vampire'?" Sue asked in disbelief.

"I did, indeed," Mildred said.

"We also don't know that," I said. "There's a lot we don't know. We should all just let the cops investigate."

"Why do you think your neighbor's housesitter is a vampire?" Sue asked, shifting from one foot to the other.

"Well for one, he never comes out during the day," Mildred explained. "He even has all the windows blocked off."

"Does he look like a vampire?" That was from one of the middle-aged women standing behind us.

"He does, actually," Mildred said.

The woman's eyes went wide as she gasped. "Really? Is he handsome?"

"Of course he is," her companion said. "If he's a vampire, he's going to be sexy."

"I don't know about 'handsome,' but he's pretty pale," Mildred said.

"Charlie, you really should be ashamed of yourself," Louise snapped.

"Me?" I was astonished.

"Yes, you. What are you doing leading an old woman astray like this?" Louise asked.

"'Old woman'?" Mildred straightened up again, clearly offended. "Watch it, young lady. I still know where your mother lives."

"I had nothing to do with this," I said.

"You just said you went to the cops," Louise said.

"I did. Because there is a missing girl and he IS acting suspicious."

"How? Other than not going out during the day?" Sue asked. Her cheeks looked a little flushed as well, and I started to almost feel sorry for Drake. I had thought the biggest danger would be a mob of people led by the Packer baseball hat guy wanting to burn Jonas's house down. But now, it was looking more likely that Drake would maybe be swarmed by a bunch of horny middle-aged women, instead.

"He's digging holes in the backyard," I said.

Sue's mouth dropped open. "Holes? As in … graves?"

"Well, he has to eat," Mildred said. "And he has to do something with the bodies after."

Louise threw up her hands. "I can't believe this is happening. Forget the vampire. The real menace is right here." She pointed at me.

"If this housesitter is digging graves in the backyard, someone needs to look into it," Sue said, ignoring Louise. "Charlie isn't the one digging graves."

"No ma'am," I confirmed.

"Fine," Louise said. "Don't listen to me. But don't come crying to me when your loved one disappears." She stalked back to her table. Jillian looked like she wanted to crawl into a hole, whereas Jessica was now happily wearing her entire bowl of macaroni and cheese. I heard Louise mutter angrily as she started pulling napkins out of the dispenser.

Mildred shook her head. "She was always a difficult child," she said to me in a low voice. "Now her brother, he had the sunniest disposition. He was always smiling and cracking jokes, but Lou …" she shook her head. "She was always a glass-half-empty kind of girl. Know what I mean?"

"I do," I said, watching Louise struggle to clean up her daughter. As frustrated and exasperated as I was with her, a part of me still missed our friendship. There had been a time where I would have helped her clean Jessica up, and we likely would have laughed at the mess she'd made.

But, that was then. Now, it appeared we were at war.

56

Chapter 7

"Did you see today's paper?" Pat asked.

I adjusted the phone receiver as I reached for my tea. "You're calling awfully early," I yawned.

"Did you see today's paper?' Pat repeated.

"I've barely made my tea," I said, watching Midnight stroll into the kitchen and stand expectantly by his food dish.

Pat huffed a sigh. "I'll be right over." The line went dead.

I blinked at the receiver for a moment before hanging it up. I took another sip of tea as I picked up Midnight's food dish and contemplated what I had in the house to feed Pat. I definitely had cookies, but it seemed early for that. Maybe there was time to make some muffins …

I paused as Pat's words finally sunk in. The paper. She was going to be right over. Oh no.

I dropped both Midnight's food dish and my mug. Luckily, I didn't break it, but the tea ended up sloshing over the side. I ignored it, hurrying to the front door much to Midnight's chagrin. The paper was in the middle of the driveway, so I threw on a windbreaker and slipped on the easiest pair of shoes I could find, which just happened to be winter boots. I clomped across the porch and down the driveway to fetch the paper, not even waiting until I got back inside to unroll it and look at the front page.

My heart sank. It was even worse than I thought.

I had just finished skimming the article when Pat arrived in her green Chevy Cavalier. She pulled over to the side of the road, failing to get close to the curb, but it really didn't matter, seeing as I lived at the end of a cul de sac and had no neighbors. She hopped out. "What are you doing out here wearing winter boots?" she asked.

"Never mind that," I said, waving the paper. "How could they write about this?"

"Are you talking about the vampire or Rowena?"

"Both!" I waved the paper some more. "This is awful."

"I told you," Pat said. "But maybe we should get you in the house before it starts snowing."

I gave Pat a look and stomped back inside. "I was going to make muffins," I said as Pat followed me in.

"I'm not going to stop you."

I yanked my boots off, hung my windbreaker on the coat rack, and marched into the kitchen, only to be greeted by an impatient meow. "I can't believe this," I muttered as I started banging around, filling the tea kettle, feeding Midnight, and pulling out the ingredients for banana muffins. "How could they even report that? They have to know that vampires don't exist."

"You have to admit, it's a pretty juicy story," Pat said. Then, she held her hands up. "Don't shoot me. I couldn't resist."

"This isn't a laughing matter," I said, dumping flour into the mixer. "This could cause a panic. A vampire living in Redemption?"

"Well, they do have a quote from Wyle that there's no evidence he's a vampire," Pat pointed out. "Or that he had anything to do with Polly's disappearance."

I eyed her. "Do you really think that's going to stop anyone from going over there? We're talking about a missing girl."

Pat dipped her head in acknowledgement. "True, but they also didn't publish where the so-called vampire lives. Nor did they mention Mildred."

I scooped up the newspaper and read from it. "'A retired schoolteacher was the first to sound the alarm about the possibility of having a vampire as a new neighbor.'"

Pat bit her lip. "Well, yeah. That does narrow down who it could be."

"People will definitely figure it out." I glared at the bananas, even though I was fairly certain they had nothing to do with the newspaper article. All I could think about was how much of a mess it was all turning into, and not just for Mildred, but Drake, too. And what if it turned out that Drake had nothing to do with any of this, which was looking more and more likely? We might have just created an absolute nightmare for him. "Especially after what happened yesterday in Aunt May's Diner," I continued. "And once they do, what's to stop them from showing up at Mildred's door? Or Drake's door? Maybe I should call her."

Pat's gaze sharpened. "What happened yesterday at Aunt May's?"

"Let me call Mildred, and then I'll tell you," I said, reaching for the phone.

"Shouldn't you wait?" Pat asked, glancing at the clock. "It's pretty early."

I frowned at her. "Seriously?"

"Well, it's you and me," Pat said. "It's never too early for us."

I hung the receiver up and went back to my baking. Pat was right; it was too early to be making calls, especially about something like this. If Mildred was having a peaceful morning, I ought to let her enjoy it, as it might be her last for a while.

I filled Pat in on what happened at both the police station and at Aunt May's as I got the muffins into the oven and made another pot of tea. Pat looked disgusted when I finished.

"That Louise," she said, shaking her head. "Why can't she let it go? I know it's terrible that her brother is missing, but to keep blaming you? She has got to move on."

"While I agree with you, that's a problem for another day," I said. I picked up my tea but didn't drink it. "Someone who was at Aunt May's must have called the paper."

"Do you think Wyle said anything?" Pat asked.

I shook my head. "Doubt it. Wyle doesn't want to talk to anyone when he's investigating."

"Okay, so it's true the paper probably found out because of what happened yesterday," Pat said. "But how did Rowena get entangled in this? Was she there?"

I pursed my lips. "I don't think so, but I can't be sure. I didn't see her, so if she was there, she was tucked away in a corner and didn't draw any attention to herself. Which I don't see happening."

"Well, maybe someone told her, too," Pat mused.

"This is turning into a disaster," I said. "Now everyone is going to know that Mildred thinks there's a vampire living next door to her, which means everyone is going to either think she has dementia, or there really *is* a vampire living next door to her. And Polly is still missing."

"Don't forget that Rowena has promised to use her psychic powers to find Polly," Pat added.

I closed my eyes. "Yeah. Like that's going to help anything. Talk about giving people false hope."

"At least Rowena said she didn't think it was the vampire who took her."

"There's that, I suppose," I said. "But still, it seems awfully irresponsible of her to claim she'll be able to find Polly in the first place. What's her angle? Does she want to become Redemption police's resident psychic?"

"It might not be a bad additional income stream," Pat said.

My eyes widened. "You think that's something they'd pay for?"

Pat shrugged. "They do in other places."

"What a racket," I muttered, opening the oven to pull out the muffins.

"Plus, it's great PR for her new business. Especially if she actually ends up finding Polly," Pat continued.

"And just in time for her big grand opening," I said, popping the muffins out of the tin and arranging them on a platter. "Pretty lucky for Madame Rowena, I would say."

"Well, she IS a psychic, after all," Pat said, reaching over to carefully pick up a hot muffin. "Maybe she looked into the future, saw this happening, and planned her grand opening accordingly."

I gave Pat a look. "Yeah, I'm sure that's precisely what happened." I heaved a sigh as I chose my own muffin. "I wonder if I need to go over and apologize to Drake about all of this?"

Pat blew on her breakfast. "Why would you apologize to him? Do you know for certain he had nothing to do with Polly?"

"No, but it appears he didn't. Wyle went over yesterday and didn't find any sign that Polly had been in the house."

Pat gave me a sharp look. "How do you know that?"

"Wyle called me," I said. Pat raised an eyebrow. "It's not like that," I said. "It was just a quick courtesy call. I'm sure Mildred received a similar one."

Pat gave me a knowing smile. "Of course. I'm sure Mildred got the same call."

I rolled my eyes as I shook my head. It really had been a short call, and Wyle sounded like he was in a foul mood. Maybe he had gotten a heads-up about the newspaper article.

"Back to Polly," Pat continued. "Maybe she wasn't in the house. Doesn't mean she's not in the backyard."

"That's a morbid thought. Although ..." I continued, blowing on my breakfast and in deep thought. "Wyle is trying to track down Jonas right now to get permission to dig up the backyard."

"He needs permission for that?"

"He does if he doesn't have a warrant," I said. "My guess is he doesn't have enough for one. Not to mention how embarrassing it would be if the police went ahead and did it only to discover that Jonas did indeed ask Drake to create a garden for him."

"That would certainly answer a lot of questions, if we knew for sure that was the case," Pat said.

"Which is why I'm hoping Wyle is able to connect with Jonas, and soon," I said. "Along with clearing up a lot of mysteries, it would also probably help put a damper on any angry mobs thinking about asking Drake a few questions themselves."

"Not to mention all the hordes of women looking for a date," Pat said.

"Yeah, well, if they're expecting Kieffer Sutherland from *The Lost Boys*, they're going to be disappointed," I said.

"I was picturing the hot vampire from *Fright Night*," Pat said, smacking her lips. "He was delicious."

"Richard will be relieved that Drake looks nothing like him, either," I said drily. Richard was Pat's husband.

"Well, that's disappointing," Pat said.

***

As it turned out, I didn't have to worry about Mildred. She loved the article and all the attention. "I can't believe how many people figured it out," she marveled. "They've been calling all day."

"I suspect what happened at Aunt May's was a big clue," I said. "How about Drake? Are people bothering him?"

"If they are, I haven't seen any signs of it," she said. "Although I wouldn't know if they've been calling or not."

I suspected Drake wouldn't answer the phone if they were. He didn't seem the extrovert type. But at least they weren't showing up at his doorstep.

Yet.

Chapter 8

"Charlie! Oh thank heaven you picked up."

"Mildred?" I glanced at the clock, the sense of dread I had woken up with intensifying in my gut. I wondered if I needed to fetch the paper again. This was becoming a worrying trend, needing to check the paper every morning to make sure Redemption hadn't blown up the night before. "What are you doing calling so early? Is everything okay?"

"No, it's not." Mildred sounded close to hysterical. "Drake killed another one."

"*What?*"

"Drake! He's still at it. The cops didn't stop him after all."

"Slow down," I said. "How do you know this?"

"Because there's a dead body in his yard."

"*What?*"

"Can you come over?"

I glanced down at Midnight, who was waiting by his food dish, tail twitching impatiently. "I'll be right there."

I banged the phone down, threw some food into Midnight's dish and some clothes onto my body, and practically flew out the door. I drove like a maniac over to Mildred's, only to discover that the cops had half the neighborhood blocked off. I had to park halfway down the block and hoof it the rest of the way, passing little knots of neighbors standing in their yards in various states of dress.

"Do you know what's going on?" one woman called out to me. She wore a pink flowered housecoat and was sporting major bedhead. I found myself wondering if she was a Thompson, Swann, or Miller.

"That's what I'm going to find out," I called back.

"Ma'am," one of the cops called out to me as I marched up Mildred's driveway. I recognized him as the one Wyle had called to take care of Mildred the day we had gone to the station. Officer Smitty, I thought his name was. "Do you have business here?"

"Mildred called me," I said. I noticed police tape blocking off Jonas's house, along with a flurry of activity.

He frowned. I had the feeling he was about to tell me I couldn't be there when Mildred threw open the front door. "Oh, thank goodness you're here. Come in."

I gave Officer Smitty a slight nod and headed to the house. He didn't look happy.

"Charlie," Mildred said as soon as she shut the door behind me. "I knew it! I knew he was a vampire, and no one believed me, and now someone else is dead!"

"Just hold on," I said, gently squeezing her arm to try and calm her. Her skin was grey and her eyes wild, and I was a little afraid she might have a heart attack or stroke. "First, let's make some tea. I haven't had a chance to have my morning cup yet. Have you?" As much as I wanted to hear the story, making sure Mildred didn't have some sort of health crisis was more important.

She swallowed hard. "No, I had started to make it, but then I saw ... I saw ..."

I squeezed her arm again. "Let's go sit down in the kitchen, and I'll make it for us."

Mildred swallowed again before nodding. She let me lead her into the kitchen, like a teacher guiding a small child.

I sat her down before going toward the stove. While looking for the sugar, I also found a half-full bottle of whiskey. After a second's hesitation, I added a healthy dollop of it to her cup, along with the sugar.

"Here you go," I said, setting the mug in front of her. "See what you think."

She grasped the cup with both hands and took a deep swallow, making a slight face. "Is that ... whiskey, in there?"

"If there was ever a time for morning whiskey, I think it's now," I said.

She pursed her lips, mulling it over before taking a second long drink. I was relieved to see the color coming back into her cheeks.

"Okay, so why don't you start from the beginning?"

Mildred nodded as she took one more sip. She placed the mug on the table, but I noticed she still kept her hands cupped around it, like she needed the warmth.

"It started like every other morning," she said. "I got up, went to get the paper, then came into the kitchen to make the tea. I put the kettle on the stove and then went to check on Drake. I wanted to see if there were any new holes in the yard, especially since I didn't see him outside last night."

"You had checked?"

She nodded. "I always do. But there was no sign of him."

"Was this different from usual?"

She thought for a moment. "Yes. Since the newspaper article came out, I haven't seen him back there very much at all."

"Okay, so this morning. What happened?"

She shivered, squeezing the mug. "I saw something in the yard. At first, I wasn't sure what it was. It was this long, thin bundle wrapped in a tarp. I was trying to figure out what it could be when the wind blew a corner of it away. And that's when I saw it." Her voice dropped at the end.

My stomach twisted in a knot. I didn't want to ask, but I knew I had to. "Saw what?"

She squeezed her eyes shut, like she was trying to block out the image that was clearly burned into her brain. "A face."

I closed my own eyes. I really didn't want to ask the next question at all.

"Polly?"

Mildred shook her head tightly, and the fist that had been squeezing my stomach lessoned slightly. "Not Polly. A man."

"A man?" That was puzzling. "Jonas?"

She shook her head again. "No, I didn't recognize him."

Even more curious. "Was he from Redemption, do you think?"

"He must be. Where else would he be from?"

Where else, indeed? I sipped my tea, wondering if I should mention that it was possible it was someone from wherever Drake had been before he became Jonas's housesitter.

"Did you hear or see anything last night?" I asked.

"I already told you, no."

"I didn't mean in the middle of the night," I said. "I was thinking earlier, like in the evening. Or even late in the afternoon."

"I wasn't home," Mildred said. "It was bridge night. I was at Phyllis's. But why? Do you think I might have seen the man hanging around?" Her eyes grew wide.

"It's possible," I said. "Maybe someone else noticed something." I found it doubtful even as I said it. I had a feeling the rest of the neighborhood left the watching to Mildred.

Mildred took another sip of tea. "I wonder why he didn't bury him. I mean, he has those graves just sitting there. Do you think it was a mistake?"

"A 'mistake'?"

"Yeah, like he killed him too late to bury him. The sun was already coming out."

"It is weird, to just leave a body in the backyard like that," I said. I had been wondering the same thing. If Drake killed that man, and he wanted to bury him in the backyard, but it was too close to sunrise, why didn't he just leave the body in the garage, or hidden somewhere until the following night? Why leave it in the middle of the yard for his nosy neighbor to see?

Something wasn't adding up.

"Ms. Schmidt?" Wyle's voice floated from the front door. "Your front door is open. Would it be okay if I came in?"

"Oh," Mildred started, pressing a hand to her chest, her eyes round. "Did I forget to shut the door?"

"It's okay, there are cops all over the place," I said, before calling out to Wyle that we were in the kitchen.

"Sorry," Wyle said appearing in the doorway. "I was just wondering if you could answer a few more questions?" He nodded a greeting at me, and I nodded back. Even though his cop face was on, his eyes were troubled, and there were signs of strain in the set of his jaw.

"I've already answered a bunch of questions," Mildred fretted.

Wyle gave her a reassuring smile, although the edges were frayed. "I know. It sucks having to answer so many questions. I promise it won't take long."

"Okay," Mildred sighed.

"Do you want some tea?" I asked Wyle.

He dipped his head. "Tea would hit the spot, thank you."

I wasn't sure if he really wanted tea, or if it was more to send me away, but I headed toward the stove, figuring Mildred could use a refill, as well.

Wyle kept his voice low as he questioned her—not that he was asking about anything she hadn't already told me. I set the tea down in front of them, and not sure what to do, resumed my spot at the table.

Wyle didn't stay long. Mildred was clearly exhausted and wasn't sharing anything useful. Finally, he took a sip of tea and stood up.

"You've had enough of a shock today," he said. "We can finish this later. You probably need to rest."

"I'm sorry I wasn't more helpful," Mildred said, her voice dejected.

"Nonsense. You are very helpful," Wyle said. "You discovered the body bright and early, which is great for us. The sooner we can get started investigating, the better. And if you think of anything, you have my number. So, why don't you take a break now? Charlie, can you walk me out?"

"Of course," I murmured. Mildred was staring into her mug.

Wyle stepped back so I could walk ahead of him. "I guess I shouldn't be surprised you're here," he said in my ear.

"Mildred called me," I said, keeping my voice just as low. "She was a mess. Of course I'd come over."

He pressed his lips together. "You both are in over your head. You need to watch yourselves."

"I'll keep an eye on her," I said. We had reached the front door, but neither of us made a move to open it. "Any ideas who the victim is?"

His eyes narrowed. "What did I just say about you being in over your head?"

"Wyle, you know we're going to find out who it is. What's the big secret?"

"Well, first off, we don't release the name until we've notified next of kin."

I put a hand over my heart. "I promise I won't tell anyone. Scout's honor."

Wyle didn't look amused. "And, second, in case you've forgotten, not only is there a dead body out there, but there's still a missing teenager."

"I haven't forgotten," I said. "I know time is of the essence to find Polly. That's why you need me. You know I can help."

Wyle stared at me, clearly frustrated. "This isn't like Claire's cabin. There's no reason for you to be involved."

"Of course there's a reason! People are disappearing and now dying, and half the town thinks there's a vampire living next door to Mildred. The sooner we get to the bottom of what's going on, the better. The last thing we want is some sort of mass hysteria taking over."

Wyle looked away. I could see a muscle in his jaw working as he struggled with himself. I stayed quiet and let him wrestle with his thoughts, although I couldn't figure out what the big deal was. Was it just his male ego? That didn't feel right to me. Wyle had never struck me as the type to care about who solved the case, just as long as the right person was charged. "I don't like this," he said.

"Who does?"

He turned back to me. "No, I mean, I don't like you being involved."

I rolled my eyes. "But you know I can help. Why are you being so stubborn?"

"Because this is getting dangerous, and I don't like the idea of you getting hurt." He glared at me, but I could see the concern in his eyes.

I chewed on my lip as I tried to frame a response. I wasn't sure how I felt about him being worried about me, but I wished I could tell him the truth—I had been in much, much more dire situations than this, and it always worked out. "I appreciate that, but honestly, I can take care of myself."

"Charlie, you live alone on the edge of town," Wyle said. "You have no close neighbors. What are you going to do if someone comes looking for you?"

"I have a mean black cat," I said.

Wyle ground his teeth. "I'm serious, Charlie."

"So am I. He's a tough cat. I'm also handy with a baseball bat. Really, you don't need to worry about me."

Wyle didn't look convinced.

I huffed a sigh. "Okay, look. I'm already involved, but even if I wasn't, we don't know who this guy would target. So, really, the best way to keep everyone safe, including me, is to get to the bottom of what's going on as quickly as possible. And you know I can help you do that."

Wyle didn't immediately respond. Instead, he ran one of his hands though his hair. "I still don't like it," he grumbled. "But you're right. The sooner we get this solved, the better."

He straightened up and looked me in the eye. "His name is Harrison Shaw."

"Never heard of him."

"He owns a rental company here in town." Wyle flipped open his notebook and read from it. "Shaw's Property Management and Rental Company."

I frowned. "Still doesn't ring a bell. But I don't understand the connection. Drake doesn't live here. He's a housesitter. Why would he be involved with the owner of a property rental company? Does Drake want to move here and is looking for a place to rent?"

"That was our thought, but Drake is claiming he's never seen Shaw before."

I chewed my lip. "So he's denying any involvement? I mean, he could of course be lying. Did he say if he saw anything suspicious last night? After all, we know he's a night owl."

"He said he hadn't noticed anything strange. It had been a quiet night."

"So, we have no idea when the body was left in the backyard?"

"As of right now, no. But we'll see if any of the other neighbors noticed anything."

That sounded like a dead end. "Okay, so what if we take Drake's word for it and assume he's never met Shaw. Is it possible Jonas is the connection? Maybe he reached out to Shaw before his vacation."

Wyle looked thoughtful. "Like maybe Jonas was interested in renting his house out?"

"Exactly. What if Jonas is considering moving, and this whole housesitting thing was just a trial run? Or maybe he's considering buying a second house and renting it out?"

Wyle pulled a pen out of his pocket to jot down a note. "Possible. We can ask him when we find him."

I looked at him in surprise. "You haven't yet?"

Wyle pressed his lips together. "It appears Jonas never showed up at the hotel he was booked at."

"*What?*"

Wyle gave me a knowing look. *Now do you get it?* "According to Jonas's coworkers, he was to spend a month driving to Colorado and exploring the state. His first stop was Aspen."

"Okay," I said. "Although it's kind of a weird time to drive to Aspen, isn't it? It's too late in the season for skiing, but it's still cold and snowy."

A faint smile touched Wyle's lips. "That's precisely why he was going now. It's the off season, so hotel prices are dirt cheap. He had made a reservation, but he never checked in."

I could feel a cold chill run down my spine. "I'm guessing he didn't call to cancel, either?"

Wyle shook his head slowly, his eyes never leaving mine. "No. He was a no- show."

I thought about what Mildred had said ... how she had never seen Jonas leave. The cold chill wrapped itself around my stomach and squeezed.

"Do you think he might have gotten into an accident on the way there?" I asked. "I mean, it's quite a drive, from Wisconsin to Colorado."

"That's what we're checking now. So far, we haven't found anything, but as you pointed out, there's a lot of miles to cover."

Despite the ice that had lodged in my stomach, my hands were sweaty, and I wiped them off on my jeans. "Okay, then. So, it's possible there's a connection between this Shaw guy and Jonas. But how does Polly fit in?"

"That's something else we're looking into."

I blew out a long breath. Considering a dead body was actually found in this case, it seemed like it should be more straightforward. Instead, it kept getting more complicated.

"Can you share more about how Shaw was killed?"

Wyle tucked his notebook back in his pocket. "Obviously, we need the ME to examine the body, but it appears he was bludgeoned to death."

"'Bludgeoned to death'? With what?"

"Again, that's for the medical examiner to say, but whatever it was, it looks like it was heavy. Also, he was hit multiple times. Whoever did it clearly wanted to be sure he was dead."

I blanched. "So, no sign of bite marks, then?"

Wyle gave me a look. "You're seriously asking me that?"

I held up both hands. "Hey. Don't blame me. You know that question is coming from more people than me."

"I thought you didn't believe in the vampire stuff."

"I don't. But at this point, who knows? Maybe Mildred was right all along, and Drake was in need of a food source."

Wyle put a hand on the doorknob. "If he was, it doesn't appear like Polly was on the menu. We'll go through the house more closely now, looking for signs of Harrison, but when we searched before, we didn't see any evidence she was ever in that home, much less killed there."

"Stranger and stranger," I mused.

He opened the door. "I have to get back, but you're going to be careful, right? Don't take any unnecessary chances. And don't you dare go into any situation that's dangerous. You call me. Promise?"

"Yes," I answered, but I was only half-listening, my mind whirling around all the possibilities.

Wyle paused, a hand on the doorframe and a scowl marring his handsome face. "Charlie! I mean it. You call me if you think there's even the slightest possibility of danger. Got it?"

"Yes, yes. I promise. I'll stay out of danger."

Wyle didn't look convinced. "And you better keep me updated as to what you find."

I smiled sweetly at him. "Of course. When haven't I?"

Wyle snorted. "I already regret this."

"Don't worry, officer. Everything is under control. I'll keep you posted."

Wyle shot me one last look before finally stepping outside.

Chapter 9

I closed the door and moved to the large living room window, carefully pulling back a corner of the drapes, so I could peer out without anyone necessarily seeing me. I watched Wyle as he headed next door, not answering the questions the crowd was peppering him with, but reassuring them that he would give them an update as soon as he could.

Drake was standing on the outside stoop, surrounded by several cops. It seemed clear they were getting ready to take him down to the station, probably for more questioning. He was wearing a black, hooded sweatshirt with the hood pulled up, black sweatpants, and black gloves. The only part of him uncovered was his face, which was making his agitation clear. While being accused of murder would likely make anyone agitated, I wondered if that was the only thing upsetting him, or if being outside in the sun was adding to it, as well. I also noticed the crowd of neighbors had grown quite a bit. Actually, it was almost intimidating now. Maybe Wyle had a point about my safety being in question.

"Look at all those people." Mildred was standing next to me, looking over my shoulder. I was relieved to see her color had nearly returned to normal.

"Well, do you blame them?" I asked. "It's not every day there's a body found in the neighborhood."

But Mildred wasn't listening. "Oh, look, there's Terri. I was meaning to talk to her about the baby." She pointed, although I wasn't sure who she was pointing at. I assumed it was the tall, rawboned woman wearing a stained green terrycloth bathrobe and holding a bundle wrapped in a blanket.

I gave her a sideways glance. "I'm not sure this is the time," I said.

Mildred waved her hand. "Oh pshaw. Of course it is. Look, it's safe now. The cops will take him into custody. I'll just go put something a little more suitable on." She took a step back, but paused, her face thoughtful. "Is that the psychic?"

My mouth dropped. "What? Where? Do you mean Madame Rowena?"

Mildred nodded. "Yeah, that's the one."

"She lives in your neighborhood?"

"Oh no. We haven't had anyone new move in for, well, years, I think. I think the Smitties were the last ones …"

I was too impatient to listen to a history of the neighborhood comings and goings. "But if she doesn't live here," I interrupted. "How did she find out about what happened?"

Mildred gave me a surprised look. "Well, Charlie, she IS psychic, after all. Of course she would know."

I opened my mouth and closed it. Clearly, asking Mildred wasn't going to get me anywhere. I needed to go to the source. And how quickly the neighborhood gossip was spreading wasn't the only thing I wanted to find out. I also wanted to suss out how much of a vulture this Madame Rowena was—whether she was planning on trying to use this situation to grow her business, like she had with Polly's disappearance.

"Why don't you go change? I'm going to talk to the psychic and see what she has to say."

Mildred's head bobbed up and down. "Excellent idea. Maybe she'll be able to tell us if Drake has any more bodies stashed away somewhere."

"I'll find out," I said drily as I moved to the door.

"And maybe get an update on Polly, too," Mildred called out.

"Definitely," I said. I put my hand on the doorknob, took a deep breath, and opened the door.

The first thing that hit me was the air. It was cool and damp, like rain was soon to follow. I wondered how that would impact the investigation next door. The sun was watery behind the clouds, which should be good news for Drake, if he really did have that allergy.

The second thing that hit me was all the eyes that turned to stare at me. I gulped, almost losing my nerve, but then I thought about Polly, Mildred, and everyone else in the town who weren't safe until someone figured out who was behind all of this. I straightened up, squared my shoulders, and walked out the door.

More eyes turned to watch me as I made my way down the driveway. "Who are you?" one woman called out, her voice sounding suspicious.

"How do you know Mildred?" another asked. I presumed it was Terri, as she was the one holding the bundle in her arms. "And is she okay?"

Rowena was unfortunately standing a little ways off, and with everyone staring at me, it would be impossible to sidle over there and have a private conversation. It also seemed unlikely I would be able to ignore them the way Wyle had, yet it wasn't like I was in any position to give an 'official' statement. Maybe if I answered a few questions, the crowd would go back to watching Drake be loaded into the police car. "Mildred is fine," I said. "She was a little shaken up, is all. She'll be out shortly."

Terri jiggled the blanket-wrapped bundle, although as far as I could tell, the baby was out like a light. "This is so awful," she said. "What is our neighborhood coming to?"

"Is it true there was a body found in Jonas's yard?" a woman asked. Unlike most of the crowd, she was carefully made up and dressed in pressed grey pants and a pink silk blouse. Her light-brown hair was slicked back in a neat ponytail.

I paused a beat, sucking in a deep breath of the fresh, cool spring air so at odds with the reality unfolding in front of us. I wished I could lie. The crowd's mood was more curious and gossipy at the moment, and I knew how quickly that could shift into something far darker.

"Yes," I said.

There was an audible gasp. "Who was it?" Terri asked.

"The cops are still investigating," I replied.

"What I don't understand is, where is Jonas?" A tall, imposing man wearing a black robe and striped pajama bottoms came toward me. He fixed his very dark-blue eyes on me, clearly waiting for an answer.

"Uh, well, it appears Jonas is on vacation," I said, wondering how I became the official spokesperson.

"Jonas is on vacation?" Pink Silk Blouse asked. "I didn't think he ever went on vacation."

"So, who are the cops arresting, then?" Terri asked, squeezing her baby tighter against her chest. *That must be one laid-back baby, to still not fuss,* I thought.

"The housesitter," I said.

"'Housesitter'?" the man wearing the black robe repeated. "Wait a minute. Are you saying this … this housesitter is the vampire the newspaper was talking about?"

"Vampire?" Terri gave a little shriek. Or maybe it was the baby. I could see it finally starting to squirm in her arms as she shushed it.

"Well, there's no such thing as vampires," I said, but my voice was drowned out by everyone talking.

"Vampire or not, he's killing people," Black Robe said. "And he's in our neighborhood! Did he kill Polly, too?"

"Polly is missing. We don't know what happened to her," I said, but I didn't think anyone was listening to me anymore. As I feared, the crowd's mood was shifting, having gone from simply wanting to be in the know to something far more dangerous.

"Calm down, everyone!" Wyle had moved to the edge of the yard and was standing there with his hands on his hips.

"Is it true?" Black Robe shouted. "Is this the vampire the newspaper was talking about?"

"And is he going to kill all of us?" Terri asked, wide-eyed.

"Vampires don't exist," Wyle insisted. "And we don't know what happened to the victim yet."

"But there WAS a victim," Black Robe said.

Wyle put his hands up, like he was trying to visibly calm the energy. "We're very early in our investigation, so there isn't much I can share, but this is what I can tell you. Yes, there was a body discovered in the backyard of Jonas Ray's house this morning. Jonas is not currently residing in his home, but the housesitter is being taken down to the police station for more questions. I promise we'll keep you updated as much as we can as the investigation continues."

"What about Polly?" Pink Silk Blouse asked. "Did the vampire kill Polly, too?"

"Okay, enough with the vampire talk," Wyle said. "There is no evidence of anyone being a vampire! There is also no evidence that Polly's disappearance is linked in any way to the murder victim."

"So, he *was* murdered?" Black Robe asked.

"Yes, we are operating under the assumption that the victim found in the backyard was murdered," Wyle said.

Another collective gasp from the crowd, this one louder than before. It appeared that Wyle saying the word "murder" made it all the more real.

"We're all going to be killed in our beds," Terri wailed, squeezing her baby, who finally had enough and let out his or her own yowl.

"Let's not be hasty," Wyle said. "You should all take precautions. Keep your doors locked, don't walk alone at night, and if you see anything or anyone suspicious, call the police immediately. Do NOT, under any circumstance, approach or confront anyone suspicious. All that said, we have no reason to believe that whoever murdered our victim is planning on killing anyone else. So, please, go about your lives … just stay aware of your surroundings, and be vigilant."

"Easy for you to say," Black Robe said. "You don't have a killer in your neighborhood."

"Again, we have no reason to believe the killer is actually residing here," Wyle said.

"You found the body in the killer's yard," Black Robe argued.

"It is still early in our investigation," Wyle said again. "Please, don't make assumptions. This case is top priority. Now, I think it's probably about time you went back to your homes and got your day started. Okay?"

Black Robe opened his mouth like he wanted to argue, but Wyle gave him a steely glare, and he closed it.

"Go on, everyone," Wyle said.

Clearly unhappy, as we could hear the disgusted mutters rolling through the crowd, people nonetheless decided to listen to Wyle and disperse. "I can't believe this," one woman said as she walked by me. "Redemption is creepy enough already. Now we have vampires to worry about, too?"

I picked my way over to Rowena, who was still standing off to the side. "Nice seeing you again," I said.

She eyed me, her expression cool. "Same." She was again wearing a lot of flowing clothes—a dark-blue silky dress with some sort of long, sparkly gold robe over it, and plenty of jewels, of course. Her hair was jet black—too black to be real—and she had it slicked back in a low bun.

"I didn't realize you live in this neighborhood," I said, keeping my voice casual.

"What happens here affects all of us in Redemption," she said.

I nodded. "True. So is that a no, you don't live here?"

She cocked her head. "I'm not sure why that matters to you, as you don't live here, either."

I looked at her in surprise. "How do you know where I live?"

"Everyone knows where you live, Charlie."

That made me pause. I hadn't figured she would remember me, but maybe she had a talent for faces and names. "Someone in this neighborhood requested I come," I said. "Did someone call you, too?"

"If that makes a difference, yes, I was called."

I raised an eyebrow. "Oh?" I pretended to look around. "I don't see you with anyone. How odd. I would think whoever called you would be here with you, too, having taken the trouble to ring you up."

She let out a sigh and put a hand on her hips. "Why are you so … *concerned* about why I'm here?"

"Because I'm worried about my friend and her safety," I said. "I'm trying to figure out how fast word is getting around."

She shrugged. "It's a small town, so pretty fast. Especially since it's about a murder."

"True. So, that's how you found out? Word is flying around town?"

She huffed another drawn-out sigh. "If you must know, the spirits called." Her voice was dramatic.

It was all I could do to not roll my eyes. Clearly, she wasn't going to tell me how she really found out. "Did the spirits say anything else? Like maybe who did it?"

"The spirits don't work that way. They reveal things in their own good time."

"That's a bummer," I said.

She gave me a sideways glance. "We're all trying to do our part to help. If my special talent can help in even a small way, I'm happy to be of service."

"I'm sure you are."

She pursed her lips, like she had bitten into a piece of rotten fruit. "I don't know why you insist on being so negative. You of all people should know how the spirit world works."

"Why? Because I live in a haunted house?"

She smiled, a small, secret smile. "No, because you're a witch."

Now I did roll my eyes. "I'm no witch."

She widened her eyes. "Oh? That's not what I hear. You have quite a high success rate with those … 'teas' you sell."

I narrowed my eyes. "What are you saying?"

Her look was innocent. "Nothing. I hear they're quite delicious. And they have done some … miraculous things."

'There's nothing miraculous about my teas," I said. "They're fresh, which is why they taste so good. And people have used teas for thousands of years to help with various aliments. If mine provide some sort of relief, I'm happy, but there's nothing more to it than that, I can promise you."

"Of course there's not."

I really didn't like the direction of the conversation at all. "Anyway, I thought you were busy helping finding Polly. Have you yet?"

She gave me another secret smile. "Not yet. But I have been assured she's alive and healthy."

I stared at her. There was something about that smile that was setting my teeth on edge. Actually, it was more than that. I was getting a very bad feeling that there was something wrong, although whether it was just about the dead body or Polly, I couldn't be sure. "If you don't know where she is, how can you possibly know that?"

Rowena started to drift away. "The spirits told me, of course. All will be revealed when it's time."

"I hope for your sake she IS alive and healthy. Otherwise, giving her parents false hope is cruel."

She continued moving away from me. "All I can do is share what the spirits have told me," she said. "They haven't let me down yet."

"Hopefully, you're right," I said, but the only feeling I had was dread.

Chapter 10

"So, let me get this straight," Pat said. We were sitting in Aunt May's with cups of coffee in front of us. After the morning I'd had, I decided I needed something stronger than tea, and Aunt May's coffee was pretty decent. My initial plan was to get it to-go, but once I walked in, I also decided I deserved a nice big breakfast. So, I went back outside to a nearby pay phone to give Pat a quick call to see if she could meet me.

I also thought it might not be a terrible idea to keep an eye on how the rest of the town would respond to the news of the murder.

Even though people were used to a more-than-normal share of bad things happening in Redemption, a dead body on top of a missing girl and a would-be vampire might be a little too much for even it to swallow.

Pat started to tick things off of one hand. "We now have a dead body, a missing girl, AND a missing homeowner. I'm still in shock. Jonas, missing! How does someone go on vacation and never arrive at his destination?"

"Obviously, something happened to him," I said.

Pat gave me a look. "I get that. But don't you think it's creepy? Jonas's first vacation in how long? I'm sure he was so looking forward to the break, but instead of relaxing by the pool with a fruity alcoholic drink, something terrible happens, and he never even makes it."

"I doubt there were pools or fruity alcohol drinks involved, where Jonas was going," I said. "But point taken. It is kind of scary. Although to be fair to Drake, he may have had nothing to do with Jonas disappearing. It's very possible something hap-pened while Jonas was on the road. Or maybe there's nothing wrong with Jonas at all, and the cops just haven't been able to track him down yet."

"That would probably be more persuasive if Polly hadn't vanished," Pat said. "Not to mention the whole vampire thing."

"*Alleged* vampire thing," I said. "I honestly don't believe Drake is a vampire."

Pat raised her eyebrows. "Well, there is something up with him. He's been here, what, less than a month, and we're up to three missing/dead people?"

I had to admit, it didn't look very good for Drake. "Maybe he's just unlucky."

Pat picked up her coffee. "If that's true, I would say it's a massive understatement."

"Well, there's got to be a connection somewhere," I said. "I don't believe in coincidences."

"Sure, there's a connection," Pat said. "He's a hungry vampire."

I made a face. "*Other* than that."

Pat tilted her head. "Why are you so convinced he's not?"

"Other than there's no such thing as vampires, you mean?"

Pat grinned. "Well, yeah. Other than that. You have to admit, if he's not one, he's doing a bang-up imitation of one."

I thought about Drake standing outside, every inch of him covered by black clothes, making his face look so white, he did resemble the undead. "Yeah, he's sure not making this any easier on himself."

"It is Redemption, after all," Pat said. "Is it so farfetched to think a vampire might have found his way here?"

"In a word, yes," I answered, spinning my coffee cup around. "But it's more than just the nonexistence of vampires. There's just … something about him. It's hard to explain, but there's something almost desperate about him."

"Well, he would be desperate, wouldn't he? He doesn't want his secret out and risk the rest of the town coming after with him pitchforks and torches."

"Yes, if he really is a vampire, that would be an issue, but …" I paused, trying to figure out how to put my feelings into words.

"Okay, look. When Mildred and I went over there, the guy was a total jerk. There was nothing all that friendly, or likable, about him. But behind that facade, I just got this sense of a scared little boy. Think about it. If he is truly allergic to the sun, and I suspect he was telling the truth about that, what a depressing way to live. He can never go outside except at night. Think of how difficult it would be for him to make friends, trapped inside all the time. Not only is he probably really lonely, but he likely doesn't have anyone in his corner. So if he WAS blamed for something, even if it wasn't his fault, what is he going to do? He'd have no one to defend him. And for all we know, this is a recurring trend in his life. People think he's weird, or worse, a vampire, and they make his life difficult until he's forced to leave and find the next place. Then, the cycle continues."

"Yeah, I guess I can see that," Pat said. "But as you pointed out, there are things he could do to make life easier on himself. Like being friendlier and more open about his condition. What if he had walked over to Mildred's shortly after he moved in to introduce himself and explain it? She probably would have been sympathetic instead of suspicious. Not that I blame her for being suspicious."

"I don't either," I said. "She's an eighty-year-old woman living alone next to a man who is acting decidedly strange. She needs to be vigilant. And I'm not going to argue with you that Drake didn't help make this mess he is now finding himself in much worse by his actions. But …" I held up my hands. "You and I both know people let their emotions control their actions. And if he's been hurt over and over, can you blame him for not wanting to take a chance on opening himself up to more rejection? Plus, how many people with conditions just randomly approach others to explain them?"

Pat sighed. "You're right. And no, I can't blame him, if that's the case."

From the corner of my eye, I saw the kitchen door swing open, and Sue appeared, holding two plates of food—what appeared to be my vegetable omelet and Pat's tall stack of pancakes. I watched her weave her way across the restaurant toward us. "Unfortunately for Drake, the best he can hope for at this point is for Wyle to discover who really killed Harrison."

"Did I hear you just say 'Harrison'?" Sue asked as she appeared at our table.

Oops. Even though Wyle had informed me right before I left Mildred's neighborhood that they had found Harrison's next of kin, I wasn't sure if that meant I ought to be the one to let everyone know who the dead body was. "Yes, I did."

"Harrison? Are you talking about Harrison Shaw?" Sue asked, depositing our plates of food in front of us.

I looked at her in surprise. "Yeah, that's him. Do you know him?"

Her lips were pressed into a straight line. "Not personally, no. But I've heard enough about him. If he was the one who was found dead in a backyard today, let's just say it doesn't surprise me."

My ears perked up. Could this be a motive? "Really?"

"Yeah, he's awful. Especially if you work for him. He's not too bad if you're a renter, and you pay your rent on time and don't ask for any special favors, but ..." she gave her head a quick shake. "I shouldn't speak so badly of him. He was a regular."

I blinked. "Really? He was in here every day?"

"Well, no. His assistant is, though. She comes in and picks it up. But you already know her."

"I do?"

Sue nodded. "Yes, it's Linda."

* * *

"You think she'll talk to us?" Pat asked as we strolled down the sidewalk toward Shaw's Property Management and Rental Company.

"I have no idea," I said. "She's not all that sociable."

"It's possible she's not even in the office," Pat said. "Or if she is, she might not even know he's dead."

"Yeah, I thought about that," I said. "So, we might have to come back. I don't think we should be the one to tell her. But we can at least re-establish a connection … see if we can get her to open up some and tell us about her boss."

"Anything would be helpful at this point," Pat said as we turned down the side street where the business was located, along with a laundromat, in a squat, dull, red-bricked building.

According to Sue, Shaw's Property Management and Rental Company managed a variety of apartment and office buildings located both in Redemption and in Riverview, but the headquarters were here. I wondered why, as Riverview was much larger than Redemption, so it seemed like it would be smarter to be centrally located there. But since Riverview was a larger city, Harrison could maybe charge higher rent, and preferred to rent out the space he would otherwise use for himself.

I pushed open the glass door, and we entered a large, plain room lit with fluorescent lights that gave everything a slightly green cast. The floors were covered with linoleum, and it was filled with cheap furniture—pressed wood desks and uncomfortable-looking chairs. It smelled musty and of old, recirculated air. Three people were working, all of whom glanced up when we walked in.

"There's Linda," I said out of the corner of my mouth as I plastered a surprised smile on my face. Linda was sitting at a desk near the back next to an open door, which led to an actual office, presumably Harrison's. She stood up quickly when she saw me wave, her expression startled, and hurried toward us.

"What are you doing here?" she asked, then immediately flushed, as if realizing how bad that sounded. "I mean, how can I help you?"

"Linda," I said. "I didn't know you worked here. What a nice surprise."

She nodded. Now that she was closer, I could see that her eyes were red and her makeup smudged. Had she been crying? Over Harrison? I thought about how Sue had talked about what a bully he was to Linda. Had Sue been wrong?

"Did you need something?" she asked again.

"Maybe. You know I sell teas and tinctures out of my home, right? I was thinking about maybe opening up an actual shop, maybe in downtown Redemption. I thought it would be great for walk-in traffic, you know, during tourist season? Anyway, everyone said I should come here and talk to Harrison, to see what's available to rent. Is he in?"

Linda's face seemed to fold in on itself, and I wondered if she was trying to hold back tears. "This isn't a good time," she said.

"What's going on?" I asked, taking a few steps toward Linda. I didn't have to fake my concern—Linda truly didn't look right. Her skin had a grey pallor, maybe because she was wearing a grey blouse paired with black pants, but there were also bluish-purple bruises under her eyes. Over her shoulder, I noticed one of the other workers, a thin, balding man wearing a light-green button-down shirt with a blue tie, watching our exchange very closely. A little too closely, for my taste.

She shook her head, dabbing at her eyes with a crumpled-up tissue. "I … I … I shouldn't be this upset."

"Upset about what?" I asked, although I could probably guess.

Linda shook her head again before glancing over her shoulder to the other worker. "Westly?"

He sighed and stood up to move toward her. "I don't think it's a secret, Linda. Word is going to get out sooner or later."

"Word about what?" I asked, hoping I looked as bewildered as someone who didn't know what was going on would. I glanced at Pat, who had widened her eyes, almost too wide, like an insane clown. I frowned at her. She quickly ducked her head and worked on rearranging her expression.

Luckily for both of us, Westly and Linda weren't paying any attention. Westly was looking at Linda, and Linda was busy taking deep breaths and dabbing at her eyes. "It's Harrison. He's … he's dead."

"Dead?" I covered my mouth with my hand. "Oh my goodness. What happened? Was he sick? Did he have an accident or something?"

"Was it a heart attack?" Pat interjected.

Linda shook her head violently. "No, he was … murdered."

She was so distraught, I didn't have to pretend to be shocked. "Here, why don't we sit down?" I asked, grabbing her elbow and guiding her to the nearest chair, which was a hard wooden one placed in a corner with two others in a weird little circle. I wondered if that was supposed to be the lobby or waiting area of the sad room with its cheap white linoleum, plain brown furniture, and beige painted walls.

Linda sat in one chair, and Pat and I took the other two. "Can we get you something? Some water, or …?" I asked.

She gulped. "There's a water cooler, but it's in Harrison's office, and I just can't …"

"I'll go," Westly said, quickly heading toward the open office door. The third worker, a middle-aged man with thick black glasses and a black beard wearing a heavy, brown, button-down shirt, ignored all of us, instead murmuring quietly into the phone.

Westly returned with a paper cup of water and a box of tissues. Linda took the water and smiled at him, which nearly took my breath away. When she smiled, the colorless waif disappeared, and her face was completely transformed … like those movies wherein the plain girl takes off her glasses and becomes instantly beautiful.

"So," I said, after she had taken a sip of water. Westly had dragged another chair over to join us in the corner. "What happened?"

"I don't know much," she said, staring into the cup resting on her lap. "The cops are still investigating, but I guess his body was found this morning. It was in a backyard somewhere."

"Wow," I said. "So, it wasn't in his own backyard?"

She shook her head, balling the tissue in her fist. "No. It's someone named … Jonas?" she squished up her face as she glanced at Westly for help. "Or was it Drake something?"

I bit my lip to keep from answering.

"I think it was Jonas who owned the house. Drake is house-sitting," Westly said.

"That was it," Linda said. "The cops wanted to know if we knew either of them, but I hadn't heard of them."

"Neither was doing business with Harrison?" I asked.

"Not to my knowledge, but of course, he didn't tell me everything." Was it my imagination, or was there a bitter note to her voice?

"You're his assistant, right?"

She nodded. "His 'executive assistant,' at least that's what he calls … err, called me."

"So, you handled his calendar? Knew his appointments?"

Another nod. "That was the idea, but of course, there were things he didn't run through me that he scheduled himself. Then it would be my fault if something fell through the cracks or got double-booked."

"Well, that's hardly fair," I said, trying to cover up the disappointment I felt when I heard he did some of his own scheduling.

She gave me a twisted smile, nothing like the one Westly had provoked. "That's Harrison." Her expression became appalled. "I shouldn't speak ill of the dead."

"Why not?" Westly asked, a touch of anger in his tone. "He was a terrible boss. His being dead doesn't change that."

"Westly," Linda gasped. "But he was murdered."

"Are you that surprised?" Westly asked. Two spots of red had appeared in his cheeks, making him look younger than I originally thought when I saw him with his prematurely balding head. Now that I got a closer look at him, he was probably younger than me. "If anyone had a target on his back, it was Harrison."

"But, still? Killing someone? That's so extreme!"

"I don't understand why you're so upset about this," Westly blurted out. He was getting more and more agitated. "Is this about Donny?"

Linda turned white. For a moment, I was afraid she was going to faint, so I reached out to squeeze her hand, which was ice cold. "Breathe," I murmured as I tried to remember who Donny was. The name rang a bell, but I couldn't place it.

Luckily, Pat could. "Donny? Are you talking about Donny Pembrook? Polly's brother?"

"That's him," Westly said darkly. Linda was violently chewing her lip.

"What does Donny have to do with Harrison?" Pat asked.

"Nothing," Linda said. "Nothing at all."

"He was one of our renters, until a couple of months ago," Westley said.

"What happened?" I asked.

"Harrison kicked him out, that's what," Westly said.

"It was all a horrible misunderstanding," Linda said. "He had nothing to do with it."

"Do with what?" I asked.

"There was a party," Westly explained. "The cops were called, and they found drugs on the premises. They arrested Donny."

"They weren't even his drugs," Linda said. "Someone else brought them."

"Nevertheless," Westly said. "That's against the terms of the lease, and Harrison evicted him."

"Wow," I said. "How did Donny take it?"

"Not well," Westly answered. "He showed up here one day to argue with Harrison, who threatened to call the cops again. So, yeah, it wasn't good."

"Harrison should have given him another chance," Linda said. "It wasn't Donny's fault. He doesn't do drugs."

"Harrison had given him a lot of chances," Westly corrected. "Donny just wasn't a good tenant. This wasn't the first time the cops had been called because of a party he was having, although as far as I know, it *was* the first time anyone had been arrested. But Donny was late with the rent a lot, too. I suspect it was the final straw for Harrison."

"So, you think Donny might have been looking for revenge?" I asked.

"No!" Linda said quickly. "I mean, yes, he was angry that day, but he wouldn't have hurt Harrison."

"He literally threatened Harrison … told him he better watch his back," Westly said.

"It was just talk," Linda said. "He wouldn't have gone through with anything."

I glanced at Pat and knew she was thinking the same thing I was—a connection between Polly and Harrison. Was it possible we had this completely wrong? That Harrison's death had nothing to do with either Jonas or Drake, and we should instead be looking more closely at the Donny-Harrison-Polly triangle?

"Did Harrison know Polly?" I asked.

Linda balked. "You think Harrison took Polly?"

"I don't know. But it's certainly a strange coincidence that Polly's brother and Harrison had such a massive falling out, especially now that Polly is missing and Harrison is dead."

"Donny had nothing to do with Polly's disappearance," Linda said quickly. "He loves his sister."

"I didn't say anything about Donny being involved with Polly's disappearance," I said carefully. "I was asking about the connection between Polly and Harrison."

"I don't know if they knew each other or not," Westly said. "I mean, if they did, it was nothing obvious, like Donny renting from Harrison. I'm not sure if Harrison knew or cared whether Donny has siblings."

"Yeah, what Westly said," Linda said, the tension oozing from her face. "I'm sorry. I'm just not myself. This has been an awful week. First Polly disappearing, and now Harrison ..."

Westly's face softened. "It has been stressful," he agreed. "Especially today, with the cops showing up. No one wants to be part of a murder investigation. Even if it is for a terrible boss."

Linda blanched at the words "murder investigation," although she didn't swoop in to defend Harrison like she had before.

"What do you do here, Westly?" I asked.

"I'm the accounting department," he said. "I do the books, make the deposits, pay the vendors, all that good stuff."

"Is the business profitable?" I asked.

He snorted. "Very. Although you wouldn't know it by looking at this dump. You'd think he could put a little money toward making this place look decent, but … well, that's Harrison for you."

"He did pay us well," Linda said.

Westly snorted again. "Of course he did. Otherwise, would either of us have put up with his crap?"

Linda looked like she was going to argue, but instead let out a sigh. "You're right. I shouldn't be so upset about Harrison being killed. He *was* awful. And he had made a lot of enemies over the years, so it's not that farfetched to think one of them could have done it. But then I start to think, what if it wasn't one of Harrison's enemies, after all?"

"You're not serious," Westly said. "Again, if anyone had a target on his back, it was Harrison."

Linda squeezed her tissue tighter. "Yes, but even so, that might not be why he was killed. What if it was for some other reason … and what if, now that Harrison is gone, we're next?" Her voice dropped, and her hand trembled slightly.

"No. I'm sure that's not the case," Westly said. His voice was firm, yet I was sure I detected a note of uncertainty. His face had gone a shade paler, as well. I wondered if there was something else he knew … maybe something in the books that would warrant a cause for alarm.

"What other reason would there be?" I asked Linda.

"I don't *know*," Linda answered, her voice revealing a touch of anguish. "That's the problem. What if Harrison was involved in some sort of shady business deal we don't know anything about? And what if whoever killed him thinks we do?"

I had to admit, that wasn't as farfetched as some of the other theories that had been bandied about. It certainly had a lot more teeth to it than a hungry vampire, no pun intended. "Was that something Harrison did? Get involved with other deals and not tell you?"

"Harrison barely kept us in the picture on THIS business, never mind what else was gong on in his life," Westly said bitterly.

"So, it's possible Harrison was involved in something disreputable, or even illegal," I said. Linda turned green.

"Yeah, unfortunately, it's very possible," Westly agreed.

"It still doesn't explain how Harrison's body ended up in Jonas's backyard though," Pat said. "Unless you think Jonas was the one involved in something illegal."

"Maybe a mail fraud ring," I contemplated. "But Pat is right. It's certainly possible, but not probable. And I wouldn't think you would be in any danger, if it were true." I gave Linda's hand a squeeze, hoping that would be enough to calm her. The last thing I wanted was for her to have a nervous breakdown, which looked more possible in the moment than some sketchy individual putting a hit out on her.

"But you just said it *is* possible," Linda said.

"I said it is possible Harrison was killed because he was involved in something fishy. I don't think it's possible they'd go after you, or Westly, or anyone else here next," I said firmly.

Linda didn't look convinced. "But …"

"No 'buts,'" I said. "Honestly, if this is about a business deal gone bad, the last thing those folks will want is to draw more attention to themselves. They're going to disappear as quickly as possible. And if you don't come across as any sort of a threat, *which you won't,* since you don't know anything, I can't imagine anything is going to happen to you."

Linda mulled over my words. I was relieved to see some color returning to her cheeks. "I suppose you have a point," she said.

Thank goodness she was starting to see reason. "All that said, this isn't to say you shouldn't be vigilant and keep an eye out for anything suspicious going on around you. I just don't think you need to lose any sleep over it. In fact, if it does turn out to be a business deal gone bad, that's probably the best scenario for everyone involved."

Linda looked surprised. "Really? Why?"

"Because it doesn't have anything to do with you or anyone else in this town, which means we'd likely not see any more murders," I said. "Harrison will be it. Plus, it's something the cops should be able to track down pretty quickly. You did tell the cops, right?"

Linda frowned. "No, but maybe I should. Officer Wyle did give me his card." She looked pensive, and I noticed Westly shifting a little uncomfortably. I wondered if Westly had said anything to Wyle about Donny.

"Yes, I think you should call him," I said. "Tell him everything you told me. He's probably going to reassure you the same as I did, which will hopefully make you feel a lot better, too."

Linda was bobbing her head up and down. "Yes, yes. That's true. I do have a dreadful habit of worrying too much. It's hard not to."

"I get it, but I think you have to try and do a better job of breaking that habit for the sake of your mental health. Maybe there's something else you can focus on, like your job. I mean, do you know what's going to happen now?"

"We don't know," Westly said. "Harrison's brother will inherit the business, assuming Harrison didn't change his will without telling anyone."

First the calendar, and now, his will. Apparently, Harrison truly didn't keep them apprised of the information they needed to do their jobs. I was also starting to wonder why Harrison even bothered with employees, if he was set on doing everything himself anyhow. "I guess you aren't kidding about Harrison keeping you in the dark a lot," I said.

"I wish I was," Westly said. "I can't tell you how much I hated reconciling the accounts at the end of each month. I would invariably have to track him down and ask him about withdrawals, and occasionally, deposits. And then, if he was in one of his moods, I'd get yelled at for not reading his mind or knowing the answers. In reality, he would write checks and take money out without telling me."

"He sounds like a peach," Pat said drily.

"Oh, that's just the half of it," Westly said.

"So, why do you stay?" I asked. "Money?"

"Pretty much," Westly said, although a faint flush had crept up his neck. "There was a reason that cheap bastard paid us so well. And trust me, he paid us very well. I'd make less than half of my current salary at a normal accounting job."

That was significant. Did he pay so well so people would keep their mouths shut? Not ask questions?

"Back to what happens to the business—if it goes to Harrison's brother, do you have any idea what he plans on doing with it?"

"It sounds like he'll keep it going, at least for now," Westly said.

Linda nodded. "He called this morning after he heard the news. He told us the cops would be by to ask us a few questions and assured us our jobs were safe, at least for the time being. He said he has no plans to do anything different with the business, and we should just keep it going like normal. But I'm not sure how we're going to do that. I mean, look at you." She gestured toward me. "You want to rent a retail space, and I'm not even sure who you should talk to. Harrison was the one who kept all that stuff in his head."

"We haven't checked his files," Westly said. "There might be something in there."

I had completely forgotten my reason for being there. "What about him?" I gestured with my head toward Black Beard, who was still on the phone.

"Ned? He's our handyman," Westly said. "Although," he made a point of raising his voice. "Why he's here and not out fixing something is beyond me."

Ned ignored him, continuing his phone conversation.

Westly shook his head. "Anyway. We're going to have to get back to you about that retail space. I hope you understand."

"Of course. Don't even worry about it," I said, waving my hand dismissively. "I'm not even sure I want a tea shop. I just thought I'd look into it and see what it would take."

Linda flashed me a tiny smile. "Thanks, Charlie. Can I give you a call once we've had a chance to figure things out?"

"Yes, yes, let me give you my number," I said, getting up to follow Linda as she made her way to her desk. "And really, no rush on any of this. This is a difficult enough time for all of you without worrying about me."

"I appreciate that," Linda said, sliding open the top drawer of her desk. I noticed how plain it was, like everything else in the office. Nothing personal anywhere, not even a framed picture.

She pulled out a notebook, plucked out a pen from her pen holder, and took down my name and number. "Also, that number is good if you just need to talk, too," I offered. "I'm here for you, okay?"

She glanced at me, her eyes shiny, and for a moment, I thought she was going to cry again. Instead, she smiled. "Thank you. That means a lot to me." I had the sudden feeling Linda didn't have very many friends, and I wondered if maybe that was part of why she seemed like a breath away from a breakdown. Between the stress of working for a massive jerk and not having a few friends to let off steam with, it must eventually take its toll.

On an impulse, I leaned over and gave her a hug. It was like hugging a baby bird—I could feel her bones under her grey silk shirt. She smelled like burnt coffee and mint gum. I wondered if she was eating decently, or just living on caffeine.

"Take care of yourself," I whispered.

She nodded against my shoulder. I gave her one last squeeze before I let her go.

Pat was already standing up and waiting for me. I headed over to join her after saying goodbye to Westly.

"Sorry we couldn't help," he said again.

"Really, don't worry about it," I repeated. I glanced over at Ned, intending to wave goodbye to him, too, but he glared at me from under his black bushy eyebrows as he continued his phone conversation.

The sun seemed brighter than normal after being in the fluorescent lights. I squinted as I fumbled for my sunglasses, breathing in big gulps of air that seemed even more fresh and clean than before.

"What do you think?" Pat asked as she stuck a pair of oversized sunglasses on her face.

"About which part?"

"About what happened to Harrison. Do you think it was some sort of shadowy figure involved in some dubious deal?"

"Maybe," I said. "But as you pointed out, that doesn't explain how his body ended up in Jonas's backyard."

"No, it doesn't. It also doesn't explain Polly … although to be fair, Polly might not have anything to do with this," Pat said.

"Yeah, but I don't know," I said, chewing on my lip. "This just seems like way too many coincidences. Since Drake started housesitting a few weeks ago, two people have gone missing, Jonas and Polly, and a third has been murdered and dumped in his backyard. Deeming them unrelated coincidences seems way too much to swallow."

Pat gave me a sideways glance. "Well, what's our next move?"

I paused as I mulled everything I knew about this case. So far, there were connections between Drake and Jonas and Harrison and Drake/Jonas's house. But, now we also had a connection between Polly and Harrison, or more specifically, Polly's *brother* and Harrison.

"I think it's time we stopped in to see how Polly's parents are doing," I said. "See if there's anything we can do to help."

Pat flashed me a knowing smile. "And if a certain brother just happens to be there?"

"You won't hear any complaining from me," I said.

Chapter 11

"Can I help you?"

The woman who answered the door looked exactly like you would expect the mother of a missing daughter would—her face was creased and puffy from lack of sleep, and a pair of glasses covered bloodshot eyes. Her hair was greasy in its partial ponytail, and her blue track suit was stained.

"Darlene?" Pat asked. "It's me, Pat Barron."

Darlene Pembrook blinked owlishly at Pat before her expression cleared. "Oh, Pat. Of course. I'm so sorry I didn't … I can't believe …"

"Don't even worry about it," Pat said quickly. "We haven't seen each other in what, three, four years now? Plus, you've had a terrible time. I'm sure I wouldn't have recognized my own husband if Barbara had gone missing when she was a teenager."

Darlene mustered a faint smile. Pat hadn't been sure Darlene would even be at the house, as she was pretty sure she had a full-time job as a school secretary, but we thought we'd give it a shot anyway.

"This is my friend Charlie Kingsley," Pat said. I smiled and held up a tin of my famous chocolate chip cookies and a bag of tea.

"Charlie sells teas. You may have heard of her?" Pat continued. "Her teas are amazing. They've pretty much cured my insomnia."

"Oh, yes, I have heard about your teas," Darlene confirmed. "Nancy has been raving about them."

"Yes, Nancy was my first customer," I said. "I know it's not much, but I thought I'd bring over my lemon-lavender blend.

It's my most popular, and it's really good at helping with anxiety and worry."

"That's really kind of you. Not necessary, of course, but thank you. Would you like to come in?" Darlene held the door open wider.

"If it's not too much trouble," Pat said.

"No, no. At this point, it's just a waiting game." Darlene sighed. "I wouldn't mind the company, quite frankly."

The sadness and loneliness in her voice cut my heart in two. Maybe Pat and I should have stopped by sooner, instead of waiting until we needed information from her. I kept my head down, not wanting her to see the guilt on my face.

Now, I was even more motivated to find Polly.

"Oh, cookies … the kids will love them," Darlene said, taking the tin from me.

"If you want, I'm happy to make us a pot of tea," I said. "Just point me in the direction of the kitchen."

"You really don't have to do that," Darlene said.

"I don't mind," I said.

"Trust me, you want her to make it," Pat said. "I don't know what fairy dust she sprinkles in it, but the difference between what she makes and other stuff is extraordinary."

"Normally, I would say to have at it," Darlene said. "But right now, the kitchen is an absolute disaster."

"Don't worry about it," I said quickly. "I'd love for you to sit down and relax for a bit."

Darlene didn't look completely convinced, but she began leading me toward the kitchen. I noticed she paused by what appeared to be a large school photo of a blonde, smiling girl.

"That's Polly," Darlene said, noticing me looking at it.

"She's lovely," I said. She was pretty in a perky, cheerleader kind of way.

Darlene nodded, ducking her head slightly. "Thank you." She turned to continue walking to the kitchen, and I hurried to catch up.

As soon as I stepped into it, I could see why Darlene was so hesitant to have us there. It was indeed a disaster—overflowing with dirty dishes, take-out cartons, and pizza boxes. I wrinkled my nose, trying not to breathe in the scents of old, greasy food.

"Oh dear," she said, surveying the mess. "It's even worse than I thought. I can do it …"

"Nonsense," I said firmly, grabbing the tea kettle and moving to the sink. "It will only take a minute to wash a few of these mugs, and I can do that while the water is boiling. Go sit down with Pat, please. I'll join you in a minute."

"But you're a guest. This isn't right," Darlene fretted.

"Trust me, I'm happy to help," I said. "Go on." I made shooing motions with my hands, and Darlene reluctantly joined Pat at the table.

"I know this is probably a ridiculous question, but how are you holding up?" Pat asked after they were both seated at the huge kitchen table.

Darlene sighed. "It's been difficult, as you can imagine."

Pat squeezed her hand. "I'm just so sorry. It must be terrible. I take it there's no news then?"

"No. There's no sign of her. The cops haven't found a single lead. There's some talk that she might have run away, but Polly wouldn't have done that. She's a good kid … she wouldn't have done that to us. No. I'm sure something must have happened to her. And …" she pressed her fingertips to her temple. "I can't stop thinking about it. What she must be going through. I almost can't stand it, the not knowing. And it makes everything even worse when I'm alone, which seems like all the time now."

Pat looked perplexed. "What do you mean? Where's Steve and the rest of the kids? And aren't you still working for the school?"

"Yes, but I'm on a two-week paid leave. The cops want someone here all the time, twenty-four hours a day, in case Polly calls or shows up, and I'm the one." Her smile was twisted.

"But the rest of your family surely must be here at night," Pat said as I brought the tea to the table.

Darlene spun the mug in her hands but didn't drink it. "Steve spends his days at the office and his nights searching for Polly. The older kids are also joining in the search, and the younger ones are with my mother. I told my mother it was fine … that I wouldn't mind having the kids here with me, but she thinks it would be better if they stayed with her for a bit."

I was starting to understand the loneliness in Darlene's eyes. "Other people aren't coming by?" I asked, sitting across from her.

Darlene shook her head. "A few do. Mostly people who are single or have grown kids. The ones with younger children …" she paused and looked down in her tea. "I can see it in their eyes. They're terrified one of their kids will go missing, too … like it's a disease they might catch from me. I know they don't mean it, and I get it. I would probably feel the same way, if I were them."

"That's rough," I said as the guilt twisted the knife in my gut a few more times. I definitely should have stopped in sooner. I made a mental note right then and there to check in with Darlene again in a few days.

"Well, you'd think with all this time on my hands, the house would be spotless, but, well, I was never very good at cleaning." It was clear she was going for light-hearted, but it fell flat.

"No one expects you to have a clean house," I said empathetically. "The important thing is, you're here … so when Polly shows up, it's not to an empty home."

"That's right," Pat said. "Clean houses are overrated, anyway."

Darlene almost laughed. "All right, all right. I'll stop worrying about it."

"Good," Pat said before nudging her mug. "Now try your tea."

Darlene obediently picked it up and took a sip. Her eyes widened. "Oh, you're right. This is really good."

"Thanks," I said.

"Hopefully, it will help keep you calm, as well," Pat said. "This is one of my favorites for helping me relax and unwind at night."

"Yeah, I definitely need help at night," Darlene said. "That's when everything gets worse, and again, there's usually no one here to talk to."

"So, these searches," I said. "Is the police department organizing them?"

"Not really," Darlene said. "They did a few of them in the beginning, but now, it's mostly Steve and Donny spearheading them."

My ears perked up at Donny's name. "What are they searching for, exactly? And where?"

"Around the lake, mostly. And the woods."

"The lake?" Pat asked. "They don't think …"

Darlene quickly shook her head. "No, no one thinks she drowned or anything like that, although the cops are talking about dragging it if there's no sign of her in the next week or so."

Pat blanched, but hid it with her cup.

"So, why are they searching there, then?" I asked. "Is there a reason to think Polly would have gotten lost in the woods? Was she real outdoorsy?"

A ghost of a smile touched Darlene's lips. "Oh, heaven's no. Polly was the girl who hated sleeping in the dirt with all the bugs and spiders. We had to drag her the few times we took her camping. She wasn't even that fond of being in a cabin. She's definitely a city girl … she can't wait to leave Redemption."

"Was there a party at The Rock the night she went missing?" Pat asked. The Rock was a popular gathering spot for teenagers, named for the giant rock standing in the middle of a clearing just off the road on top of a hill. It was surrounded by woods, and a couple of miles away was the lake. Every year, a couple of kids invariably went missing from one of these parties. Most of them were found a few hours, or even a day or so later, usually wandering around the woods or passed out under a bush.

Most of them.

But not all.

"No. At least I don't think so. Timmy said there wasn't. He's in the grade behind Polly, so he should know. And that was the first question the cops asked all the kids. They seemed satisfied there wasn't one that night," Darlene said.

"Then, why there?" I asked.

Darlene sighed. "It's those old stories," she said. "About the kids disappearing and being returned. Around the lake."

The skin at the back of my neck started to crawl. First Mildred, and now Darlene. How many missing kids' stories could there be around this town?

"What kids?" Pat asked.

"Don't you remember? The story about the girl who disappeared for a few days before they found her near the lake?"

"They said Redemption took her," I said slowly, as that crawling sensation slowly traveled down into my chest.

Darlene met my eyes. "Exactly. And Redemption brought her back."

Pat glanced at me, and I could see the concern in her eyes. We both knew the two major players in that one.

Claire.

And Louise.

"So, Steve thinks Redemption took Polly?" Pat asked.

"It's what makes the most sense," Darlene said. "Way more sense than some stranger."

Or *vampire*, I thought. Pat must have read my mind, because she made a face at me.

"So, that's why Steve is spending as much time as he can patrolling the lake and woods. When Redemption returns Polly, he wants to be there to bring her home," Darlene explained.

"What if Redemption didn't take her?" I asked.

Darlene smiled her twisted smile. "Why do you think I'm the one stuck here at home waiting for her? I'm Plan B."

Well, that explained a lot. Darlene probably thought Polly had been taken by Redemption as well, but as she was the one who had agreed to stay home, she also wouldn't be able to be one of the first to welcome her daughter once she was returned.

"Is there any other reason you think Redemption took Polly?" I asked. "Other than it makes more sense than a stranger?"

"What do you mean?" Darlene asked.

"Well, like, what was going on before Polly disappeared? Was there anything that made you suspicious? Anything you thought odd?"

"Not really. At least nothing at the time. It was a typical hectic night. The twins had tryouts for the school musical, Candy had dance practice, and Timmy had a game. I was of course trying to be in all places at once, because Steve had to work late. I'm sure Polly told me she was going to her friend's house to study."

"You're *sure?*" Pat asked. "Or is there some question about it?"

Darlene pressed her lips together in a straight line. "No one else remembers hearing it. I was sure she'd said it … that she was going to go study with Kim. Kim is her best friend, so I wouldn't think to question it. But Kim said later that she knew nothing about it. In fact, it couldn't have been her, because it was her brother's birthday, and they were having a big family party. But if she wasn't studying at Kim's house, then whose house was she at? I called her other friends, but none of them knew anything about a study night."

I met Pat's eyes and could see the same question in them. Maybe Polly had run away, after all. It sure sounded like she was planning something she didn't want her parents knowing about.

"So, Polly left and didn't come home," I said.

Darlene nodded miserably. "I didn't worry, because again, I thought she was with Kim." Her voice was almost pleading, as if begging us—or maybe herself—to understand. "Sometimes, when it's a particularly late study session, she just spends the night. I never worry about her when she's at Kim's house. I know her mother keeps a very sharp eye on the kids."

The more Darlene talked about that night, the more she seemed to collapse in on herself, almost like a deflated balloon. "I mean, she's almost seventeen years old, and she's always been so responsible. And the other kids, well, they're just more … they need me more. That night, by the time I got everyone to and from all the places they needed to be, and fed, and 'home-worked,' I was exhausted. Steve was too, as he has this huge project that has required a lot of extra hours. As soon as he gets home, he's off to bed. So, we just … well, we both assumed that Polly was fine. She'd either be home later that night after she was done studying, or she'd spend the night with Kim."

It occurred to me then that what Darlene was really saying was that she hadn't even noticed her daughter wasn't home. The guilt must be eating her up inside. No wonder why she agreed to this exile, trapped alone in the house with only her thoughts to keep her company. She was destined to be the parent who wouldn't find Polly, and she probably thought she deserved it.

"You did the best you could," I said. "That's a lot of kids to keep track of and shuttle around to different places. With Polly not only being responsible, but almost an adult, I can see why you weren't as worried about her."

"I still should have called," Darlene said. "And normally, I do. Or Kim's mother calls me. She's usually very good about that, and if we're not home, she'll leave a message. But it was …" she shook her head hard. Tears were glistening on her lashes. "I should have paid more attention. I was just so exhausted. With Steve working so much, I had to do everything, and I was just … I was just at the end of my rope. And I don't blame Steve. He's working so hard on this project, because if it goes well, he'll get a promotion. And that extra money would really help us out. We both knew it would be a sacrifice, but we also knew it would only be for a short period of time, and we thought we could handle it. But if it costs us Polly …" Darlene gulped and grabbed a paper napkin from the table to press to her face.

"Hey," Pat said, reaching over to squeeze her hand. "We don't know that yet. She could walk through that door any minute."

Darlene sucked in a deep breath as she dabbed at her eyes. "You're right. I can't lose faith."

"Pat is right," I said. "And you did discover her missing pretty quickly. What tipped you off?"

"I got a call asking how Polly was doing," Darlene said. "It was the administrative secretary at the high school. She's a good friend … we have kids who are the same age. Anyway, she had a free moment in her day and decided to give me a call. Obviously, Polly not being at school was news to me, and the rest is history."

"So, when did Steve start suspecting that Redemption took Polly?" I asked.

"When there was no sign of her," Darlene said. "It was like she disappeared into thin air. Poof." Darlene waved her hands like a magician. "No one saw anything. No one seems to know anything. If someone had taken her, surely there would be some evidence of that somewhere, right? And if she had run away, wouldn't she have told someone? Or packed a bag or something? What else could it be?"

"That is really suspicious," I agreed. "But what made Steve think about the stories of the kids disappearing?"

Darlene balled up the paper napkin and picked up her tea. "You haven't lived here very long, have you?"

I smiled. "Is it that obvious?"

"Well, if you had, or if you had grown up here, you'd know it's just what happens here. Everyone knows these stories. They're just part of … living in Redemption. Strange things happen. People disappear, never to be heard from again. And now, it's beginning to look like it's happened to Polly, too." Darlene's eyes filled with new tears, and she plunked the tea cup down onto the table, spilling some over the sides. She buried her face in her wet napkin, and her voice was so low and muffled, I almost missed what she said next.

"I just hope and pray Redemption returns her."

Chapter 12

"Poor Darlene," Pat said. We were back in my kitchen, tea in front of us again, and I was back to baking. Not only had I given Darlene the last of my cookies, but baking soothed me.

"I can't even imagine the nightmare she's going through."

I didn't immediately respond, as I was focused on sorting out the thoughts in my head. Even though I had lived in Redemption a few years, there were days when it felt as foreign as if I had moved to a different country. "So, this is what I'm still trying to get my head around," I started.

Pat smiled knowingly. "The whole 'town being responsible for people disappearing' thing is throwing you, huh?"

I couldn't help but smile back. Pat knew me too well. "Yeah. It's just when I listen to Darlene, it seems pretty obvious to me that Polly ran away. I get why the cops think that. She tells her mother she's going to the one friend's house who her mother isn't going to check up on. And her friend just happens to have a family birthday party that night, so she wouldn't be calling the house looking for Polly. It's perfect, really, for Polly to slip out and leave. She had an entire night's headstart to get wherever she was going, and she knew no one would even miss her until school the next day."

Pat nodded as she leaned against the counter. "Keep going."

"Now, maybe she didn't mean to run away. Maybe she was just going somewhere for the night … maybe she's got a boyfriend no one knows about, or maybe she wanted to see an R-rated movie. I mean, who knows what was in her head? So, it's possible something happened to her while she was out doing whatever she had planned. Or, she really did run away. Regardless, it seems clear to me what's going on. So, why on Earth are her parents making this leap to Redemption taking her? Are they just in massive denial, or is there something else going on that I'm not understanding because I'm not from here?"

Pat paused for a moment, spinning her mug in her hands. "That's a hard question to answer. So, you're right. It does sound like Polly planned this. But …" she shook her head. "Growing up here, it's almost like living under a cloud. No matter how good things are, there's always that sense that it could all disappear, just like that." Pat snapped her fingers. "The ground could just open up and swallow you, and there's no rhyme or reason to it. But even more than that, there's this very real sense that, had you not been living here, it wouldn't have happened at all. This place is the root of it, not anything you're doing or not doing."

"If that's true, why does anyone stay?"

Pat laughed. "Oh come now. You of all people know the answer to that. When Redemption wants you, you CAN'T leave. It doesn't matter how hard you try … you're not going anywhere. Just like if you want to move here and Redemption doesn't want you, it ain't happening."

I thought about my own history with Redemption. It was true—I tried everything I could to leave, yet before I knew what hit me, I found myself the proud owner of the most haunted house in town.

"Point taken. But, regardless, this is a TOWN we're talking about. Not a person. A town isn't alive or even sentient. How can a town do anything?"

Pat shrugged. "How did all those people disappear back in 1888? There's a lot of things that don't make sense."

"Okay, so what about those times when everyone thinks something was Redemption's fault, and it turns out it was a person's doing, after all?"

Pat was silent for a moment as I popped the tray of cookies into the oven. "Two things come to mind," she said. "First, not everything that's happened here can be attributed to a person. Like your haunted house. I know you've had … unexplained things that have happened here, even if you don't talk about them."

It was true. I had experienced some odd things in the house, mostly in the form of dreams and messages. But was it my subconscious talking to me, or some entity in the house?

Or even multiple entities?

I shivered despite myself and the warmth from the oven.

Pat noticed. "You know what I'm talking about."

I picked up my tea and moved to the counter. "Yes, but it's not as clear-cut as ghosts."

"Nothing is ever clear-cut. Which brings me to my second thought—just because some of the disappearances, killings, and other strange events have had a person behind them, it doesn't mean the town wasn't involved."

"What do you mean?"

"Just that the idea or motivation came from somewhere. Are we so sure the town isn't influencing people to do things they might not otherwise?"

I shivered again, thinking back to some of the things I had done in Redemption … things I wasn't particularly proud of. Things I would rather forget.

"We know for a small town, our disappearance rate is higher than it should be. Why is it such a stretch to think there isn't something else, some other entity, involved here … pulling the strings, shall we say?"

"That's creepier than just thinking the town whisks people away sometimes," I said. "The idea that the town is influencing people's behavior and actions, and not in a good way? That's really sinister."

"I didn't say it was always bad," Pat clarified. "While yes, we definitely have our share of bad things that happen here, there's good, too. Whatever is going on in Redemption, I don't think it's all bad or all good."

She had a point. I thought about my own experiences, and it was true. It did feel like there was a mixture of things happening … perhaps "tug-of-war" was more appropriate.

"Anyway," Pat shrugged again and picked up her tea. "Everything I said could be nonsense, as well. You might want to take it with a grain of salt."

"I take everything you say with a grain of salt," I joked.

Pat stuck her tongue out at me.

"Back to what Darlene was referencing—the girl who disappeared and reappeared near the lake."

"There has been more than one," Pat said. "But, yeah, my guess is she's talking about Claire's friend."

"So, you know the story," I said.

"Everyone knows the story," Pat said. "Everyone who was living here at the time, anyway. Claire's friend, whose name is escaping me, disappeared and then reappeared a few days later, and no one knows why or what happened, including Claire's friend."

"So Claire never told you the rest of the story?" I asked.

Pat's expression became more serious. "What are you talking about, Charlie?"

I bit my lip, trying to decide how much I should share and how much to keep in confidence.

Years and years ago, back when Claire and Louise—who went by Lou, at the time—were in elementary school and still friends, one of their friends had disappeared only to reappear a few days later by the lake. The girl had no recollection of what happened to her. In fact, she didn't even remember being taken or returned, and had no idea how she ended up by the lake.

All of this would be disturbing enough. But Claire and Louise, along with Louise's brother, Jesse, and Jesse's friend Jonathan, had played around with trying to communicate with Redemption. They lit candles and chanted, like they were holding a séance.

And Redemption had appeared to respond. First by taking their friend, and then, by returning her.

The whole experience had freaked them out so much, they never did anything like it again.

But the repercussions still reverberated to this day.

"I don't know how much I can share," I said. "But let's just say ... it wasn't so innocent."

Pat's expression grew more concerned. "What do you mean?"

"Well, you know they were all kids, right? They were just messing around with things they shouldn't have."

Pat stared at me. "Oh, those kids," she muttered. "I wondered if they were into something they shouldn't have been. They were the ones who found that little girl, wandering by the lake. Did Claire tell you that?"

I nodded unhappily. "She did."

"So, what? Are you thinking that Polly was involved with something she shouldn't have been, too?"

"I don't know," I said. "All I do know is IF, and that's a big 'if,' her parents are right, and this is similar to what happened with Claire's friend years ago, then Polly wasn't so innocent. She was involved somehow. But the thing is," I lowered my voice, even though there was no one in the kitchen to overhear us. "I don't know if she'd just come back on her own, if that were the case."

Pat's face was pale. "We need to talk to Claire. She's the only one who's going to be able to clear this up."

I blew the hair out of my face. "Yeah, I think I better give her a call."

* * *

"So, what's up?" Claire asked. She and Daphne, who had a fresh, warm cookie in hand, had joined me and Pat around the kitchen table. Daphne had just woken up from her nap when I called, so the timing had worked out.

I glanced at Pat. "You heard about that teenager who's missing."

"Yeah, of course. Polly, right? Terrible. Her parents must be frantic." Claire reached over to stroke Daphne's head, who moved away impatiently to focus on her cookie.

"Yeah, well, the parents have been searching for Polly around the lake and woods," I said.

Claire looked faintly surprised. "Oh. I thought she ran away. That's what the paper is reporting. At least, that seems to be what the cops think."

"Yeah, there's still some question about that. Polly didn't take anything with her, so it's not clear if she left on her own or not. But the parents are convinced that Redemption took her."

Claire sighed. "Yeah, well. It wouldn't be the first time."

"And that's why they're searching the lake. Because they think that's where they'll find Polly when Redemption returns her."

Claire stared at me. "Wait. They think it's like what happened to Gina?"

"Yes."

Claire looked between Pat and me. "You told Pat?"

"Not the details," I said.

"She didn't tell me anything that I didn't already suspect," Pat said. "That we all didn't suspect."

"What do you mean?" Claire asked.

"You really think you were the first kids to mess around with Redemption?" Pat asked. "Or, for that matter, adults who really should know better?"

I looked away. Pat definitely didn't need to hear about my own ridiculous stunt when I first moved to town.

"Well, there are always stories about that," Claire said. "But you don't know what's true or not."

Pat held up a hand. "I'm not here to judge you. That was a long time ago, and I suspect you learned your lesson. Never mess around with things you don't understand. Especially when it comes to Redemption."

Claire almost smiled. "So, why am I here?"

"Because we need to know what to look for," I explained. "If Polly was fooling around with stuff she shouldn't have been, would there be any way to tell?"

"And are there questions we should be asking?" Pat asked.

Claire pursed her lips as she thought. "Well, one question would be, was there something she wanted, or a friend of hers wanted? Especially at that age. Like, was there a boy she wanted to like her? Did she need an A in a class, or even to get into a college she wanted to attend?"

"Polly's mom said she's a city girl," I said. "Maybe she wanted a way out of Redemption?"

"Yeah, that could be," Claire said. "And if she did ask for that, then it seems she certainly has gotten her wish, right?"

My stomach seemed to twist into an icy knot, and I put my tea down. "What else? I mean, talking about leaving Redemption could also just have been a sign she wanted to run away from home, not that she was doing anything else."

"Well, if that were true, my guess is that she would have tried something else before. Maybe she tried leaving, and it didn't work. Or, like I said, there could be a friend involved, and the friend wanted something and got it, so there was a pattern of success. Also, I'm guessing there might be a little bit of desperation. Whatever she was asking for, she wanted it now, for whatever reason. I wonder if there was a specific reason leaving right away was so important."

I listened to her, wondering if I should be taking notes. "Anything else?"

Claire picked up her tea. "She was probably afraid. Along with a bit of desperation, there was probably fear. Did she seem afraid of something? That's what I would want to know."

"So, it sounds like we need to find out more about what Polly was doing before she disappeared," I said. "What she was doing, what she was talking about, her state of mind, that sort of thing."

"And if they were screwing around with anything they knew they shouldn't be," Pat said.

"Yeah, that's basically it, in a nutshell," Claire said.

"We probably need to find her friends," I said, looking at Pat. "Starting with this Kim person."

Pat nodded. "I should have asked Darlene for a last name. Ugh. I bet it was Kim Black, but I wish I knew for sure."

"I take it Darlene is Polly's mother," Claire said. "You know, you could always go back to her and ask. Then you could see if she knows the answers to some of these questions, too. I know teenagers don't always talk to their parents, but sometimes, parents can sense when something isn't right with their kids."

"I don't think Darlene would be one of them," I said. "I got the sense that Polly was the good, responsible child, and because of that, her parents were less focused on her and more on her needy siblings."

"Well, you might be surprised," Claire said. "Polly's friends would probably have a good idea, too, if they would talk to you. It's not like teenagers are all that excited to talk to any adult."

"There is that," I said. "But I think we need to start there. The fact that Polly is missing might loosen some tongues. It might have shaken them up enough that one will talk. Same with her brothers and sisters, especially if she was close to one of them."

"I agree, we need to start with the kids," Pat said. "Depending on what one of them says, we can circle back to Darlene. But for now, let's see what they say."

Pat didn't say it, but I know we were both thinking that focusing on the kids would be the best way to find Donny, as well. I still couldn't shake the feeling that everything that had been going on was somehow related, and if only I could find the right loose thread and yank it, it would all unravel.

Chapter 13

"See any sign of them?" Pat asked, craning her neck. We were sitting in my car, parked in the small parking lot by the lake. During the summer, when it was hot enough to swim, and in the middle of winter, when it was cold enough to ice skate, the lot was typically overflowing. But on a cool afternoon in early spring, we were only sharing it with one other car—a beat-up pickup truck.

I squinted at it. "That looks like something that might belong to a kid," I said. "It's probably worth it to get out and walk around a bit."

Unfortunately, Claire hadn't been very precise about the location they'd found Gina in that night so long ago. "It was by the lake, near the beach," she'd said.

"Near the woods, or the boat docs?" Pat had asked.

Claire squished up her face. "The woods. I think. She might have come out of the woods, now that I'm thinking about it."

I glanced at Pat, trying not to sigh.

"Hey," Claire said. "It was dark, and we were kids. And it was a long time ago. I can't get more specific than that."

"Well, look on the bright side … we're not necessarily looking for Polly, just the people searching for her," I said. "It will probably be easier to find them."

Pat grumbled as she zipped up her jacket. "The wind coming off the lake is going to be cold, you know," she said.

"Do you have any better ideas?" I said, zipping up my own coat.

Pat made a face at me, and we both got out of the car.

I was still debating on whether or not I should tell Pat the last thing Claire had said to me. The fact that Claire waited until Pat left the room for a quick bathroom stop made me think I should keep it to myself.

"I don't think Redemption has anything to do with Polly," she'd said, her voice low.

"How do you know?" I asked, matching her volume.

She shrugged. "It's hard to explain. The energy … it's all wrong."

"What do you mean?" While I wouldn't call Claire a 'psychic' or anything like that, she definitely had some sort of sixth sense about what was going on in Redemption. I always took what she had to say seriously, and as much as I appreciated her sharing her insights, I also wished she didn't have whatever that "gift" was. Her mother had something similar and ended up with early onset dementia. I hoped it was just a coincidence, but in my gut, I knew better.

I just kept praying I was wrong.

She frowned. "There's definitely something brewing. Something dark, almost like a storm or thundercloud. There's a lot of frenetic energy … almost violent."

My eyes widened. "Violent?" I found myself thinking about Mildred's neighborhood that morning and the mood of the crowd in the street. It hadn't been exactly angry yet, and definitely not violent, but it was certainly moving in that direction.

She saw the expression on my face and misunderstood. "I'm not saying there's someone out there attacking teenage girls like Polly," she said. "It's just … it's hard to explain. I've never felt anything like it before. It's not like the energy when the town is involved. You understand what I'm saying?"

"Yeah, I think so," I said.

"So, whatever happened to Polly, I just …" Claire squished up her face again. "I don't think the lake has anything to do with it. Or the woods. I'm not sure what happened, but it's not …" She broke off at that point, because Pat returned from the bathroom. She left soon after, before I could figure out a way for her to tell me the end of that sentence.

As we marched toward the lake, our feet crunching on the pebbles that lined the path, the damp wind picked up, carrying a fishy smell with it as it whipped through my hair. I ran through the conversation again in my head. If anyone would know if Polly had been trying to communicate with Redemption, it would be Claire. While that was good news, it also meant no one had any idea what happened to Polly.

"I think I hear something," Pat said, cocking her head. "Over there." She waved toward the woods off to the side.

I turned my head to listen. There was definitely someone walking down the path that peeked out from between the trees. Probably more than one person.

We both took a sharp turn and started down the trail, very quickly running into the small group—consisting of two girls and a boy—coming the other way.

"Oh," the girl said, her voice startled. She looked about sixteen, and other than her striking long, blonde hair, was rather plain-looking. I marveled at her neat ponytail, immediately wishing I had thought to pull my own wild hair back, too. I didn't even want to think about the tangled mess I was going to have to deal with later, thanks to the wind. "We didn't expect to see anyone else here."

"Are you looking for Polly?" I asked.

Her mouth dropped open. "How did you know?"

"Because we're looking for her, too," I said. I stuck out my hand as I inwardly crossed my fingers, hoping luck was on our side, and these were the two people we were looking for. "I'm Charlie Kingsley, and this is Pat Barron."

"I'm Kim Black," she said reaching out her hand. Jackpot! "And this is …."

"Why are you looking for Polly?" The question came from the boy in the group, and both of us dropped our hands without shaking his. He looked older than the two girls, and I wondered if he was one of Polly's brothers. He had that brooding, bad-boy look to him, which was emphasized by the ripped jeans and black leather jacket he wore.

"I'm a friend of her mother's," Pat said.

"Polly's mother?" He asked, his eyes narrowing suspiciously.

"Yes. We go back a long way," Pat said. "We stopped by her house earlier today, and she told us you were searching for Polly out here. We wanted to help."

"She told you?" His expression was disgusted. "What was she thinking? Telling the whole world what we're doing."

"Donny, I don't think that's what's going on," Kim said. "If Pat is a friend of your mother's ..."

Donny glared at her. "Oh, great. Why don't you tell the whole world what we're doing, as well? How do you expect to get to the truth of what's happening if you can't keep your mouth shut?" The last part, he yelled at the girl, his good-looking face twisted into a snarl.

Kim shrank back. "Donny, I didn't ..."

"Enough," I snapped, marching toward him. Donny glanced at me, momentarily startled. "There's no reason to yell at her. We're here to help. Usually, the more people searching, the better chance you have of finding the person, so I don't understand why you aren't welcoming us instead of yelling at her."

"Because someone is behind this," Donny said. "And I don't know who. Or why."

"That still doesn't explain why you don't want the help," I said. "Again, the more people, the better."

Donny didn't answer, instead eying me like he was trying to figure out what to say. I waited, my arms crossed over my chest. I wanted to tap my foot, but I thought that would be too much.

"We don't know who to trust," Donny said finally.

I raised an eyebrow. "So, what ... you think I'm behind Polly's disappearance? That Pat is?" I pointed at Pat.

"Maybe," he said stubbornly. "Like I said, we don't know who to trust."

"But that doesn't make sense," I said. "How is talking about what you're doing going to hurt your chances of finding her?"

"Because *none* of this makes sense," he said in exasperation. "Polly wouldn't just disappear on her own. Someone is behind it. And there's a reason why she hasn't been returned yet. If you were behind it, you could be playing some sort of mind game with us, trying to mess us up."

I studied Donny, his face defiant, and wondered if maybe this was part of the issue he had with Harrison. Was he simply obstinate, or was there something else going on? He sounded like he might be dabbling in conspiracy theories.

"So, look, I can tell you we're not a part of it, but obviously, we would probably say that even if we were," I said. "So, I don't expect you to believe us. But would you be at least willing to answer a few questions for us about Polly before she disappeared?"

His expression was suspicious. "Why?"

It was all I could do to not roll my eyes. "As I said, we're trying to help your mother by locating Polly."

"If you don't believe us, you can call your mom and ask," Pat piped in. "We were there this afternoon."

Donny glanced between us, his forehead furrowed. "Fine. What do you want to know?"

I took a deep breath. "What was her mood before she disappeared?"

Donny's expression turned into a scowl. "Her mood? You think she ran away, don't you?"

"I don't know if she did or didn't, but knowing her mood would help determine if something was going on."

"What do you mean by her 'mood'?" Kim asked.

"Was she upset or frustrated by anything? Or maybe afraid?"

"Afraid?" Donny asked.

"Yes, was she afraid?"

Kim shook her head. "No, she was fine. The same as she always was."

"Was she doing anything different, or talking about anything different?" I asked.

"You DO think she ran away," Donny said, his voice full of accusation.

"Donny, did it occur to you that maybe your sister fell into the wrong crowd, and that's why she disappeared?" I asked. "Or maybe someone was stalking her for a few days before they took her? The events leading up to when she disappeared could very well have something to do with why she disappeared, without it being her fault or because she ran away."

Donny took a step back, his expression chastened. For a moment, I saw the little boy he once was, and I wondered what had happened to turn him into the distrusting young man standing in front of me.

"I'm sorry," he said gruffly, staring at the ground. "I know people are trying to help. But something is wrong. I can't explain it, but something isn't right, and whatever is going on, I'm convinced my sister got caught up in it. Now, I have to figure out how to help her."

Donny was sounding more and more like Claire. Was that what made him paranoid? Could he sense things like Claire could? "Is that why your family thinks Redemption took Polly?" I asked. "Because it doesn't feel right?"

Donny glanced up, his dark hair falling in front of one eye. "You're making fun of me."

"I'm not. Honest. I have a friend who agrees with you. She says something is off with the energy. Maybe you're both sensing the same thing."

He nodded, ducking his head. "Yeah, the energy is off. That's a good way to put it."

"Was Polly feeling that anything was off before she disappeared?"

He frowned. "I don't think so, but I don't know for sure. That's not something Polly really talked about."

"No, she didn't," Kim said, her voice confident.

"So, you didn't notice anything different about Polly?" I asked Kim.

She shook her head firmly. "No. She was like she always was."

She sounded so sure of herself, and according to her mother, she must know, being Polly's best friend. While I wasn't surprised, especially after speaking to Claire, I was still deflated. I had hoped Kim would be able to share some nugget or tidbit that would help us find Polly.

"What about you?" I turned to the third girl in the group, who hadn't said a word. She was plump, with auburn hair that hung like a curtain in front of her face and nails that had been bitten to the quick. She looked a little startled that I addressed her, and when she took a step back, she reminded me of a fawn.

"Beth doesn't know anything," Kim said. "Right, Beth? Polly didn't say anything to you."

"Right," Beth said after a pause.

"Are you both in the same grade as Polly?" I asked.

"Beth is new," Kim said, which didn't precisely answer the question. "She just started this year."

I raised my eyebrows. "Oh. That must have been difficult, transferring to a new school in your, what, senior year?"

Beth nodded. "Yeah, it was."

"Polly was like that," Kim said with a tinkling laugh. "Always the one to befriend the stray dogs and cats in the world."

Beth shifted from one foot to another. "She was my friend."

"Well of course she was," Kim said. "She was my friend, too. Why do you think I'm out here looking for her?"

There was an awkward little pause, which made me wonder what exactly Polly's relationship was with each of them.

"We should go," Donny said. "We need to keep searching."

"Thanks for talking to us," I said. "I hope you find her."

Donny nodded and turned to walk back the way he came. Kim obediently followed after him, but Beth hesitated, glancing between them and Pat and I with uncertainty.

I quickly raised my hand and beckoned for Beth to come closer. For a moment, she didn't move, and I was sure she was going to leave with the other two, but instead, she took a few steps closer to me.

I bent my head, putting my mouth near her ear. She smelled like bubblegum lip gloss. "You know something, don't you?"

She glanced toward the path, but Kim and Donny had already disappeared into the brush. "Polly wasn't happy," she said, keeping her voice low.

I nodded. "Kim didn't know?"

Beth pressed her mouth together in a thin line. "They were drifting apart. Polly told me. Kim was more interested in Donny than Polly, and Polly was getting tired of it. That, plus Kim is pretty self-centered."

Ah. The real reason why Kim was out there trailing after Donny.

"Why wasn't Polly happy?"

Beth glanced away again. "She felt like no one cared about her. Not Kim, not her family. She was the 'invisible child.' Her words."

"I can relate," I said, thinking about my own upbringing and how I was often ignored or overlooked, especially with two older sisters who seemed to always suck the oxygen out of the room.

Beth gave a little nod. "So can I. Everyone ignores me, too. It's why Polly and I became friends. We both know what it's like to be invisible."

"It hurts to feel that way, I know," I said. "Was Polly going to do anything about it?"

Beth glanced away. "I better go." She took a step in the opposite direction.

"Beth, wait," I said quickly. "Did Polly run away? Is that what this is about?"

Beth shook her hair in front of her face. "I have to go. They're going to wonder what happened to me."

"Beth, this is important," I said, my voice urgent. "I know you know this. You have to tell someone the truth. I'll keep your name out of it, if that's what you're concerned about, but you want to help your friend, right?"

Beth chewed on her lip for a long moment, her eyes darting from behind her hair before nodding.

"Then you need to tell me the truth. Did Polly run away?"

"I don't know," Beth said. She saw my expression and probably realized how close I was to giving her a shake to see if I could jar anything loose, so she quickly continued. "That's the truth. I don't know. But there was something going on with her."

"What?"

Beth shook her head. "All I know is that she decided she was leaving Redemption. She had an acceptance letter from Riverview, but that was too close to home."

"Why did she apply then?"

"Why do you think? Because of her parents."

"Her parents wanted her to stay close to home?"

Beth shrugged. "I think it was more about the money. Riverview is close enough that Polly could either commute from Redemption or stay with a cousin who has a fairly big house in Riverview and didn't mind renting out rooms to various family members who were also students."

"What did Polly want?"

"That was the problem. She wasn't sure. She thought maybe USC. She even applied there …"

"University of Southern California?"

Beth nodded. "Yeah, there. She hadn't heard back yet, but she knew she was going to need a bunch of scholarships and financial aid if she went. She was also thinking about going to Europe and becoming an au pair."

"Wait, an au pair in Europe?" Those seemed like completely opposite goals. "She liked to work with kids?"

Another shrug. "I think it was less about the kids and more about getting away." Her voice was flat. "And, unlike going to USC, she would be paid if she went to Europe. Mostly what she wanted was a fresh start, somewhere she could reinvent herself. She wanted to be like me—move somewhere where no one knew her, so she could become whoever she wanted." Now, her voice was bitter. "I tried to tell her it didn't work like that … all she had to do was look at me. My family was constantly moving. Every few years, it seemed my dad was getting a job somewhere else. And it didn't matter. I was still the same invisible person, no matter where we moved. But I don't think she believed me. I think she thought it would be different for her."

"I think it's easier to have a fresh start if you're not in high school," I said. "Maybe that's what she was thinking?"

"She did say that a few times … that it was tougher for me starting over in high school. But whatever." She stared at the ground as she kicked a rock.

"Okay, so, she was trying to decide between USC and becoming an au pair," I said.

"Yeah, that's why she went to talk to that psychic …"

"Wait," I said, holding up my hand. "She went to Madame Rowena?"

"Yeah, I think that's her. She's the one who just started her business, right?"

"She was going to ask Rowena what she should do?" I couldn't believe what I was hearing.

"Yeah, that was the plan. She thought the psychic could give her two versions of her future, depending on which path she chose. Then, she could make her decision."

"What did she end up deciding?"

Beth shook her head. "I don't know. She never told me."

"But you're sure she went to see the psychic?"

"That's the thing. I don't know that, either. She told me that was what she was going to do. But then she wouldn't tell me what happened. Just said she had some things she had to work out first, before she decided where she was going."

"What were the things she needed to work out?"

"I don't know. She didn't tell me," Beth's voice was getting higher and more frantic. "And then she disappeared."

"Beth?" Kim's voice floated toward us. "Where are you? Are you lost?"

Beth blanched. "I have to go."

"Okay, I get it. But one last question—what do you think happened to Polly?"

"Beth?" The voice was closer.

"I'll be right there," Beth shouted back. "I don't know," she said to me, her words tumbling out as if she had held them in for so long, they just couldn't wait to escape. "I wish I did. At first, I just thought maybe she ran away. Just to clear her head or something. But then no one heard from her, and Kim told me what Donny thought happened to her … I felt like it was my fault. I should have asked her more questions or something. Did she get herself caught up in something she couldn't control? Could I have stopped it? I even went and talked to the psychic myself, but she said she didn't know what I was talking about … that Polly hadn't been in at all. So what did Polly do? Had she talked to someone else? Someone who took her? Or did she somehow get caught up, and Redemption took her? I don't know. But I had to try and find her."

"It's not your fault …" I started to say. Beth's expression was frantic, from what I could see under her curtain of hair, and the last thing I wanted was for her to blame herself for something she had no control over.

"Beth?"

"I have to go." She darted away from me, as if having emptied out the words that had been trapped inside her made her feel like she couldn't get away fast enough.

I whirled around to face Pat, who was a few steps behind me. "Did you hear all of that?"

"Not all of it." Pat's expression was grim. "I did hear Madame Rowena's name, though. How is she involved?"

"I'm not sure," I said as I started to walk toward the car. "I intend to find out, though."

Chapter 14

Unfortunately, Rowena was booked for the rest of the afternoon, so I had to make an appointment for the next day. I drove Pat back to my house, as she had left her car in my driveway. After she left, I settled in, fully intending to enjoy a quiet, relaxing night.

Midnight was waiting for me on the stairs, tail twitching, clearly expecting dinner. "I haven't even gotten my shoes off yet," I told him. "Plus, I need a cup of tea, especially after the day I just had. You can wait a few minutes. I promise that you won't starve to death."

Midnight didn't look as sure. His tail continued its impatient twitch.

"Fine," I grumbled, padding into the kitchen. I fed him before getting the water boiling, and then set to work cleaning up after Claire and Pat. I was *so* tired—all I wanted to do was collapse on the couch, or, better yet, in the bathtub.

But I also needed to figure something out for dinner. Whatever it was, it needed to be fast and easy. Maybe one of the casseroles I'd made ahead and frozen for days such as this one. I opened the freezer and fished one out. Chicken, mushrooms, and rice would do nicely.

Was it just that morning I had been at Mildred's, watching Harrison's body being loaded into the police van? It seemed like a week ago. No wonder I was exhausted.

"The real question is, how is it all related?" I said to Midnight. He glanced up at me, blinking his green eyes. "What does a missing teenage girl and the dreadful owner of a property-management company have in common? Could this all come down to her brother holding some sort of grudge after being kicked out of his apartment? And what does it have to do with

Jonas and Drake, the non-vampire? And how on Earth does Rowena the Not-So-Psychic fit into all of it?"

Midnight cleaned his whiskers as I popped the casserole into the oven.

"Maybe I need to look into a connection between Donny and Drake or Jonas," I mused as I sat down by the table, a cup of tea in hand. "Or maybe Rowena and Donny. Or Rowena and Jonas or Drake. What do we know about Rowena, anyway? Where did she come from before she moved here?" I eyed Midnight. "Think Rowena Tanveer is even her real name?"

Midnight yawned.

"Yeah, I don't think so, either." I frowned. "I wonder how I could find out. Do you think she legally changed her name, or no? If she did, there would be a paper trail. Maybe I should make a few calls."

Midnight leapt up onto the chair next to the window, curling up in the seat.

"I know. I can't assume she changed her name before doing my due diligence. I really wish I could figure out where she moved here from."

Midnight fixed his green eyes on me.

"I don't know why she bothers me so much, either. I just have a bad feeling about her."

Midnight blinked his eyes.

"Well, yes it's partly because she's a fake. I don't think that's all of it though."

Midnight stared at me.

"I just know she's a fake. Just like I know there's no such thing as vampires."

Midnight's ear twitched.

"No, vampires don't exist. I don't care how much vampire hysteria there's been throughout human history."

Midnight blinked.

"Rowena is not like Claire. First off, Claire isn't taking money for … whatever it is she does. And Claire isn't trying to fool anyone about her abilities being something they aren't."

Midnight started grooming himself.

"You're no help," I muttered as I got up to check the casserole. "I guess I'm just going to have to do everything myself. As usual."

By the time I finished eating, the sun had vanished into the night, and a full moon appeared over the horizon. I yawned again. Even though it wasn't my bedtime, I was so tired. I figured a hot bath and an early turn-in was exactly what I needed. I definitely wanted my wits about me when I saw Rowena in the morning.

I got up to refill my tea, and the phone rang.

I went to answer it, an uneasy feeling prickling at the back of my neck.

There's no reason for it. None at all, I reassured myself. It could be Pat having an a-ha moment about the day that she just couldn't wait to tell me about. Or, even more likely, one of my tea customers looking to place another order.

Really, there was no reason to think there was anything necessarily *wrong*.

Nonetheless, my trepidation increased as I picked up the receiver. "Hello?"

"Oh, thank goodness you're home." It was Mildred, her voice frantic.

The uneasy feeling turned into a five-alarm fire alert. "Why? What's going on?"

"They're outside. They're coming for him."

"Who is? And who are they coming for?" Although I already knew the answer and was snapping my head around, trying to locate my keys and purse.

"Drake. It's a bunch of people. They're outside. They're coming for him."

"I'll be right there," I said. "And call Wyle. Right now!"

I hung up without waiting for her answer and ran to the door.

*   *   *

By the time I reached Mildred's neighborhood, the crowd was starting to turn ugly, reminding me of the mobs that had driven out so-called "vampires" in the past, complete with pitchforks and lit torches.

In this case, I didn't see any pitchforks, but I did notice a few burning candles between the flashlights.

Oh, no … were they really thinking about burning down Jonas's house?

I parked as close as I could get before jumping out of my car and making a mad dash to Jonas's house. The cool night air slapped against my sweating face. The moon was so bright that I had no trouble seeing, even without the light from flashlights and flames. As I drew closer, I could more easily make out the words the crowd was chanting:

"Where's Polly?

"What did you do to Polly?"

I cut across Jonas's neighbor's yard to avoid the crowd and angled across to stand in the driveway in front of them.

"What are you doing?" I shouted as soon as I could catch my breath, waving my arms frantically. "Stop this! Right now."

The chant wavered, probably more due to the shock of my suddenly appearing in front of them.

"We want Polly back," a man yelled back. It was too dark to make out the features of his face, but he appeared to be wearing an oversized blue plaid jacket and baseball cap. In one hand, he had a flashlight he waved around, and in the other, something long and dark, like a stick or baseball bat. I wondered if he was the same belligerent guy I had run into earlier that morning. "If the cops aren't going to find her, then we are."

"Polly isn't here," I said. "The cops searched his house. You saw them this morning."

"Just because she's not here doesn't mean the vampire doesn't know where he is," a woman answered. She was carrying a thick candle that she was shielding from the wind with her other hand. Her voice was slightly slurred, as if she had enjoyed a few glasses of wine before heading out into the night to confront a vampire with a decorative candle she likely borrowed from the dining room table's centerpiece.

"Don't be ridiculous. Drake isn't a vampire," I said incredulously.

"How do you know? He killed Harrison! And we don't want his kind here," the man answered.

"We don't know for sure if he killed Harrison."

"His body was in the backyard!"

An ugly mutter rolled through the crowd. Beads of sweat dripped down my cheeks, despite how cool it was and my lack of jacket. I strained my ears, hoping to hear police sirens headed our way. Where was Wyle? What was taking him so long?

"I agree, it doesn't look good," I shouted. "But that still doesn't mean Drake killed Harrison. And even if he did, it doesn't mean he had anything to do with Polly's disappearance."

"What are you talking about?" the man yelled back. "A murderer moves into our neighborhood, and you don't think he had anything to do with a teenager suddenly going missing?"

"I don't know what to think," I answered, holding my hands out, palms up, as if I could physically calm the crowd. "But what I do know is that this isn't the answer. You have to let the police investigate."

The man snorted. "Oh, the police. What are they going to do? They're the ones who released him this afternoon. Do they really expect us to sit around waiting for this guy to go after someone else?"

Again, I wondered where Wyle was. It shouldn't take him so long. Unless … a horrible thought hit me. What if Mildred didn't call, for some reason? She was already so upset when she called me … maybe she was too flustered or distracted to make the call.

If that was the case, I hoped someone else had. Maybe Drake, although after spending half the day in the police station, he likely had his fill of police. But even he had to realize that dealing with the police would be better than whatever was brewing outside his house.

This was not good.

"Of course not," I said, still trying to pacify the crowd. "You should always keep an eye out for your loved ones and make sure they're protected. Especially since, if it isn't Drake, it's obviously someone else."

"Who else would it be? Of course it's Drake. What I don't understand is why you're defending him," the man said.

"Yeah, what are you even doing here?" the woman asked. "How would you even know this was happening … unless Drake called you?"

I could almost feel the force of the energy shifting away from the house and onto me. I took a step backward. "Drake didn't call me. Someone else did."

"Oh, who would do that?" the man scoffed. "We're the good guys here. We're protecting the neighborhood."

"Not everyone would agree with that," I said. "There is a reason vigilantism is against the law. If you attack Drake, you WILL be breaking the law."

"So what?" the man asked. "We're doing the community a favor. They'd thank us for getting rid of this garbage."

"Maybe she's his girlfriend," the woman said with a snicker.

"I'm no one's girlfriend," I said.

"What kind of man is he?" the man asked. "Letting his girlfriend come out to defend him while he cowers in his house like a little girl? Come out here like a man!" the man bellowed.

At that moment, the wail of a police siren cut through the night like a knife. I could feel the tension loosening in my chest. I didn't think I'd ever been so relieved to hear that sound.

"Charlie! I called them," Mildred shouted. She was standing by the edge of her driveway, waving at me as she hopped up and down. "They should be here any minute."

"Yes, thank you. The police are on their way," I said to the crowd. "Maybe you should all go home?"

"Not without getting rid of your boyfriend first," the man growled.

"What boyfriend? Charlie, you have a boyfriend?" Mildred asked. The sirens were getting louder.

"No, I don't have a boyfriend."

"Then why are they saying you have a boyfriend?" Mildred asked.

"Because she's out here protecting him, that's why," the man said.

"Are you talking about Drake?" Mildred asked before turning toward me. "Charlie, are you dating Drake? And you didn't tell me?" Mildred sounded legitimately betrayed.

I gaped at her. "Mildred, you were there the one and only time we met. Did it seem like we were going to start dating?"

"How should I know?" Mildred sniffed. "You young people are impossible to read. In my day, things were much clearer, but now? Who knows?"

"Busted," the man said.

"I'm not dating anyone," I said through gritted teeth as a convoy of police cars finally pulled into the street in a cloud of blaring sirens and blindingly red and blue lights, illuminating the entire street.

The crowd started to back away from Jonas's home, the murmurs sounding more confused and uncertain than before.

"It's time to go home, everyone," Wyle shouted from across the street from me, waving his arms and gesturing. "Come on, let's break it up."

More people started moving away, no doubt persuaded as additional officers appeared beside Wyle, clearly encouraging them to keep moving. But the man in the plaid jacket went the other direction, angrily stomping toward Wyle. "Why? Why should we go home? You let this monster go. How are we supposed to feel safe?"

"We let him go because there is no evidence to charge him," Wyle said calmly. "But trust me, just because we let him go doesn't mean we aren't keeping an eye on him."

Obviously not a very good one, considering the crowd in front of us, I immediately thought. But I kept my mouth shut.

The man took another menacing step toward Wyle. "That's not good enough. What about our families? How can you put them in danger like this?"

"Sir, I would advise you to step back," Wyle said. His voice was level, but the undertone of danger was evident.

The man stood firm. "Why should I? You're not doing your job. You work for me. I pay your taxes."

"Sir, if you don't step back right now, I'm going to have to take you into custody. Is that what you want?"

"Oh, great. Arrest me instead of the real monster," the man said bitterly.

"Sir, I mean it." Wyle had shifted his stance, moving one hand toward his belt.

The man must have seen that too, because he stared at Wyle for a moment longer before finally taking a step back.

"Thank you," Wyle said, straightening up. "Now, listen up. We're keeping watch. We have a patrol car regularly driving through the neighborhood to keep an eye on Drake."

"What patrol car?" The same man spread his arms out wide. "I've been out here for at least a couple of hours and have seen no patrol car."

I kind of thought Blue Plaid Guy had a point. I would have liked to think if a police car had been patrolling the neighborhood, the number of people gathering in the street would have inspired a call for backup.

Wyle eyed the guy. "But even with a patrol car keeping a close eye on things, you should of course remain vigilant in your own lives. Make sure your doors and windows are locked, and keep the phone handy, in case you see anything suspicious. We want you all to be safe."

"'Safe.'" Blue Plaid Guy spat. "That's exactly why we're out here."

"Sir, are we going to have a problem?" Wyle asked.

"Absolutely not, officer," the man said, his voice sarcastic. "I need to be home to protect my family, as it sure seems like Redemption's Finest isn't all that interested in doing it. Thanks for all of your hard work." He gave Wyle a mock salute before turning and marching off.

I continued to stand in Jonas's driveway as the crowd, energy drained, slowly disbursed. Still, as silly as it seemed even to myself, there was a part of me that almost felt like if I left the yard, the crowd would somehow magically reappear.

"You didn't have to do that."

The voice came from behind me. Startled, I whirled around. "What?"

Drake was hovering on the porch, clearly uncomfortable, despite the darkness. "You didn't have to do that."

"Well, what should I have done? Let them break into your home?"

Something shifted on his face. I couldn't quite make out the details, but I got the sense he was smiling. "I don't think they would have gone that far. I was watching pretty closely, and the moment they stepped onto Jonas's property, I was planning to call the cops."

"Next time, you might want to think about calling them earlier, before they build up enough momentum and energy to actually trespass."

He cocked his head. "Why did you do it?"

"Do what?"

"Face them like that. You don't know me. And they could have hurt you."

Suddenly, I was exhausted. All the adrenaline that had surged through me while I confronted the crowd dissipated, and all I wanted to do was get into my car and drive home to that hot bath I was about to draw for myself before Mildred called. "Because it was the right thing to do," I said. "I haven't always done the right thing in my life, so I have a lot of making up to do."

"Sooo," Mildred said, sidling up to me. "When did you start dating Drake?"

"I'm not," I said, turning to face her. I couldn't help but feel immediately embarrassed, with Drake standing just behind us in the shadows.

"Who is Charlie dating?" Wyle asked. I hadn't seen him approach and nearly jumped at the sound of his voice. Despite the silvery light of the full moon, his face was in shadow.

"I'm not dating anyone," I said again as Mildred simultaneously answered, "Drake."

"Oh this is ridiculous," I sighed, turning back to the porch. "Drake, can you tell everyone we're not dating?"

But the porch was empty.

"He was just here," I said, turning back to Wyle and Mildred.

"You were talking to Drake?" Mildred asked. "Drake doesn't talk to anyone," she said to Wyle.

"Yeah, Charlie is good at getting people to talk to her," Wyle said.

I rolled my eyes. "Oh for Pete's sake. We're not dating. In fact, the only reason I'm here is because you called me." I gestured toward Mildred.

Mildred nodded. "That's true. I did."

"You should have called *us*," Wyle said to Mildred, disapprovingly.

"I did," Mildred said.

"I mean, you should have called us first, rather than Charlie," Wyle said. "We're trained to deal with situations like this. Charlie isn't."

"I'm glad you brought that up," I said. "It took you a really long time to get here. Why? I thought you have a patrol car 'keeping an eye' on things."

Wyle's expression shifted, and he looked a bit sheepish. "We had a few … well, wires get crossed."

I raised my eyebrow. "'Wires'?"

"Yeah. Someone thought someone else was covering it, and vice versa. You know how that goes."

"So you're telling me there was a *communication* issue?"

"You have to understand … Redemption is a small town," Wyle said, his voice defensive. "We don't usually have to deal with these sorts of incidents. It's not like the big cities, where a borderline mob gathering is commonplace. This isn't something we're used to."

I shook my head, pressing my hands to my face. Man, did I want that bath. "You do realize that this communication issue could have made things end very differently … and badly."

"I know. It's not going to happen again."

I rubbed my face, trying to wake myself up. "Well, I guess that's all we can hope for. So, what about Drake? I take it you guys let him go this afternoon. Then what? Did you have a press conference announcing his arrival home?"

Wyle's mouth was a thin, flat line. "We did let him go this afternoon, yes. There's no evidence he did anything at all. We found nothing in his house, and there's no trace of anyone other than Jonas and Drake having been in it."

"What about the graves?" Mildred asked.

Wyle stared at her like he had forgotten she was there. "Graves?"

"In the backyard? He was digging graves."

Wyle sighed. "We checked it out and didn't find anything. Just more dirt."

"Maybe you didn't dig deep enough," Mildred said.

"Anyway, we had to let him go," Wyle said, ignoring the comment. "We didn't have anything to hold him on. But all the officers were under strict orders to keep it quiet."

"Well, someone ignored those orders," I said. "Although I suppose someone in the neighborhood could have seen you drop Drake off in a patrol car."

"We didn't use a marked police car for exactly that reason," Wyle said.

"Still, if someone had seen Drake come home, it wouldn't have taken a genius to figure it out," I said.

"Well, what would you have us do?" Wyle demanded. I could hear the stress cracking in his voice, and I almost felt sorry for him. But then I reminded myself that he could have prevented at least some of this from happening.

"Keep a better eye on the neighborhood," I said. "Look, it was obvious this was a powder keg. I mean, the guy had a dead body in his backyard at the same time a teenager disappeared. You had to know there was a high probability of a mob coming for him, even without the vampire nonsense. You should have been more on top of this. If you had a patrol car parked on the street, or even driving by frequently like you said you did, it's likely none of this would have happened."

Wyle let out a sigh and reached up to massage between his eyes. "You're right," he said. "This was unacceptable, and we should have been more responsive. I'm not going to give you a bunch of excuses, but the past few days since Polly has gone missing have been unprecedented in our department. But that doesn't make it right."

Despite my resolve, I could feel my heart softening toward him. He was right. There was a lot on his plate, and yes, someone at the station messed up. But if there was ever a good reason for a mess-up, it's what was going on with Drake, Polly, and Harrison.

"I'm not trying to come down on you," I said. "I get that this is a really difficult time."

"It's more than a difficult time, it's a dangerous time," Wyle said grimly. "Which is why you really need to stay out of it."

Oh for pete's sakes. Not this again. "We already had this conversation. You need the help. You know I can help. So, therefore, I should be helping."

"Yes, but you aren't trained," Wyle said. "Nor are you part of the force. We can't have citizens running around getting in over their heads. That just makes everything more complicated for us."

"I'm hardly just any 'citizen,'" I said. "You know I have a proven track record of figuring out who's guilty."

"She does," Mildred piped up to confirm.

"At this point, I would think you would be grateful for any and all help you can get," I said.

"It's too dangerous," Wyle insisted.

"Is it any more dangerous than not catching whoever is responsible for the body in the yard?" I asked.

"That's beside the point," Wyle said. "If the murderer thinks you're involved with the investigation, you'd definitely be in more danger."

"Oh, like tonight?" I asked, gesturing toward the street. "Newsflash, I'm already involved. Anyone who hears anything about tonight will hear about my involvement. You might as well benefit from my talents."

Wyle exhaled loudly from his nose. "That's precisely the problem. Do you realize what your little stunt here could have done?"

"I know it bought you enough time to get down here," I said.

Wyle shook his head, staring at the night sky. "You were lucky," he said finally. "But one day, if you keep getting involved like this, it will catch up to you, and you maybe won't be."

"Maybe," I said, thinking back over my past and the mistakes I very much needed to atone for. "But I doubt it. I suspect when my time comes, it won't have anything to do with my helping you track down killers."

"This is nuts," Wyle grumbled, staring off to the side and refusing to look at me. "I can't have this on my conscience. I just can't. If something happened to you because you were helping me … I couldn't live with myself. I don't want to be any part of the lunacy that could cause you to get hurt … or worse."

Had I heard his voice crack? I stared at Wyle, but his cop face was back, which meant his emotions were now carefully tucked away. It must have been my imagination, thinking there was something deeper being said.

Before I could gather my thoughts, he turned to face me. "It's one thing for me to put myself in danger, but quite another to have you, a civilian, face it."

"It's my decision, Wyle," I said. "As nice as it is that you're trying to protect me, it's not really your place. I'm a grown-up. I can make my own decisions and be responsible for the results of them."

"But you don't understand what those 'results' could be," Wyle said.

I looked directly into Wyle's eyes. "I do."

We stared at each other. I could feel the energy buzzing between us like an electric cord. He broke eye contact first.

"Fine," he said. "Let it be known I'm not happy about this."

"Noted," I said.

"It's just that our resources are stretched pretty thin as it is, so we really could use all the help we can get," he said.

"Thank you," I said. "I think you're making the right decision."

Wyle muttered something unintelligible.

"Look at it this way," I said. "You said you couldn't live with yourself if I got involved and something happened to me. How do you think I would feel if I didn't get involved, and someone else was killed?"

He gave me a dark look. "It's not the same thing."

Mildred was watching us, her eyes wide, as we argued back and forth. I suddenly had a bad feeling about what might fall out of her mouth (mostly likely something about boyfriends) when she spoke, and I sent her a mental message, hoping she'd keep her mouth shut. The last thing I needed was for her to say something that would derail Wyle again.

"Can I stop by tomorrow to compare notes?" I asked. "Maybe late morning?" My appointment with Rowena was set for 9:30, and the thought made me want to groan. It would have been nice to sleep in. Although, there was a killer to be caught, and I could sleep when I was dead.

He sighed. "Alright. I guess this is still better than the alternative, because you aren't going to stop either way, are you?" he continued as if the question was rhetorical. "At least this way, maybe I can help guide you, so you don't get into too much trouble."

"Keep telling yourself that," I said cheerfully.

He shot me another dark look before turning on his heel and striding away.

"Charlie, I never thought you'd be one of *those* kind of girls," Mildred said.

I eyed her. "What kind of girls?" I was already dreading the answer, but I couldn't help but ask.

"Well, juggling two men, of course." Mildred shook her head, a small coquettish smile on her lips. "You're almost as bad as I was when I was your age."

I looked at her in surprise, the question on my lips, but no. I kept my mouth shut. It was late enough … I wasn't about to dive down that rabbit hole.

Chapter 15

Stifling a yawn, I pulled open the door to Rowena's shop, noting the cheerful little tinkle of the bell. In one hand, I held a large cup of coffee, courtesy of Aunt May's. At this rate, it would be cheaper to buy myself a new coffee maker.

Helen Blackstone had left me one when she sold me the house—an ancient Mr. Coffee that didn't sound quite right every time I tried to use it. Nor did the end product look quite right. I hadn't been able to bring myself to taste it.

I should just go buy a new one and be done with it, I told myself. Especially considering how painful it had been to drag myself out of bed that morning.

Despite my complete exhaustion, I had barely slept, mostly because it took hours to relax enough to fall asleep. I had been so keyed up dealing with the crowd and Wyle, even a hot bath and pot of my special Deep Sleep tea wasn't enough to enjoy a restful night. But at least I was up, dressed, and still early for my appointment, even with the quick stop for coffee. I found myself with time to really take a close look at the new and improved shop.

Madame Rowena had certainly been busy since the last time I was in. It no longer looked like an abandoned hardware store, but instead, a true psychic shop. The walls were freshly painted with dark, almost burgundy-red and gold accents. Candles, crystals, tarot cards, books about magic and witches, and other items you'd expect to find for sale in a psychic store were displayed on the shelves. In one corner was a round table with two chairs, almost hidden by a dark-red and gold divider painted with ornate flowers and birds. A matching curtain, which smelled like incense and burnt sage, separated the main area from the back.

"One minute," a voice sang out from the behind the curtain. I didn't respond, instead continuing my perusal of the shop as I sipped my coffee.

"Welcome," Rowena said as she appeared from behind the curtain with a flourish. "You must be my ... oh."

I smiled pleasantly at Rowena. "Good morning."

Rowena rearranged her expression and gave me a professional smile that didn't quite reach her eyes. "I didn't realize it was you. When you made the appointment, you didn't use your real name."

I gave her a surprised look. "I didn't?"

"I was expecting a Charlotte," Rowena said.

"Oh, you're right. Charlotte is my legal name. I figured you would know it was me, but I probably should have gone with 'Charlie.'"

Rowena's smile turned brittle. "I'm surprised you even came back. You don't seem a believer."

"Well, I've heard some people talking about your readings, and I thought I should maybe give them another chance," I said.

Ever so slightly, Rowena straightened her shoulders. "Really? That is ever so kind. Who have you talked to, so I can thank them?"

"Beth was one," I said. "At least, I think that's her name. I only met her in passing."

A faint frown touched Rowena's face. "Of course. Beth. Come, shall we get started?" She gestured for me to move to the chairs in the corner while she went to the front door to lock it. "This way, we won't be disturbed," she said.

"Of course," I murmured. When I had stopped by the day before, there had been what looked like a high school student behind the counter—a girl with jet-black dyed hair dressed in goth style. She had destroyed the overall effect by continually snapping her gum, though. I was tempted to question her about Polly, but there were several other people in the shop as well, and I thought it better to hold my cards close to my chest. The last thing I wanted was for someone to tip off Rowena about my knowing of Polly's visit.

Rowena pulled the divider over, and we sat opposite each other. She made a big show of getting everything prepared: lighting the candle in the middle of the table, closing her eyes and taking a few deep breaths, and then running a crystal over the cards. She then placed the crystal on the table, picked up the cards, and started to shuffle. "What question do you have for the spirits?"

"What's happening in our town?" I asked. "First, Polly disappeared, and then there was a murder. What's going on? Who is responsible?"

Rowena nodded slightly, dipping her face and looking down so I couldn't see her eyes. "Yes, what's going on is very troubling," she said. "I can understand why you have questions. I think we all do. Do you have a relationship to either Polly or the victim? Perhaps a friend of the family?"

"No. I'm just a concerned citizen."

Rowena nodded again. "Yes, I understand. But wouldn't you rather ask something of a more personal nature? Say, a question about your future, or perhaps your future husband?"

I sipped my coffee, screwing up my face like I was thinking about it. "No, I don't have a question about that. Really, I'm just very worried about what's happening in this town and want to help get to the bottom of it before anything worse happens."

Rowena nodded again as she continued to shuffle. "Do you have a personal item from either victim?"

"Do I need one?"

"It helps. It's up to the spirits as to what they want to reveal, but having a personal item usually provides a stronger connection."

"I understand. Can we try without?"

Rowena finally glanced up at me, her eyes unreadable. "If that is your wish." She placed the card deck in front of me to cut, before laying them out in front of her. She took a moment to study them. "So, what I can share with you is that Polly is alive and safe."

I leaned forward slightly. "Really? Where is she? Why hasn't she come home?"

Rowena traced a perfectly manicured fingernail across the cards. I found it interesting she had chosen the French manicure, as I would have expected something more exotic. "The cards haven't revealed that yet. But I can assure you, she's safe."

"But you promised you would find her," I said. "Remember? Why haven't you?"

She shot me an unreadable look. "All in good time." She continued to trace the cards with her finger. "Also, the cards are telling me that the murder, as tragic as it was, had nothing to do with Polly."

This gave me pause. "Really? The cards say that?"

She nodded. "They do."

I wanted to ask her where, but I didn't think I would get a straight answer. I was also a little surprised she wasn't going through and explaining the different cards and what they meant like she had before. "So, who killed Harrison, then? Was it Drake?"

She shook her head. "The cards don't give a name."

"Then how can you know it has nothing to do with Polly?"

She lifted her hands helplessly. "The spirits reveal what the spirits choose. I don't control it."

"What about another victim? Is anyone else in danger?"

"That I cannot say."

"Well, what can you say, then?" I asked, a note of frustration creeping into my voice.

Rowena sat back in her chair. "I told you this may not give you the results you wanted. Without some connection to at least one of the victims, it's not that clear-cut."

"Okay, but what about Drake?"

"What about him?"

"Is he safe?"

She gave me an odd look. "I don't understand your question."

"You do realize he's being attacked, right?"

"What do you mean?"

I stared directly into her eyes. "Last night, there was a mob that nearly attacked him. The cops don't have any evidence of his being involved in Harrison's murder, but that didn't stop the mob. So, why don't you ask your spirits for some help? Or are you okay with letting an innocent man get hurt?"

She paused for a moment before crossing her arms over her chest. "Are you accusing me of not being honest?"

I shrugged. "You started this. You inserted yourself into Polly's disappearance by saying you were going to find her, even though you haven't yet. I'm just wondering why you aren't doing the same for Drake."

"Because I don't know anything about Drake."

"But you do about Polly?" I leaned forward across the table. "Is it because she came to you for a reading before she disappeared?"

Her eyes widened. "Who told you that?"

"Does it matter?"

"You make it seem like a bigger deal than it was," Rowena said.

"So she WAS here."

Rowena, realizing her mistake, shot me a murderous look. "It wasn't anything," she said again. "She had a few questions about her future, and that was it. I didn't want people to get the wrong idea, which is why I didn't say anything. However, since I had met her previously and created a connection, I'm able to sense what happened to her."

I had to give her credit—it was a nice save. "So she didn't tell you she was thinking about running away?"

"My readings are confidential," she said primly.

"You aren't a therapist," I said. "If you know something, you should tell the cops."

"And you aren't a cop," she shot back. "Nor are you related in any way to Polly, so I don't see how my discussion with her has anything to do with you."

"What happened to her?" I asked.

"I keep telling you, it hasn't …"

"It hasn't been revealed. I get it. I really do. You're at the mercy of the spirits, and it must be really frustrating to have to explain that to people who have never experienced the connection with the spirit world the way you have."

Rowena narrowed her eyes suspiciously. "Exactly."

"Which is why it would be such a shame if it got out that you did a reading for Polly before she disappeared. Of course, I get why you want to keep it confidential, because it's truly only between her and the spirit world. It's no one else's business." Here, I paused for effect. "But other people might not be so understanding."

She stared at me. "Are you threatening me?"

I widened my eyes and pressed a hand to my chest. "Me? Oh, absolutely not. I'm not into threats. I'm just simply sharing a possible scenario. After all, it's not like Polly kept the fact she was going to you for a reading a secret. It's very possible the longer this drags on and she isn't found, the more likely it is that someone, perhaps the cops, perhaps the local newspaper, may start asking more questions, and who knows what they'll find out?" I gave her a pleasant smile. "You know? This was a wonderful reading. I feel so much better. How much do I owe you?"

"Nothing," Rowena said through a forced smile and gritted teeth. "Consider it my gift to you. Especially since you weren't asking for yourself, but for the well-being of the town."

"Oh, why thank you. That's so sweet. I appreciate it."

Rowena nodded slightly. I was a little surprised she didn't tell me to never come back, but perhaps she didn't want to show that much weakness. It would be a clear admittance that I had gotten under her skin. Her eyes had darkened as she watched me, and I wondered just how dangerous of an enemy she might be.

Apparently, I was set to find out.

"Thanks again, and I hope you have a wonderful day," I called out. As I was making my way to the door, I glanced again at the curtain separating the front of the store from the back. There was something about it that just didn't sit right with me.

I whirled around. "Madame Rowena, would it be possible to use your restroom?"

She blinked at me. "It's not a public restroom."

I gave her an embarrassed smile and shifted from one foot to the next. "It's the coffee, I'm afraid. It goes right through me. I don't think I can make it home. Can I …"

Rowena looked like she wanted to refuse. "Fine," she said, her voice clipped. "It's the first door to your right. Just beyond the curtain."

"Thank you," I said, hurrying to the back of the store before she could change her mind. I quickly ducked behind it as Rowena moved to the front door to unlock it.

Right behind the curtain was a long hallway with five doors. Unlike the rest of the store, this part hadn't been redone. It was still painted off-white, and the doors were scuffed. It also smelled of sawdust and bleach. I peeked into one on the rooms on the right. Yep, it was the bathroom. Quickly, I moved to the one across the hall. It looked like Rowena's office, with a desk, filing cabinets, and bookshelf overflowing with books and paper. In fact, the whole office was messy, with stacks of paper everywhere.

I left that room and moved to the next door. It appeared to be a break room, complete with a fridge, sink, coffee maker, and microwave on one end and a couple of plastic tables surrounded by folding chairs in the middle. Along with the sawdust and bleach smell, I caught faint whiffs of coffee and … microwave pizza? Rowena didn't strike me as someone who would eat a lot of that, especially at this time in the morning. Although, I reasoned, most everything else about her seemed fake, so that assumption might be wrong, too. Nevertheless, it seemed out of place. None of her employees were there yet, so I wondered if what I was smelling was from the day before.

I left the break room and turned to the next door, glancing over my shoulder, sure that Rowena would be checking up on me soon. I found myself still marveling at how different the back of the shop looked versus the front. Like everything else in the back, nothing had been updated, and it had a gloominess about it that didn't at all match what the customers saw. I hoped, for the sake of her employees, she would eventually get around to redoing it.

I grasped the knob to turn it, but it didn't budge. Locked.

I stared at the door. It looked no different than any of the others. I wondered what was so special behind it that would necessitate a locked door. Her office was open, after all, which I assumed would have more items requiring safekeeping.

Something didn't feel right.

Maybe the more expensive merchandise was stored in there. It made sense, but still, something felt off.

I glanced again toward the curtain, feeling like I had run out of time. I hurried back to the bathroom, ducking inside to flush the toilet and turn on the water. When I emerged, Rowena was standing there, arms folded across her chest.

"Everything okay?" she asked. In the harsh fluorescent light, her complexion had a greenish tinge. She eyed the hallway up and down, as if sensing I hadn't actually needed a bathroom.

"Yes, thank you," I said, my thoughts still on the locked door. Polly's face suddenly popped into my mind.

"And thank you again for the great reading. Hopefully, the spirits will show you where Polly is soon."

Rowena looked startled. "I hope so, too," she said, gesturing with her arm toward the curtain. "Although I've learned the spirits can't be rushed. Now, if you'll excuse me ..."

"I just saw her mother the other day," I said, deliberately interrupting her. "She is really suffering right now. The whole family is. They're spending every moment they can looking for Polly."

"I'm sure they are," Rowena said. "I really need to get back ..."

"So, really, the sooner the better, to find Polly," I pushed. "Her family needs her. Badly."

"I have no doubt," Rowena said, raising the curtain and practically shooing me through it. I was getting the feeling she was pretty close to grabbing me by the arm and physically thrusting me through the doorway. "Again, there's only so much I can do. These things will be revealed in their own time. I'll do what I can to speed up the process, of course."

"I think that would be a huge blessing to everyone in this town," I said, weaving my way through the aisles toward the front door. I paused when I reached it, and turned back to Rowena. "I have no doubt how grateful everyone will be when you do finally find her."

Rowena smiled, showing an awful lot of white teeth. "That's sweet of you to say, but all the gratitude should be reserved for the spirits. They're the ones revealing things to me. I am but a messenger, doing my small part in the process. If it ends up helping even one person, that's more than I could ever ask for."

I smiled back. "Of course. Have a great day, Rowena." I pushed the door open, listening to the tinkling bell as I stepped onto the street.

The air was sweet and fresh, especially after the cloying scents of incense.

The microwaved pizza and locked door were still bothering me.

Suddenly, I wondered why I had felt compelled to stand in the hallway and talk about Polly. It wasn't like I suspected Rowena might have Polly locked in the back room of her shop. The thought was absurd.

Wasn't it?

Chapter 16

"How's the investigation going?" I asked Wyle as I sat down in the chair in front of his desk.

He frowned when he saw me. "I was hoping you might have changed your mind about helping."

"Not a chance," I said cheerfully, crossing my legs and taking another sip of coffee. I had swung by Aunt May's for a refill before heading over to see Wyle. "You should know by now you can't get rid of me so easily."

He sighed and sat back. "Alas, I do know that. But that doesn't mean I can't hope for a different outcome." He looked even more exhausted than he had the day before, black circles prominent under his eyes and cheeks that seemed thinner than normal. I wondered if he had been eating.

"When was the last time you had any time off?" I asked.

He gave me a look. "What, you're worried about me now?"

"Well, it's certainly not going to help anyone if you keel over from lack of food or sleep. When was the last time you ate a home-cooked meal?"

One side of his mouth perked up. "Are you offering?"

"Depends. Are you accepting my help and sharing what you find with me?"

He rolled his eyes. "Should have known there would be a catch."

"It's not a catch. It's a mutually beneficial relationship," I said. "And I'll be doing more than my part, because I'll share what I'm discovering with you, too."

His eyebrows went up as he began digging through the piles on his desk. "Yes, that's exactly what you should be doing. What are you finding?"

"You first," I said, sipping my coffee.

He finally located his pen and pulled his notebook out of his pocket. "No, no, no. Ladies first."

I mock sighed, although I had expected that. "Okay. Did you know that Polly had seen Madame Rowena before she disappeared?"

He glanced at me over the top of his notebook. "Madame Rowena? You mean the psychic?"

"Yes. According to one of Polly's friends, she made an appointment for a reading with her."

Wyle jotted down a note, then furrowed his brow. "She's the one who claimed she would be able to locate Polly, isn't she?"

"The one and same."

Wyle made a face. "Yeah, she's called a couple of times wanting to talk about consulting opportunities."

"I'm not surprised. Are you guys going to hire her?"

"Not if I have anything to say about it," Wyle said. "So, Polly's friend. Does he or she know what Madame Rowena told her?"

"It's a 'she,' and no. But more than that, it seems Polly didn't go to the appointment after all, which her friend thought was a little weird. A couple days after Polly disappeared, she actually went to see Rowena, who said Polly hadn't shown up."

Wyle glanced up at me. "So, Polly said she didn't have the appointment after all, and Madame Rowena denies it happened. But you think Polly actually did see her?"

"I didn't say Polly denied seeing Rowena," I answered. "I said Polly made it seem like she didn't see Rowena."

"I'm not following."

"The bottom line is, I made an appointment with Rowena this morning and got her to admit she had seen Polly after all," I said smugly.

"Of course you did," Wyle countered. "So, did Rowena tell you what they talked about?"

"Are you kidding? She claimed it was 'confidential.'" I rolled my eyes. "But we know now that Polly denied it altogether, and Rowena downplayed it. The question is, why?"

"That is a good question," Wyle said, making notes. "What's the friend's name?"

"Beth, but I didn't get a last name. She's helping Donny search for Polly, so if you find the search party, you'll probably find her."

"Where is the search party?"

"Down by the lake and in the woods."

Wyle glanced up at me, a line creased between his eyes. "Why are they searching there?"

"Do you really want to know?"

Wyle put the pen down and folded his arms across his desk. "Probably not, but you better tell me."

"They think Redemption took her."

Wyle closed his eyes briefly. "I should have guessed. Well, I guess that's better than assuming it was vampires."

"I agree. Anyway, I'm guessing you'll find Beth there, and Donny, too, should you want to chat with him."

Wyle raised his eyebrow. "*Do* I want to chat with Donny?"

I took a sip of my coffee. "You might. Did you know he was renting an apartment from Harrison, but got evicted a couple months ago?"

Wyle shook his head as he picked up his pen and made another note. "We'll look into it. Anything else?"

I paused. "Going back to Rowena, is it possible you hold off talking to her until maybe tomorrow?"

Wyle put his pen down again. "Why?"

I drank more coffee, mostly to give myself a moment to collect my thoughts. "Because I want to give her the chance to do the right thing."

Wyle gave me a blank look. "The right thing?"

I nodded. "I have a feeling Polly might be turning up very soon. Maybe this afternoon or tonight … or even first thing tomorrow morning."

Wyle eyed me. "So, you're the psychic now?"

"You could say that."

Wyle stared at me. "Charlie, if you know something …"

I held my hands up. "I don't. I swear. It's just a feeling. But if I'm right, it would be better to not push it."

"But if you're wrong, we could lose a day of searching," Wyle said.

"I know. But if I am wrong, then questioning Rowena won't matter anyhow, because she really doesn't know anything."

Wyle pressed his hands against his temples. "Wait a minute. Are you saying you think Rowena had something to do with Polly's disappearance?" Wyle was already pushing his chair back, like he was about to go track down the resident psychic.

"I don't think Rowena had anything to do with kidnapping or taking Polly," I said hastily. "But I do think she knows where she is."

"If she knows where she is, she needs to tell me," Wyle said. He was still in his chair, but his whole body vibrated with energy.

"I don't disagree, but if you go talk to her now, I seriously doubt she will."

Wyle folded his arms across his chest. "And why is that?"

I raised my hands into the air. "Because there's no proof. At all. She didn't tell me a thing."

"Then why do you think she has anything to do with Polly?"

"It's little things … like how Rowena seems so sure the 'spirits' will tell her where Polly is, for one. She doesn't strike me as someone who would make that claim unless she really knew where Polly was. And when she did my reading this morning, she was adamant that the Polly and Harrison cases weren't related."

Wyle eyed me. "*That* was the appointment you made with her this morning? For a reading?"

"Of course. How do you think I was able to talk to her? She couldn't tell me anything about Harrison or who killed him, but she was sure it was unrelated to Polly. Why? Unless she knows more about Polly's disappearance than she's letting on."

"Okay, then why aren't I heading over there right now to talk to her again?"

"Because I basically told her, though not in so many words, that I would give her a day to produce Polly before I told anyone they'd met," I said. "Think about it. She will never, ever admit it, because she knows if that came out, it would ruin her reputation. So if you go over there now, she'll deny it, and that will be that. BUT, if I'm right, she's probably in the process of tracking down Polly right now to tell her to un-disappear herself. Because she doesn't want you or anyone else showing up to ask her hard questions."

Wyle scowled. "I don't like this at all."

"I don't either, but it's the game we have to play."

He drummed his fingers on his desk. "Fine," he said. "I'll give her a day. But if Polly doesn't show up by tomorrow morning, I'm yanking Rowena into an interrogation room."

"You may want to do that regardless of whether Polly shows up or not," I said.

"Why?"

"Because there's something fishy about her that needs to be looked into."

The look Wyle shot me made me think he was starting to get a headache. "I'll think about it," he said. "In the meantime, while we wait for Rowena to do the right thing, I should go find this Beth person … see what she has to say."

I nodded. "Probably a good idea."

"I'm going to have to check the file to see if we've interviewed a 'Beth,' as well," Wyle muttered as he made a note. "I know we spoke to a bunch of Polly's friends and classmates, but no one was very forthcoming. And I'm fairly sure I didn't see anything in the files about Polly talking to a psychic before she disappeared."

"Maybe you just need to ask the right questions," I said, smiling sweetly. "What is the status of the investigation, anyway?"

Wyle picked up his coffee mug, took a sip, made a face, and put it back down. "It's going," he said neutrally. "We're following up, but there hasn't been anything new."

"Polly's mother seems to think the police assume Polly ran away."

Wyle nodded. "That seems to be the most obvious conclusion … that she left on her own, versus being taken or coerced in some way. That fact that her mother is sure Polly told her she was going to her friend's house to study, the same friend who was celebrating a family birthday party, means Polly was definitely going somewhere she didn't want her parents to know about, which points to her running away."

"But according to her mother, she didn't pack any clothes."

"That her mother knows about," Wyle corrected. "Her sister told me there's a lot of sharing of clothes, not just within the family itself, but with Polly's friends, too. For instance, Polly and Kim trade shirts and dresses frequently. So, it's really impossible to know if Polly took anything or not."

I chewed on my lip. "Her mother didn't tell me that."

"I know. Neither her mother nor her father want to believe that Polly ran away. Her sister tells a different story, though, along with a couple of her friends. Polly wasn't at all happy at home and often talked about how she couldn't wait to move away. She's really not all that surprised that Polly may have gotten fed up and just left."

"Did Kim say that?" I asked, surprised.

Wyle gave me a questioning look. "I'd have to check the file to get the specific name. Like I said, we talked to several of Polly's friends and classmates, so offhand, I don't remember which one said what. Why do you ask?"

"Because Kim was helping Donny search," I said. "I would think if she really believed Polly ran away, she wouldn't bother."

"Maybe she changed her mind," Wyle said. "Kids do that."

"Yeah, but it's more than that," I said. "Beth told me that Polly and Kim weren't as close anymore, so Kim would really have no idea what Polly was thinking or feeling."

"If that's the case, then Polly using Kim as her cover story is even more suspect," Wyle said, making a note in his notebook. "I should probably interview both of them again."

"There might be something else going on, as well," I said, thinking about the way Kim had looked at Donny and how they interacted with each other. "It wouldn't surprise me to learn that Kim has a crush on Donny, which might have hurt Polly's friendship with her."

"So, what? You're thinking that maybe Polly ran away to somehow hurt Kim and Donny?"

I shrugged. "It's possible. Although it also makes me wonder if this is somehow connected to Harrison. It bothers me that Donny is linked to both Polly and Harrison, and one is missing and the other dead."

"Yeah, I don't like it, either," Wyle said.

"The problem is, I don't see the actual connection," I mused. "Had Donny somehow escalated the conflict between he and Harrison, so Harrison took Polly for revenge? Harrison doesn't really strike me as that sort of person. He was a jerk and horrible to work for, but taking someone's sister who he doesn't even know? I feel like he would be more likely to just call the cops or slap a lawsuit on Donny."

"It depends on what Donny did to Harrison in the first place," Wyle said. "Not all of Harrison's business deals were above board, at least from what we're uncovering. If Donny somehow made the wrong person mad—one of Harrison's connections, I mean—it's possible they snatched Polly to teach Donny a lesson."

"He's really involved in the search," I said. "He's her brother, so it could be as simple as that, but if he somehow felt guilty or responsible for her disappearance, that could be another layer."

Wyle chewed on the end of his pen. "Harrison evicts Donny. Donny takes some sort of revenge on Harrison, except he inadvertently upsets one of Harrison's more unsavory business connections, who takes Polly. Donny shows up at Harrison's house to demand he return Polly, but Harrison refuses … or maybe Harrison legitimately doesn't know where Polly is … and Donny doesn't believe him, so in a fit of rage, Donny kills him and drags the body to Drake's house to try and pin the blame on the new 'vampire.'"

"Harrison was killed at home?" I asked.

Wyle gave me a look. "Keep it to yourself. We don't want it getting out. But yes, Harrison was killed at home, which is also partly why we released Drake. We could see no earthly reason why Drake would go to Harrison's house, bludgeon him, and then drag his body back to the house he's housesitting at and leave it displayed out in the middle of the backyard. Nor could we find any evidence that Drake even knew who Harrison was. We're still digging through Harrison's business files and checking phone records, but as of right now, there's nothing."

"Yeah, that theory definitely doesn't make sense," I said. "And you're absolutely sure Harrison was killed at home?"

"We found bloodstains in Harrison's living room that match his blood type," Wyle said. "We're still waiting for the DNA test to know for sure, but it seems highly doubtful there would be blood from someone else with the same blood type in Harrison's house. The murder weapon was found in the living room next to the blood, and it appears to have belonged to Harrison."

"Could someone have taken the murder weapon, used it to kill Harrison, and then returned it to his house?" I asked, thinking maybe it was something like a fireplace poker … something easy to take that would probably not be missed. If it was Drake, maybe he tried to set up the scene later, so it only looked like Harrison was killed in his house. Even as I thought it, I knew it was probably a long shot.

Wyle looked at me from over his notebook. "It was a lamp."

"Oh. Yeah, that's probably not the first thing a would-be murderer would take as a murder weapon," I said. "So, someone broke into Harrison's house and hit Harrison on the head with his own lamp, and then dragged his body to Jonas's house?"

"Pretty much," Wyle said. "Except it doesn't look like whoever did it broke in."

"Harrison let the person in? You think he knew his killer?"

Wyle nodded. "Yep. There's no sign of any break-in. That's why we were thinking it was a business deal gone bad. Whoever it was came to Harrison's house, and Harrison let him or her in, presumably to talk. But the talk didn't go very well, and the killer ended up grabbing a lamp and hitting Harrison on the head. Once he was dead, the killer panicked and decided to hide the body by leaving it out in the open at Jonas's, thereby hopefully diverting the investigation."

"That theory works with Donny, too," I said. "In fact, it might fit Donny even more than one of Harrison's shady business partners. He likely would have come more prepared, in case things went south."

"Yes, another chat with Donny is also on the list," Wyle said.

"I wonder how Rowena fits into all of this," I said thoughtfully. "Is she renting her shop from Harrison?"

Wyle frowned. "I don't know. But even if she is, it doesn't mean anything. Harrison has lots of renters."

"I'm sure he does, but that might be another connection between Harrison and Polly," I said. "I wasn't thinking Rowena took Polly, but maybe … maybe she did."

Wyle gave me a skeptical look. "Why would she? Because Harrison asked? Do you think he said 'please'?"

"Maybe that's all it would take," I said. "Like I said, there's something off with her that needs to be investigated. Other than she isn't a psychic and her name probably isn't Rowena Tanveer, we don't know anything about her. Where was she before she moved to Redemption? What shady deals are in her past? Maybe she knew Harrison from before, and he was the reason she moved to Redemption in the first place."

Wyle eyed me. "You really don't like Rowena, do you?"

"What, and you do?" I asked.

"I don't know her enough to make a decision one way or another."

"Well, there's something about her that bothers me," I said. "Someone really needs to look into her background." I gave Wyle a pointed look.

"Fine," Wyle said with a sigh. "I guess I'll make a few calls. Anything else?"

"Actually, I was also wondering about Jonas," I said. "Were you able to find him?"

Wyle shook his head. "No, we still can't locate him. There's no record of him anywhere after leaving Redemption. We've got a trace on his credit cards, but there's been no activity, and there are no police reports on any accidents anywhere. It's like he just … vanished."

Vanished. Like Polly. No trace of either of them. I could feel the hair on the back of my neck stand up. "Do you think there's any connection between Jonas and Harrison and/or Polly?"

"We didn't find one between Jonas and Harrison, but I will admit we haven't looked for one with Polly," Wyle said.

"You know, it IS really weird that Jonas decided to go on this vacation and have a housesitter move in right before all of this other stuff happened," I said. "I mean, as far as I can tell, Jonas doesn't go anywhere. For years, he's lived in the same house and had the same job … he doesn't even take day trips to Riverview. But the one time he happens to leave for a real vacation, all hell breaks loose?"

"I don't like it, either," Wyle said. "And believe me, I haven't forgotten about him. I'm still following up."

"Okay, I guess I better leave you to it," I said, getting to my feet.

"So, what time do you want me over?" he asked, his face suspiciously bland.

I gave him a blank look. "Over for what?"

Wyle widened his eyes in mock surprise. "Dinner, of course! You promised me a home-cooked meal if I shared, and I did."

I stared at him. "You can't be serious."

His mouth quirked up. "I'm extremely serious about home-cooked meals."

I couldn't think of what to say. My mind had gone blank—actually, it was more jumbled than blank … like a box of jigsaw puzzle pieces. Was this some sort of backwards way of asking me for a date? Except what kind of date was it really, if I had to do the cooking?

He raised an eyebrow. "Well? You did promise."

I ground my teeth. Argh. He was right. I did. "Fine. Would 7:00 work?" *Maybe this will end up being a good thing,* I reassured myself. *I could get an update on all his to-dos.*

"Perfect," he said. "I'll see you then." He busied himself at his desk. Clearly, I was dismissed. Ugh.

"Don't be late," I said, turning on my heel and marching out the door. I thought I could hear him chuckle as I strode through the station, which made me grind my teeth even more.

As if everything going on wasn't bad enough, I now had to figure out what I was going to make for dinner.

Chapter 17

I was busy in my kitchen, putting the finishing touches on a slow-cooked pot roast—which I was going to serve with mashed potatoes, homemade biscuits, and a salad—and still fussing about what to bake for dessert when the doorbell rang.

Oh boy. It was probably Pat, which would normally be a good thing, especially since I had a lot to share with her. But in this case, I didn't want to have to explain to her why I had a pot roast in a slow cooker. She would probably make all sorts of assumptions that were just not true, so I was already busy trying to get my explanations sorted out in my head when I discovered Drake on my front porch.

For a moment, I could only stare at him. I was so sure it would be Pat, and equally sure I would never see Drake outside his house, that for a moment, I thought I was hallucinating.

He wore the same black hoodie (with the hood up) and black sweatpants that he'd worn to the police station. My porch was covered with a roof, and therefore, there was no chance of the sun bothering him. Yet his head remained bowed down, as if he was so used to keeping the sun off his face, it had become a habit every time he ventured outside.

"Can I come in?" he asked. Well, it was more like a mutter, as he was staring at the ground.

Wordlessly, I opened the door wider to allow him inside. It was only when I was closing it behind him that I realized how stupid I was being.

I had no idea who this man was. While he didn't appear to have anything to do with the dead body in his backyard, that wasn't a sure thing. And even if he didn't have anything to do with Harrison's murder, it didn't mean he was harmless.

The worst part was, no one even knew he was in the house with me.

Other than Midnight, that is, who took that moment to stroll into the living room. I realized it only because Drake blanched and then sneezed.

"Cats," he said. "I'm allergic."

I turned around to see Midnight sitting on the bottom stair, calmly cleaning himself.

"Yeah, well, you know. Cats always know when someone is allergic," I said weakly, thinking to myself there was no way I was putting Midnight away anywhere. If Drake was truly allergic, it would hopefully keep his visit short.

He sneezed again and dug a tissue out of his pocket. "I won't be long," he said.

"How did you find me?" I asked.

"The phone book," he said, blowing his nose. "You told me your full name the day you introduced yourself."

Oh yes. I did, didn't I? That was part of the challenge of having a business out of your home—people could easily discover where you lived. *Although this is Redemption,* I had to remind myself. Everyone already knew I lived in the most haunted house in town. It wouldn't be that difficult to find me regardless.

"I'm surprised to see you here at this hour," I said.

He finished with his nose and tucked the tissue back into his pocket. "Yeah, I rarely go anywhere during the day."

There was a long pause. Even though Drake had moved inside the house where there was definitely no sunlight, he was still staring at the ground. I was wondering if I was going to need to nudge Midnight closer to see if that would encourage Drake to get to the point of his visit when he finally cleared his throat.

"You didn't have to do that," he said.

"I didn't have to do what?"

"What you did last night," he said. "You don't know me, and you put yourself in danger to defend me."

I was mystified. "You came all the way out here during the day to tell me this? You already said it last night."

"I know, but no one's ever done that for me before." He raised his head to look me in the eye, and the pain I saw there nearly took my breath away.

"As I told you last night, I have a lot to make up for," I said gently. "Trust me when I say I've made a ton of mistakes in my life. A ton. I'm no saint. I'm just an average person trying to balance the ledger of my life, even though I know it will never be."

"You're not average," he said, his gaze intense. "Average people don't do what you did."

There was no point in arguing with him, as I had no intention of delving into my past mistakes. Instead, I changed the subject. "What's the real reason you're here?"

His mouth curved into a smile, but there was something rusty about it, as if it didn't happen much and he had almost forgotten how. "I wanted to tell you the truth."

"The truth?" Oh no. If he said he was really a vampire …

"About Jonas."

That got my attention. "What about Jonas?" As much as I wanted the truth, I was also hoping I wasn't about to hear a confession. I also started to wonder where my baseball bat was. I had a sinking suspicion it was upstairs in my office. Argh. I decided I needed to invest in more of them to place in various locations around the house.

"I wanted to tell you why he left. The real reason."

"Which is …"

Drake paused to take a deep breath. "He wants to move."

Move? For a moment, I wasn't sure I heard him correctly. "Did you say … 'move'?"

Drake nodded.

This couldn't be right. All of this mess, when all Jonas wanted was to leave Redemption? "I don't understand."

Drake sighed. "He swore me to secrecy."

"I still don't understand. So what, if people know he wants to move?"

Drake started waving his arms around. "You know the stories, right? You live here. Redemption decides who stays and who goes."

I nodded, the pieces starting to assemble themselves in my brain.

"Jonas had been unhappy for a long time, but he wasn't able to leave. At first, he did what people normally do—apply for transfers. But all of those fell through. After a while, he decided he was unhappy enough to not care if he lost his pension, so he started applying for other non-government jobs. But that didn't work out, either. Finally, he decided he was just going to quit, pack up his stuff, and leave, but the day he was going to turn in his notice, his supervisor had a heart attack, and he ended up being promoted. That's when he realized Redemption was never going to let him go. So, he came up with this scheme to take a month-long 'vacation,'" Drake placed air quotes around "vacation" with his fingers. "And never come back."

"So, this was all planned?"

Drake nodded. "Yeah, and very hush-hush. He wouldn't have even told me, if he hadn't needed someone to stay behind to fix up the house and sell it for him."

"So, you really ARE fixing up the backyard then?"

"Along with other things. Jonas was trying not to tip Redemption off, so he didn't even want to start the home improvement projects himself."

"And he thought all this pretending would somehow 'trick' the town?" I asked, my tone full of disbelief. "Didn't he realize that, if what everyone thinks about the town is true, it would know what he was planning?"

"He took a lot of precautions," Drake said. "We weren't allowed to discuss him not returning in the house or even in Redemption. We met at a coffee shop in Riverview instead. He loaded up on cash, so his credit cards wouldn't be tracked. He thought of everything."

Everything except a dead body appearing in his backyard and the rest of the town assuming his housesitter was a vampire, I guessed. "So, why are you telling me now? It can't just be because I helped you yesterday."

Drake ducked his head, shuffling from one foot to the next. "No, it's not." He sighed. "I need your help. I know everyone thinks I had something to do with that murder, but I swear, I've never even met that Harrison guy. I can sense the cops trying to pin it on me, and the fact that no one knows where Jonas is, is a problem."

"Do you know where he is?"

Drake shook his head. "The plan was for him to establish himself somewhere and then reach out to me about selling the house. He wasn't sure what to expect … as far as he knew, no one had tried anything like this before, so he thought it might take a few months or even a year before it would be safe for him to contact me. In the meantime, someone would be living in the house and getting it ready to sell once it seemed clear that Redemption was no longer interested in keeping him."

"That may end up being longer than he thinks," I said drily. "I don't know how well a house with a dead body recently found in the backyard is going to sell."

Drake rubbed his face with his palms. "I know. This is such a mess. I don't know what to do."

"So, why are you here talking to me instead of the cops?"

"Because I don't think the cops will believe me," he said.

"And you think they'll listen to me?"

"At least that one will," he said. "Officer Wyle, I think his name is. I was watching you two last night."

"I'm not sure what you think you saw, but there's nothing there," I said. "Wyle and I aren't even friends. At best, he tolerates me helping with his investigations." The aroma of pot roast wafted into the living room, as if it was calling me a liar. I shifted uncomfortably, although I told myself I was being silly. It's not like Drake would connect the smell of dinner with Wyle coming over for a strictly platonic note-comparing session.

"That's a step up from what he thinks of me, as a murder suspect," Drake said. "But I think you're selling yourself short."

"Trust me, I'm not," I said, even as the scent of the pot roast seemed to grow stronger. "But regardless, if you want me to talk to Wyle for you, I can do that."

Drake looked relieved. "Thank you."

"I'm not done yet," I said, holding up a finger. "I need something more. Like some cities where Jonas might be considering moving to or something, so the cops can track him down. It would really help if they could find Jonas and have him corroborate your story. Me just saying it is going to sound just as crazy as you telling them, and Wyle is going to need something solid to go on."

Drake's expression of relief disappeared almost as quickly as it had appeared, and he looked deflated. "I was afraid you might say that. I really don't know."

"You must know something," I urged. "Something he said. Even if it was in passing."

Drake shook his head. "He was afraid of jinxing anything. But maybe you could talk to his cousin."

"His cousin?"

"Yeah, the one who introduced us. He might have more of an idea of where Jonas would want to move to. I can give you his name and number."

"Well, that's a start," I said, as I looked around for a pen and paper. "Anything else?"

"I know Jonas is looking for a job," Drake said. "That's part of how he wanted to establish himself."

I handed him an envelope to write on, along with a pen. "What kind of job?"

"That's the thing. I think he was planning on looking for something off-the-books … at least initially, until he was sure Redemption would let him go. I asked him how handy he is, but it doesn't seem like a skill he has. So, my guess is he'll be doing something like washing dishes for a restaurant, or maybe some sort of day laborer."

This wasn't boding well at all for Wyle being able to find him.

"Is that something you know about?"

His expression was embarrassed as he finished scribbling a name and number before handing the envelope back to me. "I've had my share of off-the-books jobs. It's tough, when people don't understand your medical condition. For me, it was more about not being *able* to land a normal job. That said, I didn't get the sense that Jonas is the type of guy who would be able to disappear for very long. Yes, he might find some sort of job where they pay cash, but he's probably going to have a lease somewhere, or a utility bill or two in his name."

"I don't understand," I said. "It seems like he's going through a lot of trouble to hide. So why would he have things like leases and utility bills in his name?"

"Because he's not trying to hide from the law, or anything like that," Drake said. "He just wanted to throw anyone off his trail, like his boss, or maybe your friend, the nosy neighbor. So, they look for him where he said he would be vacationing, and when he's not there, maybe they search other hotels and vacation spots. When they still don't find him, maybe they think something happened to him. By then, the trail would likely be cold, and they'll end up moving on. He's not trying to hide forever … just long enough for Redemption to let him go. Eventually, he planned to resurface, if only to finalize the sale of his house. So, my guess is, if the cops investigate that way, they'll be able to find him."

"Makes sense," I said, tucking the envelope in the back pocket of my jeans. "Okay, I'll share all of this with Wyle, and we'll see. Hopefully, he'll be able to find Jonas."

"Hopefully," Drake said, his voice glum. "I'd like this to work out, so I can stay here at least until the house is sold. It's a good gig for me. I'd hate to have to leave."

Even though he continued to keep his gaze down, I still could see the loneliness and sadness on his face, and I felt my heart go out to him again. "I promise, I'll do what I can to keep that from happening," I said.

Chapter 18

Pat was already waiting for me at The Tipsy Cow, the local bar and grill. When she heard I had been at last night's mob scene, she insisted we meet there rather than our usual Aunt May's late lunch date. "This calls for a glass of wine," she said.

"It's the middle of the day," I protested, despite the fact that a glass of wine sounded like exactly what I needed.

"With everything that's happened since yesterday, it doesn't matter what the clock says," Pat said.

After I hung up, I realized she had a point. Not to mention that wine was sounding better and better.

Pat waved at me from one of the corner booths, two glasses of white already on the table. I wove my way around the wooden and scarred tables and chairs that smelled like beer, bourbon, and cigarettes toward her, relieved again she had immediately insisted on eating out rather than coming over. In that case, I would have been stuck trying to explain why I was making pot roast.

"I want every single detail," she said the moment I slid into my seat. "Don't leave anything out. I can't believe you didn't call me."

"It was after 8:00 p.m. Did you really want me to call you, so you could come face down a mob with me?" I asked.

Her eyes widened. "You faced down the mob? Spill it! I need to hear everything. And yes, I want you to call me for such things!"

"Well, it all happened really fast. Mildred called, and all I could think about was getting out there …"

"Start at the beginning," Pat broke in, interrupting me as she picked up her glass of wine.

I did, starting with Mildred calling me and ending with Drake on my doorstep. The only thing I didn't share was how Wyle finagled a dinner invitation that night. Even though I knew it didn't mean anything more than a bribe for more information, it felt like too much effort to try and explain it.

Pat stared at me as I finished, a fry dangling from her hand. It had taken me so long to go through everything, we had not only ordered, but gotten our food. Pat had chosen the chicken club with fries, and I decided on the Cobb salad, which was remarkably good for a bar and grill. Plus, with the dinner I was cooking, I figured a lighter lunch was in order. "I don't even know where to start," she said.

I picked up my wine to take a sip. "I know. It's a little nuts, everything that happened."

"I guess I'll start at the end, with what Drake told you. Have you told Wyle yet?"

I shook my head. "I'll tell him later. I know he's looking into Polly right now, and that feels more urgent than Jonas. Especially if it's as Drake says, and Jonas disappeared on his own accord. If it takes Wyle a day or two to dig into Jonas's whereabouts, it won't change much."

"That's probably true," Pat said, munching on a fry. "So, let's talk about Polly and Rowena. You seriously think she's somehow involved with Polly's disappearance?"

"I have no idea, but I think she's a better bet than Drake," I said, putting my wine glass down and picking up my fork. "If one of the reasons you think Drake is involved is because all of this started happening after he arrived, well, guess what? Rowena just arrived, as well."

"Yeah, but Rowena didn't have a dead body in her yard."

I pointed at Pat with my fork. "But she DID say she was going to use her psychic gifts to find Polly. Why would she do that, unless she knew where Polly was? She was risking incredible embarrassment, as well as her professional reputation."

"But I'm sure the cops asked her about it," Pat said.

"What would they say? 'Are you making this prediction because you know where Polly is?' 'I have no idea where Polly is, but the spirits know, and I know how to talk to the spirits, and I'm sure they'll tell me.' If Rowena actually comes up with something, then I think the cops will have something to go on, but right now, it's just her empty promises."

"Well, if she is involved, especially if it's because of something shady in her past, don't you think she'd be keeping it quiet? Why make such a public declaration, if she didn't want the cops poking into her past?"

"She might think she's protected herself well enough," I said. "It's also possible she thinks it won't lead back to her. Until Polly comes home and tells us what happened, we don't know how Rowena will spin this so she somehow gets the credit and avoids any issues. The only thing we can be sure of is that she WILL spin this."

Pat cocked her head. "You really don't like her, do you?"

"There's something off with her," I said, stabbing at my salad. "Don't you feel it, too?"

"I don't think I know her well enough to have any feelings about her one way or another," Pat said.

It was on the tip of my tongue to tell her she sounded like Wyle, but then I would have to explain how I was talking to Wyle, and I didn't particularly want to get into all of that.

"She claiming to be a psychic when she clearly isn't."

"Again, we don't know that," Pat said. "We just heard one reading from her, and she probably knew we weren't serious, so who knows what she's saying to people who have legitimate questions? It's possible whatever she's doing is on the up and up. Some people are good at reading others, which could be all this is."

"I can't believe you're defending her," I said.

"I'm not," Pat protested. "I'm just saying we should keep an open mind. Kind of like how you want people to have an open mind about Drake."

I could feel my cheeks getting hot. "That's different."

"Is it?"

"It is," I said firmly, even though a part of me was starting to wonder. "First off, I never said Drake was innocent of anything other than being a vampire. It may come out that he killed

Harrison, and maybe even Jonas for that matter, and he's using me to send the police on a wild goose chase. As for Rowena, it's possible she had nothing to do with Polly, but she's sure not acting like it."

"You're also sure she's a fake," Pat said. "But you haven't shared any evidence as to why."

I pressed my lips tightly together. "Okay, fine," I said. "Maybe I'm jumping to conclusions about Rowena. But there's something off with her. I can feel it. I don't believe she's trying to help anyone but herself."

Pat picked up her sandwich to take a bite. "I guess we'll see if Polly magically reappears or not."

I forked up a bite of salad as Pat craned her head. "Hey, is that Linda?"

I turned to see Linda standing by the bar, chatting with the bartender. I glanced at my watch. "Shouldn't she be working?"

"Maybe she's not working anymore," Pat said.

"Maybe not," I said. From what I could tell, Linda certainly looked different. She seemed more relaxed and was actually smiling at the bartender, who looked about her age.

I slid out of the booth. "I'll go find out and report back."

"I'll make sure no one takes your wine glass," Pat said. "It's a tough job, but someone has to do it."

I headed over to the bar, studying Linda as I went. She was still dressed the same as before, in a white silk blouse with a huge bow at the neck and a beige skirt that didn't suit her any better than any of her other outfits. I had a feeling she would look fabulous in pastels, something like soft pinks or lavenders, instead of these stark black, white, and brown disasters, but of course, she wasn't asking for my opinion. However, unlike those other times, she had make-up on, which helped add some color to her sallow skin tone and gave some definition to her thin lips.

"Linda," I said. "Fancy meeting you here."

She turned and smiled one of her million-watt smiles, causing me to catch my breath again. "Charlie! So nice to see you again."

"What are you doing here? Isn't it a little early for a drink?" I winked as I said it.

She giggled a little, and it was all I could do to not let my mouth fall open in shock. Linda hadn't struck me as the giggling type. "I'm here to pick up lunch, not drink."

"So no Aunt May's today?"

"Nah. I like Aunt May's, but it's nice to have a little break." She leaned closer to me, and I caught a whiff of mint like before. "And I like the Cobb salad here better," she finished in a mock whisper.

The bartender heard her and grinned. He was a big, beefy guy with a shaved head and broken nose, like a boxer. Very different from the skinny, slouchy Donny, I noted.

"So, you're still working at the same place then?" I asked.

"I am. Graham, that's Harrison's brother, put Westly in charge."

"Westly?" I pictured the thin, fussy-looking, prematurely balding man in my head. He didn't seem the manager type, especially when I thought about how the maintenance guy seemed to ignore him. Although maybe that was because Westly didn't have any authority at that point. That might change, now.

Plus, he certainly seemed to know Harrison's business inside and out. Graham could do far worse for a manager.

"Yeah. Graham is going to take care of the Riverview office, as he's already settled there with another business and has no intention of ever moving to Redemption. So, we just need to handle Redemption."

"Sounds like it's all working out, then?"

She smiled and nodded. "Oh, yes. I mean, I don't want to speak ill of the dead. I know Harrison ... well, *he tried*. But it's so much less stressful now! I feel like a huge weight has been lifted off my shoulders."

"I can imagine," I said, picturing Harrison's tombstone. He tried. I supposed there were worse epitaphs.

"Here you go, Linda," the beefy bartender said, handing her two Styrofoam boxes.

Linda thanked him and smiled brilliantly, causing him to busy himself by wiping down the counters. I wondered if Linda had any idea of the power of that smile.

"I should let you go," I said. "But I'm really glad it's working out so well for you."

She bobbed her head. "It is. It's just all such a relief. Working in such a relaxed office. Knowing that Donny had nothing to do with Harrison's murder. I'm just so …"

"Wait a minute," I interrupted. "What do you mean, about Donny? Did the cops arrest someone for Harrison's murder, and I just haven't heard about it?"

She looked startled and pressed a hand to her mouth. "Oh! I shouldn't have said anything."

"About what? Do the cops know who did it?"

Linda shook her head as she shrunk back into herself, transforming right in front of me into the mouse-like Linda of old. "No. It's not like that. It's just …" her eyes darted nervously around the bar to see if anyone was near before she leaned in closer to me. "Westly has been doing some digging," she said. "In Harrison's old files. And he's found some names of some of Harrison's past … 'associates.' Bad people. Red was one of them. Remember him?"

I did indeed remember Red. He was the owner of the Lone Man Standing bar before it burned down. He disappeared a couple years ago. Everyone presumed he had died in the fire, but I wasn't so sure.

There were a lot of rumors swirling around the Lone Man Standing—drugs, gangs, prostitution … and Red was at the center of it all. No one could prove anything, though. I had endured a few run-ins with him before he disappeared, and as far as I was concerned, it was good riddance.

"I remember," I said. "But no one has seen Red since the fire." Surely, Linda wasn't saying Red was back in Redemption and gearing up his crime ring. I knew there had been some rumors of drug gangs moving back into the area, after having disappeared along with Red and the bar, but that didn't necessarily mean Red himself was back.

"I didn't mean to imply that Red murdered Harrison. I was giving you an example of the kind of people Harrison was doing business with," she said. Then, she shivered. "It gives me the creeps, even though Westly has been sharing the files with the police and Graham, and no one thinks we're in danger. Especially since we don't know anything. Westly already turned everything he found over to the authorities, so that's good news."

"That *is* good news," I agreed, wondering how any of that possibly exonerated Donny.

"Westly also discovered that Harrison had a couple of meetings with Jonas."

I did a double take. "Really?"

"Yeah. A few months before he disappeared, and the vampire moved into his house."

An uneasy feeling stirred in my stomach. "Linda, you know there's no such thing as vampires."

Linda chuckled uncomfortably. "Well, yes. Of course. But there's still something not quite right about him, don't you think? Never going out into the sun, digging graves in the backyard …"

"He's digging a garden, not graves," I corrected. "And he doesn't go out into the sun because he has an allergy to it."

She gave me an uncomprehending look. "An allergy to the sun? That sounds exactly like a vampire."

"No, it's an actual medical condition. It's rare, but it's real."

She didn't look convinced. "Well, whatever. The point is, it's looking more and more like it was the vamp … I mean the housesitter, after all, which means it couldn't have been Donny."

I stared at her, my mind whirling. Suddenly, Drake showing up unexpectedly at my home felt completely different.

Was it possible Drake knew this connection between Jonas and Harrison was bound to be found, and he was trying to get in front of it?

I pictured his face as he told me he had never met or heard of Harrison. He seemed completely sincere. Of course, Harrison and Jonas could have met at some point without Drake knowing. And whatever Jonas and Harrison had discussed could very well have had nothing to do with either Drake or Harrison's murder.

"Do you know why Harrison and Jonas were meeting?" I asked.

"Harrison wasn't great about taking notes," she said. "I don't know if there was much in the file. Oh, speaking of Westly, I better run. He's probably hungry for his lunch."

I watched her go before heading back to Pat, who had nearly finished her sandwich. She glanced at my face and frowned. "This can't be good."

"I don't know if it is or isn't," I said.

I filled her in on what Linda told me, and her eyes grew wide. "Jonas and Harrison were doing business together?"

"Linda didn't say that, exactly. Just that they had met, and she wasn't sure why."

"So, Drake may have actually had a motive to kill Harrison?"

"Maybe, but I can't think of what it would be." I chewed on my lip. "Setting aside how incredibly dumb it would be to kill someone in his house and then drag his body to your own backyard, why would Drake be threatened by Harrison having a business relationship with Jonas?"

"Well, what if Jonas was going to sell the house to Harrison? That would mean Drake would be out," Pat theorized.

I frowned. "Maybe. But Jonas isn't here right now."

"That doesn't mean Harrison wasn't taking steps to purchase Jonas's house."

"If he was, it was a huge secret. Neither Westly nor Linda knew anything about it when Harrison was alive."

Pat squished up her face. "Hmm. Is it possible that Harrison knew something, or had something, on Drake?"

"Like what?"

Pat shrugged. "I don't know. Maybe Drake had been in trouble with the law? Or something else that he wouldn't want Jonas knowing, as he was staying in Jonas's house?"

"That's possible," I said. Again, I could see Drake standing in front of me, begging me to talk to Wyle and tell him Jonas was alive and well and just wanted to move away from Redemption without any further issues. "Or, what if Drake had something to do with Jonas's disappearance after all, and either Harrison knows something, or Drake suspected he knew something, and wanted to silence him?"

"I thought you told me Drake wanted Wyle to find Jonas."

"He did, but that doesn't mean Wyle is actually going to locate him. It's not like Drake gave me a lot to go on. But just opening the door that Jonas is hiding out somewhere waiting for the right time to sell his house could be enough to plant reasonable doubt."

Pat traced the top of her nearly empty wine glass. "Hmm, Drake as a master manipulator. I guess if that's the case, then maybe he moved Harrison's body to his backyard to throw everyone off. As you pointed out, it's incredibly stupid to do something like that if you are the one responsible. Therefore, people would think he couldn't possibly have done it, because no one is that stupid."

"Wouldn't that be something?" I asked. "The killer right in front of our noses the whole time, but it was so obvious, we all overlooked it."

Pat started to smile, but then twisted her head. "Hang on. There's something going on over there." She pointed, and I turned around to watch. There was a knot of people talking excitedly, but I was too far away to hear what they were saying.

"My turn," Pat said, sliding out of the booth. "Besides, you need to finish your food."

"Okay, I'll keep an eye on the wine," I said, picking up my fork.

Between bites, I watched Pat join them, and after a few minutes, she hurried back to me, her expression one of absolute disbelief.

"You're not going to believe this," she said as she settled back into her seat. She nodded at my salad. "You may want to hurry up and finish your lunch."

"Why?" I asked.

"They found Polly.

Chapter 19

It was actually Donny, not Rowena, who found Polly. Sure enough, she was wandering around the woods near the lake, and he had taken her straight to the hospital.

"Is she okay?" I asked.

"I'm not sure," Pat said. "No one was very clear. But it does seem like she had some injuries."

Injuries? I hadn't expected that. I was so sure she had orchestrated her own disappearance, I didn't imagine she'd be injured.

Once Pat and I had gobbled down the rest of our lunches and paid the bill, we immediately headed off to the hospital. "I don't know if they'll let us in, since we aren't family," Pat said.

"We have to at least try," I said.

I had assumed there would be a huge crowd of people in the waiting room, but there wasn't. Things seemed perfectly normal. It took a bit of sleuthing to find Polly's room, as I didn't want to draw attention to ourselves by asking. So, we did our own search, and it was actually more luck than anything that we found it, as we just happened to spot Donny exiting one of the patient rooms.

"Donny!" I called out, waving at him. He stopped and stared at us, confusion on his face.

"What are *you* doing here?" he asked.

"We're seeing a friend," I answered. "What are you doing here? Did you find Polly?"

"Yes, she's here." He pointed to the room he'd just left.

"Oh, that's wonderful news! Is she okay?"

"I think so. It's hard to tell." He seemed pensive—definitely not as happy as I would expect after finally finding his sister.

"What do you mean, 'It's hard to tell'?"

He looked at his shoes, his hair falling into his face. "I don't know. I can't really explain it. She's just … she doesn't seem happy to be back."

I almost reached out to put a hand on his arm, but I drew back, not sure how he would take it. "Depending on what happened to her, it can be difficult," I said. "She might have been drugged, or traumatized, or both. Plus, she's probably exhausted and may not have had enough food or water. Give her a little time to rest. I'm sure she'll bounce back."

"Yeah, that's what the doctors said, too, but I don't know. There's something not right with her."

I glanced at the door, wondering if there was a way I could get a peek inside to see her for myself. "Do you know what happened to her?"

"Not exactly. She had gone to Riverview for some sort of frat party, but something happened, and the next thing she knew, she found herself wandering around out by the lake."

"What do you mean, 'something happened'?"

"That's the thing. She doesn't know. She can't even remember if she made it to the party or not. My parents are convinced that means Redemption did take her, especially since I found her in the woods. My dad especially is feeling vindicated. But …" he hesitated.

"What?"

He glanced around the hallway, as if looking to see if anyone was watching before moving closer to us. "I found drugs in her pocket," he said, his voice low.

Immediately, my mind flashed to Red. Was it possible he actually was back? "Drugs? What kind of drugs?" I asked, keeping my voice equally low.

He avoided my eyes. "I'm not sure. A few different types."

I had a feeling he was lying, but I didn't want to press it. "Was she into drugs?"

"No! I've never seen her take anything but aspirin."

"Where did she get them?"

"I don't know, but I'm guessing at the party."

"Has she gone to parties like this before? Where there are drugs available?"

Donny shook his head violently. "No! None of this is Polly. She was always the good girl … never smoked, never drank … certainly didn't do anything harder. I don't understand what's going on. It doesn't make sense." The words tumbled out of him, like he had been holding everything inside for way too long.

I glanced at the door to Polly's room again. "What did she say about it?"

"That she doesn't know anything about it."

"What do the doctors say?"

Donny ducked his head again and didn't answer.

"Donny? What's going on?"

His voice was barely audible. "The doctors don't know."

"What do you mean? Why not?"

"I didn't tell them."

"But you have to! It could be really important."

He finally looked up at me, staring directly into my eyes. They were a startling dark blue, framed with long, thick lashes wasted on a boy. "But she could be arrested and thrown in jail."

"Yes, that's possible," I admitted. "But it's highly unlikely. It's her first offense, right? And she's under eighteen, so chances are, nothing will happen to her legally. More importantly, the doctors really need to know in order to treat her properly."

He was shaking his head firmly. "No, I can't risk it."

I sighed, glancing at the door again. "What if I talk to the cops and see if I can get some sort of guarantee she won't go to jail? Would that help?"

He eyed me suspiciously. "I don't know."

"You want to do the right thing by Polly, right? I can tell you do. It's really important to be honest with the doctors."

He looked away from me, his jaw set. I wanted to sigh.

"How did you even find the drugs on her?" I asked, wondering if there might be another way to convince him.

He didn't say anything, and for a moment, I was afraid he was done talking—that my suggestion to ask the police was a bridge too far, but after a deep breath, he began speaking. "I found her in the woods. She was sitting under a tree, staring at nothing. Her clothes were dirty and torn, and her hair was a tangled mess. She had a bruise under her eye. I dropped to my knees and hugged her, but it was like hugging a mannequin. There was just nothing … no emotion, no anything. I started asking her questions, but she didn't have any answers. She just kept shaking her head and saying she didn't know what happened. So I got her to her feet, and as I did, I felt something in her jacket pocket. I looked, thinking maybe whatever it was would shine a light on where she'd been, but it was the drugs. I asked her about them, but she just stared at me … said she didn't know what they were. I didn't want her getting in trouble, so I took them." He turned to me, an almost desperate expression in his eyes. "I would have told the doctors if it was important. Honestly. But other than her memory loss, they say she's perfectly healthy and likely just suffering from exhaustion and stress. I'm sure she didn't take any of them."

"What do they think is causing her memory loss?"

He screwed up his face. "They think it's likely some sort of fugue state, and that it's temporary. Once she gets some good food and sleep, she'll remember what happened."

"I'm familiar with fugue states," I said. "They're not generally well understood, but they're usually caused by trauma, which fits Polly's situation. But Donny, what if she did take some of the drugs? That could be what's behind her memory loss, and by not telling the doctors, it could affect her recovery."

"No, the doctors are sure it's stress and exhaustion," he insisted. "Once she gets some rest, her memory should return, and she should go back to normal."

I wasn't sure if I believed him or not. I wished there was a way I could talk to the doctor myself and see if that were true. I could understand wanting to protect his sister, but I also thought the doctors needed to have all the information to treat her properly.

Before I could figure out how to answer Donny, the door to Polly's room opened, and Wyle came out. He saw me with Donny, our eyes locking for a moment, before he turned away and strode down the hall.

Donny had turned when the door opened, and seeing Wyle, he whirled back to me. "Don't you dare say anything," he hissed.

"But Donny, I honestly think …"

"No! Do NOT tell him. If you do, I'll deny ever saying anything." His gaze shifted back and forth between Pat and me, his eyes glittering.

It was clear he meant it, and even though he didn't say it, he would likely destroy the drugs he took from Polly, so the doctors still wouldn't know what she might have taken. My only hope was to agree now and see if there was another way to let the doctors know. Maybe it would be possible to go directly to Polly, although if Donny were to be believed, she wasn't talking to anyone … at least at this point.

"Okay," I said quietly. "I won't say anything."

"You promise?"

"Yes."

He turned to Pat, who also nodded.

"Just as long as we understand each other," he said before darting forward toward Polly's room. I glanced at Pat and saw she had the same idea I had, and we both scurried after him. I had no idea if we would be thrown out or not, but it was worth a try.

Polly was propped up in the hospital bed, looking exhausted and filthy. I did a double take—the golden-haired child I had seen in the picture in Darlene's hallway was gone. Whoever was in the bed looked to be about a decade older and a whole lot harder. She stared at me, her eyes listless. Darlene was sitting beside her, holding her hand tightly, while on the other side of the bed, a nurse in a crisp white uniform stood holding a folder.

Darlene glanced over at us, her expression mirroring the same confusion Donny's had. "Pat! And …. is it 'Charlie'? What are you doing here?"

"We were visiting a friend and ran into Donny," Pat said smoothly as she hurried forward to hold Darlene's other hand.

Donny stepped in front of the nurse to sit at the other side of his sister's bed. "We're so grateful Polly has been found!"

"Yes, it's a miracle," Darlene said, looking back at her daughter. Polly seemed to be gazing at the corner of the room, focused on nothing. The nurse, finishing her duties, melted out of the room, and I quietly took her place.

"Is there anything we can do?" Pat asked. "Can we get you anything? A cup of coffee or maybe something to eat?"

"No, no. Steve is getting us something," Darlene said absently.

"Polly, how are you doing?" Pat asked.

Polly didn't respond. Instead, she continued staring off into the corner.

"Polly?" Darlene asked. "Are you doing okay?"

Polly didn't make any indication she had heard either her mother or Pat.

"She's just tired," Darlene said to Pat, although it sounded like she was really trying to convince herself. "The doctors said she might need some time to rest … I'm sure some home-cooked dinners will help, too. Right, Polly?"

Polly still didn't respond, but the more I looked at her, the more I thought there was something off.

Something in her eyes, even as she tried to hide it.

Pat was reassuring Darlene that of course Polly just needed some time to recover when Steve, Polly's father, walked in carrying a tray of coffee and a plate of cookies. He looked startled to see Polly had visitors and asked us to go as soon as Darlene finished introducing us.

"Of course! We didn't mean to intrude," Pat said. "We just wanted to see if there was anything we could do."

"We appreciate that," Steve said as he handed out coffees and cookies. "But right now, we just need some family time. The rest of our kids will be here shortly, and it's going to get pretty crowded in here. I'm sure you understand."

At the mention of Polly's other siblings, Polly's face snapped toward her father. She still didn't say anything, but for a moment, it was like the mask dropped from her eyes, showing her real emotion.

Fear.

As fast as the mask dropped, it returned. Polly blinked her eyes and shifted her gaze back to staring at nothing. I glanced around at the rest of the room, but it didn't seem like anyone else had noticed as they busied themselves with their refreshments.

As I pondered Polly's reaction, Pat assured Steve that we of course understood his wanting family time, and we quickly headed out the door.

"So, what do you think?" Pat asked out of the corner of her mouth as we passed nurses, orderlies, and other patients in the hallway.

"Something isn't adding up," I said just as quietly. "I'm just not sure what it is yet." My mind flashed to Wyle and the look he gave me as he left the room. "Luckily, I know someone who can help."

Chapter 20

I called Wyle the moment I got home, after assuring Pat that yes, I would call her as soon as I learned anything. She needed to get dinner on the table for Richard, which was a good thing, or she might have insisted on accompanying me to track down Wyle. I told her I was going to start by calling him, which she found disappointing.

"I think you should stop by the station," she grumbled as she unlocked her car door.

"I don't even know if he'd be there. He might be out investigating where Polly was found. I'll start with a phone call and go from there."

She gave me a look as she tucked herself into her car. I didn't tell her that part of the reason I didn't want to go to the station was because I thought there might be a good chance Wyle was already headed to my house.

"Are you going to tell him about the drugs?"

"Not officially," I said.

She half-smiled.

"I have to figure out another way, though," I continued. "I'm definitely worried about Polly. Donny was right. She doesn't look right."

The smile disappeared from Pat's face. "There's definitely something wrong," she said. "Do you think something more serious happened to her, and she's just pretending to have amnesia because she doesn't want to tell anyone the truth?"

I hadn't thought about that, but I could feel the goosebumps rise on my forearms when Pat said it. Was it possible? Could Polly be hiding something even worse from her family?

"If she is, it's probably because Rowena is involved," I said.

"Okay, I grant you that Polly suddenly appearing after you gave Rowena your ultimatum is … suspicious, and more than a bit disturbing. But I'm still having trouble believing Rowena would be involved in something that truly hurt Polly. Yes," Pat held up her hand. "I can believe she's a fake psychic. But to be involved with people who would kidnap a teenage girl and do who knows what to her? That seems like a very big stretch."

"Someone gave her the drugs," I said. "If you believe Donny, that is."

"We have no evidence that Rowena was that person," Pat countered. "I haven't seen any evidence of Rowena dealing drugs or taking drugs. Have you?"

"It's too much of a coincidence, Pat. Polly magically appears after I give Rowena a day before telling the cops about her reading with Polly. So she knew they would be coming to talk to her. I'm sure she's involved. I just have to figure out how." My mind kept turning around something Donny had said—not just about the drugs, but how Polly was admitting she had tricked her parents in order to go to the party. "Is it possible what happened wasn't the plan after all?" I asked.

Pat cocked her head. "What do you mean?"

"Well, this whole thing is just feeling really confusing and disjointed," I explained. "Polly says she is going to talk to Rowena. Then, after she does, she denies and downplays it. She also stops talking about wanting to leave town. Then, she disappears, and it seems like she was taken. She didn't pack any clothes or take any extra money. Rowena comes out and makes this big announcement that she's going to find her, but then the days stretch by, and she doesn't. And when Polly does turn up, she admits she had set the stage so she could go to a college party in Riverview, apparently by herself. Who goes to a college party by herself, especially as a high schooler? And even more especially, someone who doesn't seem like the partying type. Which leads me to the drugs in her pocket. Again, she doesn't seem the type. And it wasn't just her brother who gave me that impression about her. The rest of her family and friends didn't describe her that way, either. She was the good girl. So why does she have drugs? To maybe provide an explanation for the amnesia?"

"That's an interesting point," Pat said.

"Not that I want to give Rowena the benefit of the doubt, but it's possible she is involved, but didn't want to hurt Polly," I said. "What if this is somehow connected to Harrison? Rowena arranges this … 'taking' of Polly, or whatever it was, but Polly wasn't supposed to get hurt. But then Harrison is murdered by one of his business partners, and suddenly, all bets are off when it comes to Polly."

"That would explain why it took so long for Polly to re-ap-pear," Pat said. "Harrison died, and the rules changed."

"And it was only because Rowena told whoever was holding Polly that, if they didn't release her, the cops were going to be on to them," I said. "Maybe that was the leverage she needed to free Polly."

"Oh, so, what? Are you saying you're a hero now?" Pat asked with a grin.

I smirked. "Okay, I didn't mean it like that. I don't think I'm a hero at all. Rowena could have figured it out on her own, too. She just got the idea faster after our talk."

"Maybe," Pat mused. "Although what you just said makes the most sense. The next step is to figure out how to prove it."

"Yeah, and that's the hardest part," I said.

"So, where are you going to start?"

"Probably with how we began this conversation," I said. "By tracking down Wyle."

Unfortunately, he wasn't at the police station when I called, and I didn't bother to leave a message. I figured when he had a moment, he would find me. He was probably as anxious to talk to me as I was him.

I just wasn't sure if he was going to call or stop by. And if he stopped by, was it going to be for dinner anymore? Or "official" business?

As time ticked by and 7:00 came and went, my stomach was growling, and I wondered if I should go ahead and eat. Yes, it would be rude if he showed up, considering I'd invited him, but this seemed like extraordinary circumstances.

I had just about decided to start when the doorbell rang.

"Sorry I'm late," Wyle said. He was still in his uniform, but I couldn't see his face, as it was hidden in the shadows of the porch. "Also, sorry I didn't call to tell you I was going to be late. I meant to, but …" he raised his hands helplessly. "It's been one thing after another today. And I'm even more sorry I can't stay."

"Do you want to at least come in for a few minutes?" I asked. "The pot roast is ready. I can make you a sandwich, if you want to take it with you."

He stepped inside "I really shouldn't," he said. "I still have so much to do tonight."

"You gotta eat," I said. "Don't they at least allow you 15 minutes for dinner?"

One side of his mouth quirked up, which seemed to highlight his exhaustion even more. "Actually, it might be as much as 20."

"Oh, a whole twenty minutes," I mocked, taking a few steps toward the kitchen. "I was about to fix a plate for myself. Why don't you sit down for 20 minutes? If it helps, we can talk about all the cases you have going on, and I can share a few things I learned today."

He perked up then—whether at the mention of food or information, I wasn't sure, but he followed me into the kitchen.

"So, what did you find out?" he asked, leaning against the side of the door as I took a second plate out of the cupboard and began dishing up pot roast, mashed potatoes, and gravy.

I eyed him under my lashes. "What, no small talk? I cook you a homemade meal, and you don't even ask about my day?"

His mouth quirked up again. "You know I only have 20 minutes. I don't have time for pleasantries."

"Well, let's do this, then. Why not tell me what YOU discovered today, as I'm getting the food ready, and then, while you're eating, I'll tell you what I discovered. Fair enough?"

"Fine," he said, in a mock grumble. "You drive a hard bargain. What do you want to know?"

"Well, to start, what's going on with Polly?"

"She's been found, by her brother. But you know that."

I put both plates on the table and went back for the salad, biscuits, and silverware. "Yes, I'm aware of that. Is she actually suffering from a fugue state, or no?"

"That was one diagnosis the doctors threw out," Wyle said, taking a seat in front one of the plates. "Other than her memory loss, which the doctors are saying is temporary, she seems healthy enough. Physically, that is. She's a little dehydrated and appears to have lost some weight, but that's about it. There's no sign of her being abused or hurt or anything. She does have a bruise on her face, but it's pretty minor … the doctors think she could have fallen down, at some point. So, physically, she's fine. Mentally," he shook his head. "Of course, Polly isn't giving them much to go on."

"What do you mean?"

"She's pretty non-responsive. Not answering any questions, not doing much of anything. We didn't get much out of her other than she did leave on her own, but she wasn't trying to run away. She wanted to go to some sort of college party in Riverview, but she couldn't remember where it was or who was hosting it."

"Donny said it was a frat party," I offered, handing Wyle silverware and a napkin. "Want something to drink?"

"Tea, I presume?"

"I have Coke, too," I said, bemused. "And water."

"I'll take a Coke," he said. "I need the caffeine."

I went to grab a can out of the fridge as Wyle continued. "That was the assumption, that it was a fraternity party. But Polly didn't actually confirm it."

"And she went by herself?" I asked, sliding into the seat across from Wyle.

Wyle nodded. "So it seems. But, as I said, she's not being very responsive, so it's hard to know if that's true or not. None of her friends have said anything about a college party, and I did call the Riverview Police and requested they ask around about any that might have been going on the night she disappeared."

"Do you believe her? That she did all of this to go to a college party?" I asked.

Wyle picked up his fork and scooped up some mashed potatoes. "I don't know what to think at this point," he said. "Now, your turn. What did Donny tell you?"

I paused, trying to decide how much I should reveal. He noticed my pause and stopped eating, the fork halfway to his mouth. "What did he say?"

"I can't tell you," I said.

He stared at me before dropping his fork. It made a clattering sound on his plate. "You can't what?"

"I promised. But more than that, he's going to deny it, if I do."

Wyle folded his arms across his chest. "I can't believe this."

A sudden inspiration struck me. "But what if I were to tell you hypothetically? What he might have told me?" I asked.

Wyle unfolded his arms. "Go on."

"I'm just spitballing," I said. "You understand."

Wyle picked up his fork and gestured for me to continue. "Of course. We're just having a pleasant dinner conversation."

"Well, with this type of memory loss, there seems to be a few potential causes," I said. "One is trauma or stress, which is what it seems like the doctors are pointing to now."

Wyle nodded.

"Another is that Redemption took her. I know that's what her parents think, and the fact that Donny found Polly in the woods made them believe it. And, if I recall, when the town does take people, they do claim not to remember."

Wyle sighed. "Yes, that is what the parents are maintaining at this point. That is was the town, not anything that was Polly's fault."

I gave Wyle a sharp look. "Are they telling you not to investigate?"

"No, I wouldn't say that. They want me to look into it. But they seem … I guess satisfied with the explanation that it was Redemption. At least that's the way it seems now. It's possible they're just so relieved to have Polly home right now, and maybe after a day or two, they'll change their minds and decide they want a more in-depth investigation. But at least for the moment, they're not pushing."

"Hmm. For the record, Donny doesn't appear to be buying that explanation," I said.

Wyle's eyes narrowed. "What does he think happened?"

"He doesn't know, but he thinks there's something wrong with Polly. As he put it, she's not herself, and nothing about this is anything that Polly would do, including sneaking off to go to a party on her own."

Wyle looked thoughtful. "Is that what he would deny?"

"Not exactly." I took a deep breath. "Going back to the reasons someone might lose her memory, a third is because of drug or alcohol impairment."

Wyle stopped eating. "She was taking drugs?"

"This is all hypothetical, remember," I said. "And there's no evidence she was taking drugs, nor does it seem like she was on drugs when Donny found her."

"Then why are we talking about Polly possibly being impaired by drugs or alcohol?"

"Well, it's just if you were to maybe find some drugs in someone's pocket, it's not a stretch to think that might have been what caused her memory loss."

Wyle went very still. "Do we have a hypothetical type of drug?"

"Unfortunately, no." Red popped into my mind again, and my mouth went dry. I reached for my tea.

"I'm no doctor," Wyle said. "But it's certainly possible drugs could cause memory loss. And speaking of doctors, it would probably be good for them to know. Is there a reason why all of this is hypothetical?"

"Because it's against the law."

"As in Polly could be arrested?"

"Something like that."

Wyle frowned and took a bite of food. "Would it help to pass on that that's not likely to happen?"

"I already tried, but Donny is a little, shall we say, untrusting. And protective."

"Hmm." Wyle paused.

"Since we're on the subject of hypothetical drugs, do you have any idea where someone might get them?"

Wyle gave me a curious look. "It depends on what we're talking about. There are drugs in Redemption. I know it's a small town, but there are some things you simply can't get away from. Riverview is close, and people can pretty much get anything they want there."

"I was thinking more about drug gangs," I said. "I know we didn't have any for a while, but I had heard a few rumors they were back."

Wyle reached for his Coke. "Yeah, we are seeing some increasing activity that does point to some of that. Why? Is there some hypothetical tip you'd like to share, too?"

"Not really. It's just I saw Linda, and she mentioned that Harrison had done business with Red."

Wyle eyed me. "Red is dead."

"So they say."

"You don't think so?"

"I think Red knows how to take care of himself," I said.

Wyle thought about it as he polished off the last of the pot roast. "His body was found in the bar the night it burned."

"*A* body was found," I said. "Actually, two. But they were too far gone to be conclusively identified."

"True, but he's also never been seen again after that night. His bank accounts weren't touched, and nothing was taken from his residence. If he did survive, he clearly wanted to disappear, and I doubt he would come back."

Unless he had some unfinished business, I thought. Although I couldn't imagine what that could be. He had wanted to buy my house, but Helen refused to sell to him, so he tried to get me to. He also loved that bar. I couldn't imagine how he could either rebuild his bar or figure out how to buy my house from me now without revealing his identity.

So, maybe Wyle was right, and Red was either dead or gone, never to return, and I was just letting old fears get in the way.

"Linda also told me Westly discovered that Jonas and Harrison had met," I said.

Wyle nodded. "Yes. Westly handed over some files relating to Harrison's unsavory business connections and included that, as well."

"What were in those files?"

"Not much. Basically, a few notes about following up to see if the house would be a good fit for a rental."

My eyes widened. "So, Jonas *was* looking to sell to Harrison?"

"Maybe. But it's equally as likely that Jonas was looking to keep the house and have Harrison manage the renters. That's most of Harrison's business … managing other people's properties."

"How do you think that would impact Drake?"

"Well, I imagine if Jonas actually handed over property management to Harrison, Harrison would kick Drake out. There doesn't seem to be any sort of contract between Drake and Jonas, so it's just Drake's word that he's supposed to be there, housesitting for Jonas. However, there's also no contract between Harrison and Jonas, and no evidence Jonas was actually planning to hire Harrison for property management. It's just a couple of scrawled notes that could mean anything."

"What if I were to tell you that Drake came to see me earlier today?"

Wyle stopped chewing and stared at me. "Is this hypothetical, as well?"

"No, Drake asked me to tell you something."

"Tell me what?"

"That Jonas is hiding out somewhere so he can escape from Redemption."

Wyle blinked before fumbling for his notebook in his front pocket. "You better start from the beginning."

So I did. Wyle didn't say a word as I talked, as he was rather focused on scribbling notes.

"We'll look into it," he said when I finished. "It would definitely help if we could locate Jonas and get his side of the story."

"Not to mention how it would help to confirm that Drake didn't kill Jonas," I added.

Wyle's mouth curled up in that half-smile again. "Well, there's no evidence of that, but yeah, it would sure help eliminate some possibilities." He pocketed his notepad and mechanical pencil and glanced at the clock on the wall. "Anything else I should know before I get back to work?"

"Not at this point," I said. "But who knows? That might all change in an hour or so."

Wyle fully smiled as he got to his feet. "Well, I better get myself in gear then and see how much I can get done, as it seems every time I talk to you, my to-do list grows. At this rate, I may never sleep again."

Chapter 21

"I hope this works," Pat muttered next to me as we stepped onto the Pembrook's front porch. I was carrying tea, and Pat had a casserole I'd made for the family.

"So do I," I said as I reached for the doorbell.

That morning, Pat called the hospital to see if Polly was still there, but she had already been discharged. While I expected Polly and Darlene would both be home, I wasn't so sure about the rest of the family—Steve, in particular. I had a feeling that, if he had decided to stay home from work, our visit wouldn't be long. We might not even be able to get inside.

We listened to the footsteps coming toward the door. I glanced at Pat, and she nodded slightly. They were lighter than a man's, so hopefully, we were in luck.

The door opened, and Darlene stood there, a smile on her face. "Pat, Charlie. How nice of you to drop by."

"Well, of course we wanted to check on you," Pat said. "Is this a good time?"

"Yes, yes," Darlene said, taking a step back. "I was just about to make some tea."

"Oh, then I got here just in time," I joked, waving the two bags of tea I held. "I brought two types—this one is my most popular, Lemon Lavender, and it's great for calming nerves. This one, I created especially for Polly. It's a brain-boosting combination, to help with cognitive function."

Darlene looked surprised. "Really? There is such a thing?"

"Plants and herbs have long been used to treat medical conditions," I said as we followed Darlene into the kitchen.

"There's an herb for everything," Pat added.

"Also, the herbs I used will help with stress and anxiety, too," I said. "Of course, this isn't to replace anything her doctors gave her."

"They didn't prescribe anything but a sedative that she refused to take," Darlene said with a forced smile. "I considered taking it instead, if I'm honest. Didn't want it to go to waste."

The joke fell flat, but both Pat and I smiled. "Oh, my Lemon Lavender tea is perfect then," I said. "Let me go make a pot of it for you and Pat, and I can make a cup of Polly's tea for her."

"Oh, you don't have to go through all that trouble," Darlene said, but I waved her off.

"No trouble. Polly is here, right?"

"Yes, she's in her bedroom." Darlene shifted from one foot to the next. "She's been in there all morning. Wouldn't come out for breakfast, so I brought her a tray, but I don't think she ate much."

Pat put the casserole on the counter and wrapped an arm around Darlene's shoulder. "She's going to be okay," she said. "Just give her a little time."

Darlene gave her a watery smile. "That's what the doctors said."

"It's tough. I know. It breaks your heart to watch it."

Darlene screwed up her face as Pat hugged her. As quietly as I could, I finished making the tea and put it on the table while Darlene cried in Pat's arms.

When her tears started to slow, I picked up the mug I made for Polly and moved into her line of sight. "Is it okay if I bring this to Polly?" I asked.

Darlene hiccupped and nodded. I met Pat's eyes, who nodded slightly to me as well, and disappeared down the hall.

There was only one closed door, and I guessed Polly was likely behind it. I gently knocked. No response. I turned the knob and gently pushed it open.

The first thing that hit me was the smell. The room stunk of old sweat and body odor. I breathed shallowly through my mouth and peered inside, waiting for my eyes to adjust. It was darker than the rest of the house, as all the shades were drawn.

There were twin beds, one on each side of the room. Polly was in the one furthest from the door. She was lying on top of the covers, staring at the ceiling, her eyes barely blinking. "Polly?" I asked, nudging the door wider. "My name is Charlie Kingsley, and I'm a friend of your mother's. Can I come in?"

Polly didn't respond. I waited a moment before stepping inside anyway and shutting the door behind me.

"I make teas and tinctures," I said, slowly walking toward the bed. "A lot of what I use, I grow myself. I made this blend especially for you."

The smell grew worse as I moved closer to her, but I did my best to not let the repulsion show on my face. My tea, at least, smelled wonderful, and I held it as close to my nose as I could.

Finally, Polly slowly turned her head to look at me. She still looked as filthy as she was when I'd seen her in the hospital, but the blue sweatpants and oversized white T-shirt she had on were reasonably clean. It appeared all she had done when she had gotten home was put on different clothes and climb into bed.

"Do you want to try it?" I held the cup out to her.

She stared at me. A small tongue darted out to lick her lips. "What is it?"

Her voice was raspy, as if she hadn't used it much. Or, she hadn't been drinking much. I glanced at the nightstand next to her bed and saw an untouched glass of water.

"It's got lots of good things in it, like ginger, turmeric, and lemon balm. I put a little honey in, as well. Do you want to try it?"

I held out the tea again. She didn't move at first, but I could see her nostrils flair. If I did say so myself, it smelled wonderful, and nearly covered up the disgusting odor.

The struggle was plain on her face. She clearly wanted to refuse, to continue to deny herself—maybe "punish" herself was the right word—but the lure of the tea was too strong. Either that, or she was too exhausted and weak to fight herself anymore. Slowly, she pulled herself into a seated position and held out her hand. I gave her the tea, and she took a sip, her eyes never leaving me.

"It's good," she said.

"Thank you."

She took another sip before holding it in her lap. "Why would you make me tea?"

"I wanted to help."

She twisted her face. "Why?"

"Because you've been hurt," I said gently. "I wanted to do what I could for you."

She dropped her head to stare into her tea. "I don't deserve it."

"Why would you say that?"

She shook her head, dislodging chunks of matted, oily blonde hair, causing it to fall into her face.

"Do you remember what happened?"

A slight hesitation before another head shake.

"Then why do you say you don't deserve it?"

She didn't answer … just continued to stare into her mug.

I watched her for a moment before lowering myself to sit at the side of her bed.

"You know, it's sometimes easier to talk to a stranger about things," I said.

"There's nothing to talk about," she muttered.

I said nothing, figuring it better to simply sit and wait.

It took a bit, but she eventually looked up at me. "I don't remember," she said.

"Okay."

"I don't," she insisted.

"I get it," I said. "Do you want to tell me what you do remember?"

She looked away. There was another long pause while she took another sip.

"I snuck out of the house. And I lied to my mother, so I could go to a fraternity party. That's why it's my fault."

"How did you hear about that party?"

She jerked back to look at me, clearly surprised by the question. "What do you mean?"

"How did you find out? Did someone tell you about it, or did you see a flyer, or … ?"

"I don't remember," she mumbled. "Someone told me, I think."

"Who told you?"

"I said I don't remember," she repeated.

"Okay. You don't remember. Do you remember why you decided to go to a fraternity by yourself?"

"Because I wanted to go to a party."

"I get that. What I don't understand is why you would go by yourself. I don't know any girls who would go to a frat party alone."

She looked away again. "I just … I just wanted to party."

"Did you often want to party?"

Her head twisted back to me. "Why are you asking me all these questions?"

"I'm just trying to help you remember."

"Well, I don't. I don't remember anything."

She was clearly lying. "But you do remember lying to your mother and sneaking out because you wanted to go to a party?"

"I told you I did." She was also clearly getting flustered. "Why are you doing this? I want you to leave."

"I'm not trying to upset you," I said gently. "I'm trying to help."

"Well, you're not." She turned back to the wall. "Thank you for the tea."

I let out a sigh. I should have known it wouldn't be easy, but I did have one last card to play. "I'll leave," I said. "But there's actually another reason I'm asking you questions. Do you want to know what it is first?"

She kept her gaze firmly glued to the wall. I waited a moment, but she didn't respond, so I took it as a "yes."

"Because I don't think it was your idea. The party, the disappearance … I don't think any of it was your idea. I think you were manipulated by someone else. And none of it is your fault."

I saw something flicker across her face, but she didn't turn her head. I watched her for another moment, but she didn't move, so I stood back up and began walking across the room to the door.

I just about reached it when she spoke. "You're wrong."

I turned back to her. "What am I wrong about?"

"It IS my fault."

I leaned against the door, folding my arms across my chest. "I don't believe it."

Her eyes widened in surprise. "What do you mean, you 'don't believe it'?"

"Just that. I don't believe you."

She struggled to comprehend. "But I was the one there. I should know."

"Then prove it. Tell me why it's your fault."

"But I told you, I don't remember."

"If you don't remember, then how are you so sure it was your fault?"

"I … I …" Her jaw worked as she tried to formulate an answer. "You don't understand," she finally said, her voice breaking.

I took a few steps away from the door and toward the bed. "What don't I understand?" I kept my tone soft and gentle.

Her shoulders heaved like she was about to cry, but her eyes remained dry. "It wasn't supposed to be this way," she whispered.

It was all I could do to remain calm as excitement surged through my veins. I knew she remembered. I slowly lowered myself back onto the edge of her bed. "What wasn't supposed to be this way?"

She was breathing hard through her nose. I waited, hardly daring to breathe myself, less it break the spell and cause her to clam up again.

"You have to promise you won't tell my parents," she said. She turned to look me directly in the eye. "Do you promise?"

Inwardly, I winced. I didn't particularly like being in a situation that would prevent me from being honest with her parents, but someone had to get the truth out of her. And maybe I would be able to talk her into telling her parents herself, which was likely a better solution, anyway. "I promise."

She held my gaze for another heartbeat as if debating whether or not she believed me before dropping it to stare into her tea again. "I was the invisible child," she said, her voice so low, I had to strain to hear it. "The lost child. Yes, I know that's part of what happens when you're in the middle of nine kids, but I couldn't even meet the low bar. My parents always said I was the child they never had to worry about. I was the good girl, the one who always did the right thing. And I was. For most of my life, that was what I did, because I thought it was the only way to get their love. I got good grades; I always did my homework; I kept my room neat; I never snuck out. I did everything right.

"And I hated it."

She paused and licked her lips. "It took years for me to realize how much I hated and resented being the kid they never worried about. My sisters and brothers always got their attention before me. If I went up to my mom and said I needed to talk to her, the response was always the same—"Of course we can talk, but first, I have to take care of Candy … and Danny, and Jackie, and whoever else. Or, she was too tired, and would ask if it could wait until the next day. Eventually, I stopped asking, because it was just too painful.

"As time went on, I decided I needed to just leave town. It was clear I wouldn't be missed. I wasn't even sure anyone would notice my disappearance. At first, my plan was to leave once I graduated, but the resentment kept growing and growing. So then, a friend suggested maybe I shouldn't wait. Maybe I should run away now, and then I could see if they missed me or not. Then, I would know for sure."

I felt the hairs on the back of my neck stand up at the mention of a "friend." "What friend?" I asked.

"Just a … a friend. No one special. Anyway, the more I thought about it, the more I liked the idea. A test, you understand, just to see if I was as invisible as I felt. And now seemed to be a great time to do it, since that weird vampire moved to Redemption …"

"Wait a minute," I broke in again, unable to control myself. "Vampire? What are you talking about?"

"You know. I guess he's housesitting, or something. He's the one who killed that guy."

My mind raced to put all the new pieces together. "Are you talking about Drake Crimson?"

"Yeah, I think that's his name."

"So, you thought you'd disappear now because you wanted people to think he took you?"

Polly's cheeks flushed red. "I didn't want to get him in trouble," she mumbled. "I WAS going to turn up, you see. I wasn't going to let him get arrested or anything like that. But he was a convenient reason for my disappearance."

I was trying to work out the timeline in my head. "You disappeared before Harrison was murdered," I said.

"Yes, and that's when everything went wrong," she said.

I was trying to follow her logic. "What do you mean? What went wrong?"

"I was just going to hide for a few days and see how long it took for my parents to even notice I was missing and what they did when the realization came. I really thought they would just say, 'Oh, well, Polly has such a good head on her shoulders … I'm sure she's fine.' I honestly didn't think they would worry much about me. But then I started to see that they really WERE upset, so I was going to go home. But then that man was murdered, and I couldn't."

"Why couldn't you?"

She looked at me like I was an idiot. "Because I would have to admit I ran away. I couldn't do that. Finally, FINALLY my parents were focused on me. On ME! And if they knew I ran away on purpose, they would hate me. Don't you see?" Her voice cracked and her chest heaved. "It would ruin everything.

I couldn't bear it. I finally saw that my parents loved me, and I couldn't risk that changing already."

A couple tears trickled down her cheeks, and she buried her face in one of her hands while still holding her tea in the other. It sloshed over and onto her lap, but I didn't say anything. I simply let her cry as I plucked a tissue from the tissue box and laid it on her lap.

After a few moments, she got herself under control and plucked up the tissue to blow her nose. "Thanks," she said. "Sorry for crying."

"There's nothing to be sorry for," I said. "Although I'm still a little confused. I understand why you didn't want your parents to think you did this on purpose, but I'm still not getting why Harrison being murdered changed all of that."

She sucked in a deep, shuddering breath. "Because the cops were investigating him," she said.

"You mean Drake, who you're calling a 'vampire,' but who isn't one," I said.

"Yeah, him. The cops would know he didn't have anything to do with my disappearance once they investigated, so I no longer had an excuse for it."

"But didn't you say you weren't going to blame him?"

Her head bobbed. "Yes. I was going to say someone took me, but I didn't know who, and after a few days, I was able to escape. People might assume it was the vampire, but there wouldn't be any proof, and as he was here housesitting, I fig-ured he'd be gone in a few weeks, so it wouldn't matter."

It was difficult for me to wrap my head around her reason-ing—that it was somehow not hurting Drake if people thought he took a teenage girl. For a girl who was supposedly so good, it felt very cold to set someone up that way.

Unless … it wasn't her idea.

"How did you even know about Drake?" I asked.

Her expression was wary. "What do you mean?"

"Well, no one really knew about Drake until after you disap-peared and Harrison was murdered. That's when it hit the paper, and people started talking about it. So, how did you find out about him?"

"Oh." Her cheeks were stained pink again. "People still knew. They must have. People talk. It's a small town. I'm sure I heard it from someone."

It's true that Redemption was a small town. Still, I felt sure that there wasn't that much talk about Drake until everything happened with Polly and Harrison. I wondered if Mildred had told someone. I made a mental note to ask her.

"Okay, so back to your story. Harrison was murdered, and you had to change your plan," I said.

Polly stared at her lap. "Yeah. I didn't know what to do, so I didn't do anything. For days. I was so upset, I could barely eat, drink, or sleep."

That explained the dehydration and weight loss.

"Eventually, I couldn't stand it anymore, so I … I went to the woods, so Donny could find me. I had to come up with something, which is why I invented the frat party."

"What about the drugs in your pocket?"

Polly blanched. "I … I bought them from a drug dealer. I'm not even sure what they are, but I figured having them would help explain my memory loss, if my parents didn't believe Redemption did it."

She was lying, at least about the drug dealer. I was sure Polly would have no idea how to even find one. I suspected her "friend" (aka Rowena) gave her the drugs, but I doubted she would ever admit it. I decided to try a different tact. "What if the police find out there wasn't a frat party that night?" I asked.

She hung her head. "It wasn't the best excuse, I know … but there had to be a party somewhere, right? I figured I could just say I was confused about whether it had been an actual frat party or not, if that came up. I mean, what other choice did I have? At that point, I didn't want to bring anyone else into it. I nearly had a murderer blamed for my disappearance. What if he realized I made it up? Would he come after me for real?" She blanched.

"The cops didn't find any evidence that Drake killed any-one," I said. "If anything, he is an alleged murderer, but he's not even that, as he hasn't been charged with anything."

"Well, even so, I didn't want to bring anyone else into this. I'm so ashamed and embarrassed about what I did." She turned her head toward the wall so I couldn't see her face. Her whole body seemed to crumble and fold into herself.

Looking at her, I was torn. Part of me wanted to shake her. How could she possibly think it was okay to cause people to blame an innocent man?

But another part of me wanted to hug her. She looked so completely broken, hunched over in bed, her shoulders continuing to heave even though she was out of tears. It was clear she knew she had messed up, and the guilt had been weighing heavily on her. It's probably why she finally broke down and told me—she just had to tell someone. Plus, she was only a kid … a kid who had never felt loved or seen by her parents, ultimately leading her to this incredibly stupid plan.

"You really should tell your mom," I said.

Her head jerked around, horror on her face. "No! You can't tell them! You promised."

"And I won't," I said. "Because they should hear it from you."

"I can't! I already told you, I can't tell them the truth! They'll hate me."

"They won't hate you," I said.

"You don't know that."

"I do know that," I said calmly. "I spoke to your mother while you were missing. She needs to hear the truth. Not only about what you did, but why." I leaned forward, my voice urgent. "If you want your parents to treat you differently, to pay attention to you, then something has to change. I guarantee they have no idea how much their actions have hurt you over the years. I'm not saying they won't be angry about what you did. They might even punish you. But you're never going to build a loving, trusting relationship with them by hiding the truth about this."

She was shaking her head. "I can't. You don't understand. I just can't."

She was done. I had pushed her as far as I was able. Hopefully, I had at least planted the seed, and it would eventually take root and grow, leading her to the right choice. I reached over to squeeze her leg. "Think about it. And if you need to talk to me again, my number is on the tea bag."

She didn't answer, instead turning back to the wall, the fingers of one hand plucking obsessively at her quilt.

Quietly, I got up and let myself out of her room.

Chapter 22

"So she did plan it all," Pat said. We were sitting in the car after leaving the Pembrook's house. I had just given her a quick snapshot of what I'd learned from Polly.

"Well, I don't know about that," I said. "Yes, she made herself disappear, but I'm not convinced she was the one who did the planning."

"Who then? Rowena, perhaps?"

"It makes sense," I argued. "The timing fits. Before her appointment with Rowena, her plan was to leave town after she graduated. But then, she talks to Rowena, and poof. Everything changed. When you add that to the other pieces, like Rowena claiming to be able to find Polly and how that plan doesn't really sound like something Polly would come up with, it all starts to come together."

"But how can you be sure Polly didn't come up with it?" Pat asked. "You barely know her."

"True, but it's pretty callous for a teenager to want to subtly blame an innocent man for her disappearance."

Pat eyed me. "Didn't you watch *Heathers?* And since when have teenage girls not been capable of all sorts of callous and cruel things?"

"I didn't mean all teenage girls. I'm talking about Polly, specifically," I said. "She's known for being a good girl, and I think for the most part, she is. Look how she befriended Beth. Plus, it's clear that what she did is eating her up inside."

"Maybe," Pat said. "But before you get too convinced that Rowena is at the bottom of this, you should know that Darlene has nothing but good things to say about her."

"Really?"

"Yes. Apparently, Rowena called her a few times while Polly was missing to tell her that while she didn't have any specific details, she was sure that Polly was alive and relatively safe and would come home soon."

My eyes widened. "And you think that exonerates Rowena? Again, how would she know that unless she knew where Polly was this whole time?"

"I'm saying that you aren't going to get any support from Darlene when it comes to Rowena being the mastermind behind her daughter's disappearance. She's very grateful to Rowena."

I shook my head. "I can't believe how Rowena is able to manipulate so many people. Polly refused to tell me it was her. She just said it was a 'friend.' And she's apparently got Darlene wrapped around her little finger."

"Putting aside the possibility that maybe the reason Polly didn't tell you it was Rowena was because it wasn't Rowena … why would Rowena do all of this? What could she possibly gain from convincing a teenager to run away from home, but pretend someone took her?"

"To 'prove' she's psychic," I said. "Think about it, if she had told the world where to find Polly, and Polly was there, wouldn't that be strong proof she really is a psychic? Talk about a boost to her business."

"Okay," Pat said. "Assuming that's true, why didn't Rowena carry it out? Why didn't she make a big announcement that Polly was in the woods?"

"I don't know," I said, frowning. "That's been bothering me, too. I can only think something must have gone wrong. Polly did say, 'None of this was supposed to happen.' So I suspect for some reason, when Harrison's body was found in Jonas's backyard, it threw the original plan out of whack. Polly did say she was going to blame some sort of 'shadowy figure' on her disappearance, with the idea being that everyone would assume it was Drake, but they couldn't do that anymore once the police started investigating Drake. At that point, there probably wasn't a good way for Rowena to interject herself. If it came out that Polly did this to herself and was hiding somewhere, maybe Rowena was concerned people would put two and two together and realize she did have something to do with it after all. Speaking of hiding somewhere … where WAS Polly hiding all this time?"

"Are you saying Rowena was not only the mastermind behind Polly's disappearance, but that she was also providing the hiding place?"

"There was that locked room in Rowena's shop," I said.

"Which could have been locked for any number of reasons," Pat said. "It seems unlikely she was hiding Polly there."

"Well, Polly had to be hanging out somewhere, and who would look for her in the back of Rowena's shop?"

Pat shook her head. "I think that's a bit of a stretch."

"It's also a stretch that Polly would be able to successfully hide somewhere in Redemption for several days without help," I said. "Maybe she wasn't in the back of Rowena's shop, but I'd bet a month's worth of homemade cookies that Rowena was hiding her somewhere."

"I would love to take that bet," Pat said and made a face. "Except I would be afraid to lose. Then, I would be the one baking."

"You already know you can have as many cookies as you want." I drummed my fingers against the steering wheel. "But back to these two cases. Rowena isn't the only thing bothering me. Why does Drake keep coming up?"

"Oh, I don't know. Maybe because a dead body was found in his backyard?" Pat said.

"So, yes, that makes sense, in Harrison's case. But not in Polly's. On the surface, she has nothing to do with Drake, and yet here she is talking about him being a vampire, just like Linda was."

"Well, of course people are going to mention the vampire thing," Pat said. "Do you honestly expect them not to?"

"No, but what I don't understand is how Polly knew about it before she disappeared," I said. "The only person who was talking about it at all was Mildred. So how did she find out?"

"Mildred was probably telling people," Pat said. "She told you."

"That's probably it, but I don't know. Something doesn't feel right," I said as I started the car. "Maybe I need to call her."

"That's a good idea," Pat said. "Depending on who she told, we might be able to track down who told Polly, which might give us a better idea of who put this whole disappearance plan into her head."

* * *

Mildred swore up and down she didn't tell anyone but me.

But she *might* have mentioned it to Terri when asking about her false labor. And maybe the Thompson wife … but probably not her.

Needless to say, it wasn't a satisfying conversation. I couldn't see any of Mildred's neighbors having a direct line to Polly, even if they had decided to repeat the vampire rumor. So who had told Polly?

While I talked it over with Midnight, who was tolerating the conversation only because I was getting his dinner, the phone rang again. It was Wyle.

"We found Jonas."

"What?" I was so surprised, I put Midnight's food down on the counter. Equally surprised, he meowed impatiently, and I placed his dish on the floor.

"Yeah, it was exactly like Drake said," Wyle said. "We found him in Cedar Falls."

"Iowa?"

"Yep."

"So Jonas really is looking for a place to move?"

"He is, yes."

It took me a moment to process the information. After discovering Jonas and Harrison had met, I was half-convinced Drake had been lying to me in order to save his own skin. "And Harrison?"

"Yeah, I guess they did have a meeting, but it was a couple years ago, when Jonas was still trying to figure out how to leave Redemption without Redemption stopping him. He was thinking if he didn't sell his house and just had Harrison rent it out, it wouldn't 'count.' Or something like that. Needless to say, that fell through as well, but Jonas couldn't remember the exact details anymore. It was clear he hadn't thought about Harrison or that conversation in a long time."

"So, Drake killing Harrison because of Jonas …"

"Is unlikely," Wyle finished. "Jonas didn't even remember the meeting right away. Had to think about it, so it clearly didn't make much of an impression."

"Okay, so it sounds like Jonas and Drake weren't connected to Harrison's death," I said. "What about Rowena? Did you find a connection between her and Harrison?"

"Nope," Wyle said, his voice muffled as though he had just taken a bite of something. "At least nothing obvious," he said in between chews. "It appears she moved here from a suburb of Northern California, around San Francisco."

"What? What is she doing here?"

There was a rattling of paper. "It's complicated, and I wasn't able to get all the details. The court sealed the case."

"Court?"

"Yeah, there were some sort of legal issues regarding a business. I'm not sure if she owned the business or how she was involved, but whatever happened, it seems clear she wanted a fresh start. Along with moving to Redemption, she changed her name."

"I knew it. Rowena Tanveer had to be made up."

"Well, as it turns out, you were right about that."

"So, what is her real name?"

More paper shuffling. "Margaret Townsend."

"Margaret Townsend? That definitely doesn't sound like a psychic's name. No wonder she changed it."

"Yeah. Anyway, we can't find any connection between her and Harrison. Not when she was in California or here."

"What about her business? Who is she renting it from?"

"She's renting it directly from the owner, who isn't Harrison. Hold on." He covered the receiver with one of his hands, and I could hear him having a muffled conversation with someone. "I have to go," he said. "I'll call you later."

I still had questions about Rowena, or 'Margaret,' plus I had planned to tell Wyle about my conversation with Polly. But clearly, all of that was going to have to wait.

I hung up and went back into the kitchen to figure out my own dinner. Midnight had finished eating and looked up at me, licking his whiskers.

"I'm missing something," I said to him. "Something obvious."

He blinked at me, as if to say he wasn't surprised.

"Oh, you're so smart," I said. "Maybe you should tell me, then."

Midnight flicked his tail.

"It's like the pieces are all there, but they're just not fitting together," I said. "I know I'm missing something, but I can't figure out what."

Midnight yawned and stood up to find a soft pillow to take a nap, as if to say if I was going to be that stupid, he wasn't going to waste his time with me anymore.

"You're a lot of help," I called out.

Chapter 23

I pushed open the door to Shaw's Property Management and Rental Company and was greeted with the tinkling of a little bell. That was new.

And it wasn't the only thing that was new. It appeared the entire office had undergone a makeover. There was a new waiting area with a black leather couch and matching chairs grouped around a glass-topped coffee table filled with magazines. There were new desks, as well—instead of cheap, pressed wood, they were made from oak and complemented by comfy executive chairs. The walls were newly painted a soft, dove grey. It even smelled like new paint. The only thing that hadn't changed was the cheap linoleum floors.

Actually, that wasn't the only thing that hadn't changed. Linda was still wearing the same unflattering outfits as before, although she didn't look nearly as awful as she had. I suspected at least some of that had to do with her new makeup routine.

She was standing next to Westly, their heads quite close together while discussing something, but when they heard the tinkle of the bell, they both jumped apart, in an almost guilty manner. Westly busied himself with some files on the desk while Linda turned toward me, a faint pink staining her cheeks. The moment she recognized me, she smiled her million-watt smile and came forward, arms outstretched.

"Charlie! So good to see you again. Are you here for business, or just to say hi?"

"Both."

Her face lit up even more, which didn't seem possible. "Wonderful. Are you ready to discuss options for renting a storefront?"

I was impressed she had remembered my little white lie from before. "I am. But first, I really love the new look." I spread my arms wide.

"I know. It's great, isn't it? It was a gift from Graham for sticking around and helping get the business back on track. He gave Westly and me both a bonus and told us to redecorate without worry about the cost." She frowned as she studied the floor. "The hardwood floor will have to come later, unfortunately, as there were too many files we needed to go through, and it would have been way too disruptive. I can't wait … it's going to look so awesome."

"Wow, hardwood floors. That will look fabulous."

"Oh, I can't wait," she said again. "I'll make sure to call you when it's done, so you can come see the finished product."

"Definitely. I would love to."

Linda looked around the room one last time, as if seeing her new floors in her mind's eye before turning back to me. "So, enough about my redecorating. Let's talk about you and a new tea store. I bet you're excited."

"I'd love to talk about it. And you're the one I should talk to, right? Or would that be Westly?" I had my fingers crossed she would answer "Westly."

"Westly," Linda said. *Perfect,* I thought. I also noticed the pink darkening on her cheeks again. "I think he's free now, but I can check for you."

"Sure, but first," I said, taking a step closer and ducking my head. "Is there something going on between you two?"

She blushed. "I don't know. It's all very new," she said, keeping her voice low. "We were working late last week, as there's just been so much to do. Harrison was so unorganized. Anyway, we were talking, and then … I don't know … it was like one thing led to another, I guess."

"I'm happy for you," I said, thinking back to when I first saw her and Westly together. It was clear Westly had a thing for her, but Linda was clearly caught up in Donny. I was happy she had apparently moved on to a more adult relationship, but I could also feel my stomach twist in a sad knot for her, knowing what was coming. "It would be great to chat with him, if he has time now."

"Sure. Let me go check." She headed over to Westly, who was still messing around with the files on the desk. He looked up as she walked over, his eyes following her. She paused a couple of feet away to ask him if he could see me. I saw him nod before he glanced over toward me to wave me over.

Like the office and Linda's makeup routine, Westly had had a makeover, as well. He had traded in his pastel colors for bold, brighter colors—a blue and red plaid shirt and red tie. It suited him.

"Great to see you again, Charlie," he said, shaking my hand and gesturing toward his desk, which while a nice upgrade from before, was still right out in the open.

"Actually, I was hoping we could talk a little more privately," I said. I had noticed that Harrison's old office had been converted into a conference room, and with its large glass windows, it would be perfect.

He raised his eyebrows but didn't comment, instead leading me into the room and shutting the door behind him.

"You have nothing to worry about," he said as he ushered me to a seat. "Everything you say is confidential, and that includes anything you say to Linda."

"I'm so glad to hear that," I said, carefully setting my purse on the table.

He gave me a small, professional smile and smoothed his tie. "So, how can I help you?"

"Well, first off, I have a confession to make."

He raised one eyebrow but didn't say anything.

"I'm not here to talk about renting a shop."

His eyebrows knit together in confusion. "I don't understand. Then why *are* you here?"

"You probably don't know this, but I'm helping out the police with their investigations."

"No, I didn't. Are you are on the force, or undercover?"

"Something like that," I said. "I wanted to swing by because I have a few questions for you."

He was still looking puzzled. "Oh. Why didn't Wyle come?"

"Well, he's slammed," I said. "All that paperwork you've given him, which is great, by the way. It's given him so many leads. It's truly incredible how helpful you've been, but he's just so busy. So, I thought I'd volunteer to swing by and help out."

I could see his expression smooth out and transform into something that looked more like false modesty as I talked. He straightened his shoulders. "Of course. I completely understand. I know I gave him a lot."

"You did," I assured him.

"Well, unfortunately, I think it speaks more to Harrison's character than my own." He sighed, a little dramatically. "Harrison was a busy guy."

"Yeah, that seems pretty obvious," I said. "However, the questions I have are about what is likely the only legitimate business dealing in the pile you sent over … with Jonas."

"Oh." He shifted in his chair. "Yes, Jonas was legitimate. I don't know how much I can help, though. I couldn't find much else other than what I already turned over."

"Actually, it's more about Drake than Jonas," I said. "Now that we know Jonas and Harrison had at least one business meeting, are you absolutely sure Harrison and Drake never met?"

"Well, I can't be absolutely certain," Westly said. "It's possible they had a meeting, and Harrison just didn't make a record of it anywhere. You can see how unorganized he was. He kept so much in his head, which was another reason it was so difficult to work for him. But I combed through pretty much everything and wasn't able to find any notes about it."

"Yeah, that's what I thought. Is it possible that even if Drake didn't meet Harrison, he still somehow learned about the meeting he had with Jonas and decided to do something about it?"

Westly bobbed his head up and down. "It's possible. Harrison is in the phone book, so if Drake knew about Harrison and Jonas, he could have found his address and showed up at his house."

"Yes, I can totally see that," I said. "But here's the thing that I don't understand: why? What could Jonas and Harrison have talked about that would cause Drake to want to kill Harrison?"

"Well, I've been thinking about that." Westly shifted the chair closer to the table. "Drake has that … that condition, right? Makes him look like a vampire …"

"Yes, he's allergic to the sun," I said.

"Yes, and that's got to be really difficult for him, only being able to come out at night. It must be hard to work a regular job. But if Jonas was serious about wanting to rent out his home, and maybe even rent out a few other homes, maybe Drake thought he could be Jonas's property manager. Clearly, he knows Jonas, so maybe he thought Jonas would be fine with him working odd hours."

"You really think Drake killed Harrison over a job?"

"Well, it would have been more about money than a job," Westly corrected. "Isn't it true that nearly all murders are committed over money or love? This would certainly be about money. Drake probably thought he had a sweet deal locked up, and when he realized it was all slipping away, he panicked."

"Hmm." I frowned. "What you say does make sense …"

Westly sat back in his chair, a big smile on his face.

"Except that we were able to locate Jonas."

The smile disappeared. Westly swallowed. "Jonas is back?"

"No, not exactly. Drake is still housesitting. But what was weird was that while Jonas confirmed he'd met with Harrison, he said it was a couple years ago. That he had no intention of moving forward with any sort of arrangement with Shaw's Property Management and Rental Company."

"Oh." Westly swallowed again. "Well, you know, maybe Drake knew Harrison from before. Maybe Drake isn't even his real name, and he's in those files. Like I said, it had to be tough for him trying to find work with his condition."

"Yeah, about his condition," I mused. "I'm curious …. when did you find out about it?"

Westly gave me a wary look. "What do you mean?"

"When did you find out that people thought he was a vampire?"

"I don't know. I probably read it in the paper. Or maybe I heard one of our clients or Linda talk about it. What does it matter?"

I smiled. "It might not. But I got to thinking that Linda was at Aunt May's the day Mildred announced to the town, at least it felt like the entire town, that Drake was a vampire. My guess is, Linda said something about it."

Westly licked his lips. "Yes, now that I think about it, that is probably when I first heard about it."

"Yeah, and knowing there was this, well, let's face it, this strange man living here ... I mean," I let out a little chuckle. "Everyone was becoming convinced he was a vampire. So, I'm just wondering if that was when you decided to kill Harrison."

Westly blinked at me. "Excuse me?"

I held my hands out. "Look, I don't blame you. Harrison was a crappy boss, that's clear. And he treated Linda horribly, and that was pretty clear, as well. Even I could see it, and I'd just barely met her. She was terrified of him. I could also see how much you care for her, so of course you would want to protect her, and what better way to do that than get rid of Harrison? The guy was the scum of the Earth. Really, you've done the world a favor."

"I ... I," Westly licked his lips again. "I think you should leave."

"So, what did you do? Show up at Harrison's doorstep one night? Or ..." I tapped my finger against the table. "Maybe you didn't mean to kill him. Maybe you just wanted to threaten him. So, you showed up at his house one night legitimately wanting to talk to him, thinking you could get through to him. But what did he do? I bet he laughed at you, didn't he? Told you what a loser you are. And then he turned his back on you. Clearly, he didn't think you were a threat. And that was probably the last straw, wasn't it? That's why you killed him."

I could tell Westly was getting more and more agitated the longer I talked. His face was becoming red, and he was breathing harder. It suddenly occurred to me that maybe this wasn't the smartest idea—accusing a murderer while alone with him in a room.

He must have been thinking the same, because he glanced up at me, his eyes full of rage. It was all I could do not to shrink back in my seat.

But then he looked away from me, toward the big glass windows. I followed his gaze and saw what he saw—Linda, working at her desk. She was typing something, and her eyes were narrowed in concentration. She must have sensed us looking at her, because her head turned, and her face lit up when she saw Westly's gaze.

Westly's breath caught in his throat. There was a long pause that seemed to stretch out for hours.

Then, suddenly, abruptly, he jumped to his feet, knocking the chair behind him to the floor. He stormed out of the conference room and past Linda's desk. Linda's expression faded as she watched him come toward her, obviously understanding that something was very wrong. She got to her feet as well, and put a hand out toward him. I could see her lips moving as she asked him what had happened, but he kept going, across the room and out the door, even as she called after him.

I reached into my purse to click off the little tape recorder that had been recording. I was hoping it would be enough—especially the part about him knowing Harrison had been killed at home. Between that and how he doctored the dates of Jonas's meeting notes, it should hopefully be enough to get a confession out of him.

"What happened?" Linda was standing in the doorway, her eyes full of accusation.

I sighed. "I promise I'll tell you, but before I do, we need to call the cops."

Chapter 24

"Wow … Westly," Pat said, eyeing the chocolate chip cookies I had set out in the middle of the kitchen table but not taking one. "He was the one who killed Harrison?"

"He was indeed," I said, picking up my tea. "He confessed everything."

As it turned out, Wyle didn't even need my recording. The moment they got Westly into the interrogation room, he started to talk and didn't stop.

Also, I had apparently been right about all but one thing: Westly HAD showed up at Harrison's intending to kill him. He had even brought a gun, which he pointed at Harrison once he was in Harrison's living room.

Harrison's response was to laugh and basically tell him he was too much of a coward to pull the trigger. He even turned his back on Westly, which, after years of Harrison's abuse, immediately infuriated him. Shooting him would be too quick, too easy. Instead, Westly snatched up the first thing he could—a lamp on a coffee table—and smashed it over Harrison's head. Harrison went down, and Westly hit him a few more times in a complete fit of rage.

And just as Westly had come prepared to kill Harrison, he was also prepared to dispose of the body. He actually brought a dolly with him, which he used to not only get Harrison out of his house, but also into Jonas's backyard.

"So, he really thought he could pin this on Drake based on those old notes?" Pat asked.

"My feeling is that the notes may have been a backup plan," I said. "I think Westly initially wanted to shift the blame to Harrison's shady business associates, but he saw an opportunity with Drake to make things even more convoluted for the police. The more leads they had to follow up, the longer it would take, and the colder the trail would become."

"If that's the case, why did he fall apart so quickly when Jonas was located?" Pat asked. "I mean, Westly must have known all along Jonas was going to eventually show up. Even though we now know that Jonas had no intention of returning at the time, he had told everyone he was on a month-long vacation."

"My guess is, Harrison knew more about Jonas's plans than the notes let on," I said. "Despite all of Harrison's faults, he seemed like he had a good head for business. He probably followed up with Jonas, and eventually, Jonas told him his plans. Or, maybe Jonas asked Harrison what to do, and Harrison gave him the idea. Who knows? I'm guessing Westly found out somehow. Maybe Harrison mentioned something, or maybe he overheard a phone conversation and didn't think anything of it until Linda came back from lunch talking about a vampire. It wouldn't have taken much research to realize the vampire was Jonas's housesitter, and once he did, he probably saw his opportunity to further complicate the suspect pool. Especially if it took a year or more for Jonas to resurface."

Pat finally gave in to temptation and picked up a cookie. "Poor Drake. First Polly wants to have him blamed for her disappearance, and then Westly wants to pin a murder on him."

"All because of his medical condition," I said.

Pat shook her head. "If this is how other communities treated Drake, no wonder he avoids human contact and only comes out at night."

"Even worse, I have to wonder how much of this is my fault," I said.

Pat stared at me. "Your fault? How is any of this your fault?"

"Because if we hadn't gone into Rowena's that first day for a reading, we wouldn't have alerted her to something dark that might be brewing," I said. "Whether she started poking around to see what we were talking about or someone mentioned something and she put two and two together, I don't know, but us going in there likely gave her the ... well, maybe 'idea' is strong, but the seed for the idea. And then, when Polly showed up for her reading, it all fell into place."

Pat made a face at her cookie. "Man, I was just coming to terms with Rowena being behind Polly's disappearance, and now you're telling me *all* of this happened because I thought it might be fun to have a psychic reading."

"It's both our faults," I said. "And let's not forget we paid for the privilege."

Pat groaned.

"Regardless, it makes the most sense," I said. "Polly 'disappears' for a few days, and Rowena gets to become the psychic hero. Everyone wins. Rowena must have thought she won the lottery when it all fell into her lap like that."

Pat sighed. "Okay, so I get how we're to blame for Polly. Are you going to explain how we're to blame for Harrison, as well?"

"Well, continue the timeline," I said. "Polly disappears, Mildred and I go report it to the cops and stop for lunch at Aunt May's, and …"

Pat dropped her head in her hands. "I just thought it would be some funny story," she wailed. "How was I to know it was going to start this chain reaction?"

"If it makes you feel any better, I suspect Westly would have eventually murdered Harrison anyhow," I said. "And if not Westly, then someone else. But Harrison's days were numbered. As for Polly, she would have probably tried some other hairbrained thing to prove whether her parents love her. In this case, it backfired so spectacularly, Polly might have learned a bigger lesson than she intended."

Pat tilted her head, blinking at me. "So it was a good thing we visited Rowena?"

"I don't know if I would go that far," I said. "And even though things might have run a similar course for Harrison and Polly, I suspect Drake was worse off than he'd have been if we had never stopped in."

Pat rolled her eyes. "Great pep talk."

*　*　*

I was cleaning up the kitchen after Pat left when the doorbell rang. It was Drake.

"This is a surprise," I said, glancing at the late afternoon sun. "I'm happy to give you my phone number if calling would be easier."

"I'm okay," he said. He was still wearing his black get-up, which made me wonder how okay he was. "This won't take long."

"Do you want to come in?" I held the door open wider.

He shook his head. "I just wanted to thank you again. And tell you I owe you."

"You don't owe me anything," I said. "I'm just glad Wyle was able to find Jonas."

"No, I do owe you," he said, lifting his head to look me in the eyes. His were such a pale, light blue. "If it wasn't for you, the cops wouldn't have tracked down Jonas, and that guy who worked for Harrison would have ended up successfully framing me."

"I think you're giving me too much credit," I said. "Wyle is a good cop. He wouldn't have charged you without a lot more evidence."

He shook his head firmly. "Trust me. I know Wyle is your boyfriend and all, so of course you're going to defend him, but I've had more than my share of experiences with cops. You stepping in made all the difference."

"He's not my boyfriend," I said automatically.

"Or whatever he is," Drake said, but the tone of his voice made it clear that he didn't believe me.

I wanted to argue the point, but I forced myself to close my mouth. I wasn't going to change his mind about it or the fact that I actually had very little to do with him not being charged. "I'm glad it all worked out in the end."

"Yes, because of you." He continued to stare into my eyes. "I mean it. I owe you one."

"You don't …"

"I do," he interrupted. "So, the next time you need something, you come find me. Okay?"

Even though I still didn't think I did anything that remarkable, it was clear he wasn't taking "no" for an answer. "Okay," I said. "Does this mean you're staying in Redemption?"

"For a while," he said. "It appears Jonas has found himself a job he likes, and things are going pretty well for him, but he doesn't want to upset anything yet by selling the house. For at least the next several months, if not year, I'll be staying put."

"That's good," I said. "I'm happy it's working out for you."

He half-smiled. "Yeah. I'm a bit surprised myself. Not much in my life has, but so far, fingers crossed."

"Well, maybe Redemption is willing to let people go after all," I said. "I mean, the cat is out of the bag now. If Redemption didn't know before where Jonas was, it does now."

Drake didn't look convinced.

It wasn't until later that evening, long after Drake had left, that it occurred to me that maybe Redemption had moved on from Jonas.

And now, it wanted Drake to stay.

* * *

I was in the kitchen getting my tea orders ready for the day's delivery when the doorbell rang.

I didn't think it was Pat. She usually called before she came over, especially if it was morning. It could be a customer or new prospect, I figured.

It was none of the above.

It was Rowena.

I blinked at her. "Rowena. I'm … I didn't expect you."

She smiled, and I was immediately reminded of a snake. "I'm so sorry to drop by so early, but with my store hours, I don't have a lot of flexibility."

"It's fine," I said. "I was working myself. Do you … ah, want to come in?"

I didn't particularly want to invite her inside, but I wasn't sure how I could avoid it.

Her smiled widened. "Thank you. That would be lovely." She stepped inside, bringing with her a cloud of incense and perfume.

"Would you like some tea?" I asked.

"I was hoping you would offer," she said. "Everyone has been raving about your tea, telling me I simply must try it."

"That's nice to hear," I said, leading her into the kitchen. As much as I didn't particularly want her in my home, I was also curious about why she had come.

Midnight was on his usual chair, which is where he normally settled himself after his breakfast while I worked in the kitchen, either baking or making tea. He sat up the moment he saw Rowena, his tail twitching angrily.

"Oh, you have a black cat," Rowena said. She gave me a mischievous smile. "I thought you said you weren't a witch."

"I'm not," I said. Midnight's tail continued lashing. "My cat doesn't make me a witch."

"As you say," she said, sitting down at the table without waiting for me to ask. Midnight continued to watch her, his eyes narrowing.

I brought two mugs of tea to the table. "So, what brings you to my house this early?"

She paused for a minute, taking a long sip of tea. "Oh, everyone was right," she said. "This is heavenly."

"Thank you," I said. "It's one of my most popular."

"I can see why," she said, taking another sip.

I wanted to ask her again why she was there, but clearly, she was going to take her own sweet time before saying anything. So, I sipped my own tea in silence.

After a moment, she put the mug down. "Well, as we're both busy businesswomen, I'll get right to the point."

"Please," I said, setting my own mug down.

"We both have similar … 'talents,' shall we say, I thought it might make sense for us to work together."

I stared at her. "Work together?"

"You know, team up."

I gave my head a quick shake. "I'm sorry … how would we do that, exactly? And what are these similar talents we share?"

"Well, you know …" she waved at my bags of teas. "You make teas, and I give readings, but it's all the same."

"My teas are nothing like a tarot card reading," I said. "They might have some health benefits, but they're nothing more than that. Mostly, they just taste good, and people enjoy drinking them."

"Of course," she said, winking at me. "Just like my readings are entertainment."

"You're admitting your readings aren't real?"

She gave me a long look. "I came here in the spirit of letting bygones be bygones, Charlie. I think we maybe got off on the wrong foot and could make a fresh start," she said, her voice a little less bright than it was. "I would think you would like that, as well."

"Anything is possible," I said. I toyed with the idea of calling her "Margaret," but decided it was better not to show my hand yet.

"As far as I see, we have three choices," she said. "First, we could partner up. Maybe I sell your teas in my store, and maybe you include a coupon for a discount on a reading with your teas. The opportunities are endless."

"I'll consider it," I said, even though I had no intention of doing anything of the sort. Still, I was curious about her other two options. "And the second?"

"We stay out of each other's way," she said. "You do your thing. I do my thing. Everyone is happy. Although, I will add, especially now that I've tried your tea, I do hope you take me up on the first option, as I would dearly love to carry a local Redemption tea brand in my store."

"I appreciate that," I said.

She took another sip, eying me over the mug. "You know, it's curious," she said. "Since I've moved in, I've noticed you really inspire a great deal of … well, let's call it 'passion.'" She laughed, although it sounded as fake as her name. "People either love you or hate you. There's really no in-between."

"Yeah, I have that effect," I said.

She half-smiled before taking one last sip and placing the mug on the table. I noticed it was stained with her dark-red lipstick. "Well, look at the time. I better be off."

I also stood up. "You didn't tell me the third option."

"Oh, I didn't?" She sounded surprised. "I was sure I did. It would truly be so much better if we partnered up, wouldn't you say? Goodness, I better be off. I'll see you around?"

"Definitely," I said, smiling a wide, toothy smile at her.

She breezed out the door, but left behind the lingering scent of incense and perfume. As soon as she was gone, Midnight relaxed.

"You're a lot of help," I said to him. "You could have at least hissed."

He fixed his green eyes on me.

"Yes, I appreciated that you stayed here and kept an eye on her." I picked up her mug. "It sure seems like she thinks she's going to be a formidable enemy. I guess we'll have to see whether that's true or not."

Midnight flicked his tail.

"How could I forget?" I asked, moving to the sink to wash—and perhaps sterilize—the mug. "Having you on my side is clearly my secret weapon."

A Word From Michele

Can't get enough of Charlie? I've got you covered. Keep going with book 4, *Murder Among Friends*.

Five friends went into the woods. Only four return. Can Charlie get to the bottom of what happened and why?

Grab your copy right here:

MPWnovels.com/book/murder-among-friends

* * *

You can also check out exclusive bonus content for *Murder Next Door* right here:

MPWNovels.com/r/q/murder-next-door-bonus

The bonus content reveals hints, clues, and sneak peeks you won't get just by reading the books, so you'll definitely want to take a look. You're going to discover a side of Redemption that is only available at the link/QRcode above.

* * *

If you enjoyed Murder Next Door, it would be wonderful if you would take a few minutes to leave a review and rating on Goodreads:

www.goodreads.com/book/show/60749909-murder-next-door

or Bookbub:

www.bookbub.com/books/murder-next-door-charlie-kingsley-mysteries-book-3-by-michele-pw-pariza-wacek

(Feel free to follow me on any of those platforms as well.) I thank you and other readers will thank you (as your reviews will help other readers find my books.)

The *Charlie Kingsley Mysteries* series is a spin-off from my award-winning *Secrets of Redemption* series. *Secrets of Redemption* is a little different from the *Charlie Kingsley Mysteries*, as it's more psychological suspense, but it's still clean like a cozy.

You can learn more about both series, including how they fit together, at MPWNovels.com, along with lots of other fun things such as short stories, deleted scenes, giveaways, recipes, puzzles and more.

I've also included a sneak peek of *Murder Among Friends*, just turn the page to get started.

Murder Among Friends - Chapter 1

Heading down Main Street to drop off my next tea order, I was enjoying another beautiful summer day in Redemption when I saw the girl crumple to the ground.

I dashed over, hoping to catch her before she hit the curb, but I didn't make it. She fell almost gracefully, folding in on herself before landing in a heap.

I squatted down beside her, gently grasping her shoulders and praying she wasn't having a seizure or something equally serious. I didn't think it was weather-related—while it was definitely warm and humid, which was typical of a Wisconsin summer, it wasn't overly hot. "Are you okay? Do you need me to call an ambulance?"

Her eyelids were fluttering, and I started to worry she was having a seizure when her eyes popped open. She blinked confusedly at me. "What the ... what happened?"

"I'm not entirely sure. You just collapsed. Here, take it easy." I helped her sit up, propping her against the silver car she had fallen next to. "Do you need me to call someone? A doctor?"

She shook her head. "No, I'm sure I'll be fine." She was probably in her mid-twenties, with straight, long, nut-brown hair and bangs. Her eyes were also a deep brown, framed with thick lashes that made them seem even more huge than they actually were, although they may have appeared so because the rest of her features were more petite. She was dressed simply, in a white V-neck tee shirt and jeans, and she smelled like tangerines and cherry-flavored lip balm.

I gave her a skeptical look. "Are you sure? It might not be a bad idea to get yourself checked out."

"I'm positive." She shot me a weak smile. "It's probably because I haven't eaten today."

"You definitely need to eat. There's a diner right down the street. I can walk you there, if you'd like," I offered.

She made a face. "Ugh. You're right. I should eat, but I also get horrible motion sickness, so right now, I don't think I can."

"Motion sickness? I have a tea that can help," I said. "I'll need to run home and get it, but I don't live that far away. Less than fifteen minutes."

"Oh, you don't have to go through all that trouble," she said. "I'm sure it will pass. Eventually." She made a slight face and rubbed her stomach.

"It's no trouble," I assured her. "I've had bouts of nausea and motion sickness myself. I know how miserable it can be. I'm happy to do it."

"Honestly, I'm sure I'll be fine. Now that we're here and I'm out of the car, I should recover quickly."

"It still might take a little while … especially without the tea." I thought about taking off right then to fetch it for her, but I didn't feel right leaving her there on the street, either. It was still troubling me that she'd fainted. Someone her age shouldn't be collapsing the way she did, even if she had skipped breakfast *and* lunch. I wondered if there was something else going on. "Where are you from?"

"Riverview," she said before rolling her eyes. "I know … it's less than an hour away. I would have been fine, if we had driven straight from there to here. But no. We of course had to make a million stops."

"We?"

"Yeah, I'm here with my friends. They're all in there." She tilted her head toward the Psychic Readings by Madame Rowena sign, and it was all I could do not to roll *my* eyes. Of course it would be a fake psychic's shop that lured her friends away. Not that I knew for sure she was fake, as my best friend Pat was quick to remind me, but I knew something was off with her.

"You didn't want to see if Madame Rowena could cure your motion sickness?" I asked, raising my eyebrow.

She laughed. "Actually, it was more because of the overwhelming smell those shops usually have. Like way too much incense burning. I figured that was the last thing I needed, as I was already feeling so sick. I didn't want to end up losing it on one of the crystal displays."

Now it was my turn to laugh. "No, I don't think Madame Rowena would appreciate that very much. It was probably better you stayed out here." Although I did find myself wondering what kind of friends would leave someone who clearly wasn't feeling well outside by herself while they poked around a psychic shop. "Do you often see psychics?"

Her face was bemused. "Not by choice. Lynette loves them."

"Lynette?"

"My best friend. We're practically sisters. We grew up together."

"Oh, that's nice to still be so close with one of your childhood friends."

She nodded. "Yeah, we basically lived together."

"Really? Were you neighbors?"

She laughed a little. "Not quite. We lived in a house on her property."

"Property?" I glanced up at the silver car the girl was leaning against. I hadn't paid much attention to it before. I wasn't all that into cars, but even if I was, my focus was on the girl and making sure she was okay. But in taking a second look, I realized it was a Mercedes Benz.

The girl noticed. "Yeah, that's Lynette's car. Brand new. Just got it this year. Her parents are loaded. I mean, really loaded. Her mom is related to the Duckworths."

The Duckworths were one of the richest families in Riverview. Along with owning and managing a number of businesses, a couple of family members were also heavily involved in local and state politics. Pretty much everyone in southern Wisconsin had heard of them. "How did you end up living on their property? Does one of your parents work for them?"

"It's just my mom and my younger brother," she answered. Her smile was a little sheepish. "It's kind of a complicated story. My mom and Janice, that's Lynette's mom, have been friends forever. My mom hasn't had … well, the best of luck with men, shall we say. Or life. My father bailed on her while she was pregnant with me. I have no idea who he even is. Then, after my stepdad died when I was nine, my mother wasn't able to function, so Janice moved us onto her property. It was supposed to be temporary, until my mother was able to get back on her feet. But then Janice had some issues with one of her staff, so my mother stepped in to help, and she's been working for her ever since."

"I guess it was a good thing your mother had a friend like Janice," I said.

The girl started twisting a ring around one of her fingers. "Yes. It was a blessing. Janice has been helping my mother for as long as I can remember. She helped her get a job as a secretary after my father bailed, and she'd have Lynette's nanny watch both of us. My mother didn't have to pay a dime, which was also a blessing. My mom's an orphan—both of her parents died when she was a teenager—so there was no one for her to turn to. Honestly, I don't know what would have happened to us without Janice."

"That's horrible," I said. "Your mother really did have it rough."

The girl nodded, her hair swinging in front of her face. "Yeah, she did."

"So, is that why Janice was so generous? Because of your mother's circumstances?"

"That's probably some of it. But apparently, my mother saved Janice's life when they were kids, too. So, I guess she also felt like she owed her."

"Naomi!" A female voice called out behind us, and I turned to look. Another young woman was standing there, who appeared to be the same age as Naomi. Her white-blonde hair was cut in a short pixie cut, and she wore stone-washed jeans, an oversized pale-pink shirt over a white tank top, and several clunky necklaces. A large, white tote bag was slung over one of her shoulders. She was with a second girl, who couldn't look more different—long, very straight, dark hair and dressed all in black. White-Blonde hurried over to us, pulling off her expensive sunglasses and revealing shockingly green eyes. "What happened? Why are you on the ground?"

"Are you hurt?" the second girl asked, trailing just behind White-Blonde.

"I'm fine," Naomi said, struggling to her feet. I grabbed one of her arms to help her up as the newcomer took the other. "I just ... I guess I just fainted."

"Fainted?" White-Blonde's eyes widened. "I told you that you should have eaten breakfast today. This is exactly why you should have listened to me."

"You were right," Naomi said resignedly before turning to me. "This is Lynette, by the way." She waved toward White-Blonde. "And this is Sloane." The dark-haired girl nodded at me. "And I'm Naomi, although you probably figured that out. But I don't know your name."

"Charlie," I said. "Nice to meet you all."

"Nice to meet you," Lynette said, cocking her head as she studied me. The sun glinted on what looked like diamond studs in her ears. "Did you see her faint?"

"I did. I don't think she hit her head or anything like that," I answered.

"I'm so glad you were here," Lynette said before turning back to Naomi. "We need to get some food in you."

"Ugh," Naomi uttered, making a face.

"There's a diner just down the street," I said. "It's called Aunt May's. They have pretty good food."

"Perfect. We'll all go there. The boys are probably hungry anyway," Lynette announced, putting her sunglasses back on as she turned around, presumably looking for "the boys."

"Honestly, I'm not all that hungry," Naomi said.

"Still, you should try to eat something," Sloane interjected. She had sharp features and a pointed chin, reminding me of a fox.

"Let's do this," I offered. "You go to Aunt May's, and I'll run home and get you some of that tea I was telling you about. I promise you it will help calm your stomach, so you can eat a little something."

"Really, you don't have to go through all that trouble," Naomi protested again.

"It's no trouble," I said. "I'm happy to help. And I agree with your friends. You need to eat."

"You sell tea?" Lynette asked, her focus back on me.

"Yes, I sell teas and tinctures out of my home," I said.

"You make them yourself?" Lynette asked.

"Yes. I grow a lot of the herbs and flowers that I use, as well."

"Wow. That's really cool," Lynette said. "I'd love to try some."

"I'd be happy to bring you some samples," I said. "Just tell the waitress Charlie is bringing tea, and she'll set you up."

"Perfect," Lynette said with a smile.

Naomi held up her hands in mock surrender. "Okay, then. I guess I'm outnumbered."

"Great. I'll be back in fifteen minutes … twenty tops," I said.

"We'll be there," Lynette called out as I turned to hurry back to my car.

Murder Among Friends - Chapter 2

Aunt May's was a cute, 50s-style diner with a black-and-white checkered floor, red booths, and menu that featured all sorts of comfort food. It was popular among both the locals and the tourists, and even in the middle of the afternoon, between the lunch and dinner rush, it was still a quarter full.

I found Naomi with her friends in the big corner booth. Sloane and Lynette were there, along with two guys who I assumed were "the boys."

Lynette was the first to spot me, and she waved me over. "Charlie! Thank you so much for doing this. Can we treat you to something? A snack or a meal?" I noticed her white tote bag balanced awkwardly on her lap.

"I'll just have some tea," I said as I caught the eye of Sue, one of the waitresses, and pointed at one of the mugs on the table. If I wasn't meeting potential clients at home for a tasting, I would often bring them to the diner, so Sue knew what I was asking for. I also always made sure we ordered food to go along with the tea, so it worked out for everyone.

"Guys, this is Charlie, the one I was telling you about," Lynette said as I slid into the booth next to Naomi, who already had an empty mug and silver pot filled with hot water in front of her. "Charlie, this is Mace and Raymond."

"Nice to meet you both," I said. Mace had that bad-boy vibe, with his longish, dirty-blonde hair, soulful dark eyes, and ripped black Nirvana tee shirt. Raymond was far cleaner-cut, with short, sandy-brown hair and a Riverview University tee shirt.

"I still think Naomi should get checked out by a doctor," Raymond said as Sue placed an empty mug and the hot water pot in front of me. "It's not normal to just collapse, or faint, or whatever. It's not like she was drinking or anything."

"Honestly, I'm fine," Naomi said.

Sloane rolled her eyes. "You worry too much." She leaned into Raymond as she squeezed his arm, the gesture more possessive than affectionate. "But it's still sweet of you to be so concerned."

"Let's get some food into Naomi, and then we can reassess," I suggested.

"That sounds like a plan," Lynette agreed. "If only we could get her to actually order something." She shot Naomi a side-eye, while Naomi seemed to turn a little green.

"It's going to be okay," I said, hoping to comfort her. "Would it be alright if I prepared the tea for you? You don't have to drink it, but let me at least make it for you, and you can decide."

Naomi didn't look convinced, but she nodded. I pulled her cup and hot water toward me.

Lynette craned her neck. "What's in it?"

"It's a special blend that can help soothe an upset stomach," I said as I measured the tea. "It has ginger and peppermint in it. It's very refreshing."

"Sounds like it," Lynette said.

"I also brought one of my most popular teas, a lemon lavender." I pushed the small bag toward Lynette.

"Oh look … 'Charlie's Concoctions'! What a cute name," Lynette said, admiring my little logo on the side of the bag. "And is that a caldron?"

"Yep."

Lynette continued to study it. "Like a witch's caldron?"

"It's a joke," I said, unable to stop my smile. I had decided that the best way to handle half the town accusing me of being a witch was straight on, complete with a logo. "It's a loose tea," I explained. "But I included a tea strainer in the bag."

"That's the type I love," Lynette said excitedly, opening the bag to take a sniff.

"Next, you're going to ask if she can read your tea leaves," Mace joked.

Lynette jerked her head up. "Can you?"

"Absolutely not," I said.

Lynette's face fell. "Bummer. How about a love potion?" She nudged Naomi, who looked uncomfortable.

"I don't need a love potion," Naomi said.

"I *absolutely* don't do love potions, or any other type of potions, for that matter," I said firmly.

Lynette sighed dramatically. "Foiled again." She nudged Naomi a second time. "Hey, I'm just kidding. Trying to lighten the mood a bit. You gave us all a scare."

Naomi gave her a flat smile that didn't reach her eyes. "Of course."

"Here, see if this helps," I said, pushing the tea in front of Naomi. "Just breathe it in, to start. See if that doesn't start settling your stomach."

Naomi nodded as Lynette leaned closer. "Mmm, that does smell good. I may need to taste it, as well. You wouldn't mind, would you Naomi?"

Before Naomi could answer, the bag in Lynette's lap trembled, and a miniature white poodle head popped out of the top.

I started. "What … is that a … poodle?"

"This is Tiki," Lynette said. "Tiki, meet Charlie. Oooh, Tiki probably wants some tea, too. It smells really good, doesn't it?"

"I … ah, I don't know if tea is all that good for dogs," I said as Tiki gazed at me, tilting her head. She was elegantly groomed and sported two pink bows, one over each poofy ear. She also appeared to be wearing a pink shirt that matched Lynette's. "Is she … is Tiki wearing a shirt the same color as yours?"

Lynette beamed as she reached into the side pocket for a dog treat. "Isn't it great? I was so excited when I found this shirt for her. We don't always dress the same, but sometimes, it's fun! Isn't it, Tiki?" Tiki was definitely more interested in the treat than the fashion discussion.

I glanced around the restaurant, wondering if anyone else had noticed the small dog head poking out of the purse, but as there weren't that many people there and we were in the corner, no one seemed to be paying any attention. "Uh, you know, it's probably not a great idea to bring a dog into a restaurant. Violates health codes and all that."

"Oh, Tiki doesn't violate any health codes," Lynette said.

"Yeah, because she's not really a dog," Mace joked. "She's a hamster."

Lynette punched him on the shoulder, a little harder than what I would consider a love tap. "Will you stop it already? She's very sensitive."

Mace rolled his eyes. "No self-respecting dog lives in a purse."

Lynette glared at him. "Don't listen to him," she said to Tiki, covering her ears. Tiki panted happily. "She's a poodle," Lynette said to me. "They're hypoallergenic, you know. Perfectly safe for people with allergies."

"I, uh, don't think the health-code violations are allergy-related," I said.

"Well, it certainly has nothing to do with Tiki," Lynette said firmly. "Look how tiny she is. She's no threat to anyone. And besides, restaurants let seeing-eye dogs in all the time, and those dogs are much bigger than sweet little Tiki. They probably aren't hypoallergenic, either. Not like my little one," she cooed to the dog.

"But that would be discrimination ..." I started to say, but Sloane caught my eye and gave me a quick head shake, as if to tell me not to bother.

"But it's not discrimination against people with dog allergies?" Lynette asked. "If you're deathly allergic to dogs, but the restaurant allows a blind person to bring in a seeing-eye dog, then who exactly is being discriminated against, hmmm?"

"I don't think people dying from dog allergies is a thing," Mace said. "But an allergy to a rodent is a whole different story."

Lynette's eyes narrowed, but otherwise, she ignored Mace. "None of this matters anyway, as Tiki spends most of her time sleeping, don't you?" She pushed the little dog's head down. "See? No one is any the wiser."

Unless I wanted to turn her into the dog police, the subject was closed. I decided to leave it alone, figuring if Sue got a look at Tiki and wanted to kick Lynette and her pint-sized sidekick out, that was her business. "Are you all from Riverview?" I was curious about the dynamics of this little group of friends.

"Naomi and I are," Lynette said. "We grew up in Riverview, and we both decided to stay there to go to school."

"Riverview is one of the best schools in the country, so it made sense to stay," Naomi said.

"Including the theater department," Lynette said. "Believe it or not, we've had several famous actors attend Riverview."

"I've heard great things about it," I said. "What about the rest of you?"

"I'm originally from Chicago," Sloane said. "And you likely haven't heard of the town Raymond is from."

"It's a small farming community," Raymond explained.

"And Mace here is from Milwaukee," Lynette said.

"So, you all went to school in Riverview and decided to stay?" I asked.

"Actually, we're not staying," Lynette said. "That's part of what this trip is about. Mace and I are headed to LA in a few weeks to break into the film industry."

"You're an actor, too?" I asked Mace.

He shook his head. "Cinematography and maybe directing. Documentaries, especially."

"Wow, documentaries," I said. "That's difficult to break into."

"And it shouldn't be," Mace said disgustedly. "Blow something up, and you make millions, but if you want to create a piece of art that has the potential to change the world, no one wants anything to do with it."

"That's why we need to go to LA," Lynette said. "Mace has been working on his masterpiece here. He's very talented, but he hasn't been able to get any bites from distributors. We need connections. Plus, as an actress, LA is where I need to be."

"Yeah, I'm surprised you're not already there," I said.

Something unpleasant flickered across Lynette's face, but it disappeared as quickly as it appeared, making me wonder if I had imagined it. "It's a tough business," she said, her voice smooth, like nothing had happened. "And I was lucky enough to land a couple of juicy roles for the United Players Theatre. I played Lady MacBeth in *MacBeth* and Amanda in *The Glass Menagerie.*"

"That is impressive," I said. The United Players Theatre was one of the most prestigious theater companies in southern Wisconsin, best known for its Shakespeare in the Park productions.

"Along with being a great resume-builder, it was also a blast," Lynette said, her expression wistful. "But it's time to spread my wings and hit the big league now."

"Well, I hope you make it," I said.

"Yeah, so we can all say we knew her when," Sloane said, pressing both hands against her heart and fluttering her eyelids.

Lynette threw her napkin at Sloane. "You're just jealous you're stuck here."

"Stuck?" I asked Sloane.

Sloane made a face. "I'm still in grad school. Psychology."

"Ah," I said.

"And yes, they're all leaving me," she confirmed, dramatically flinging her hand to press her wrist to her forehead.

"You're *all* leaving?" I asked, looking around. Naomi, I was pleased to see, was sipping her tea and already looking much better. She nodded.

"Yep, Naomi is coming to LA with us," Lynette said.

"I'm apparently going to be the one with a regular job while these two try and make it," she said drily.

"Oh, stop," Lynette said. "You know how much I need you around. And once I make it big, it will all be worth it."

"Yeah, I know," Naomi said. "I'm just kidding." The two exchanged a look I couldn't read. I couldn't put my finger on their relationship, but it almost felt like a sibling energy—they were close, yet there was a competitiveness between them, too. I turned to Raymond.

"What about you?" I asked.

"He's the worst of all. He's leaving the country," Sloane said mournfully.

"The country? Where are you going?" I asked.

"He's going to build schools in Africa," Naomi answered for him.

"Truly? That's what you're doing? That's inspiring," I said.

He ducked his head. "It's not like that. I'm no one to look up to."

Sloane sighed as she shook her head. "That's our Raymond. Takes humility to a fault." There was a sharp edge to her voice that belied her words, and I found myself wondering about their relationship. If they were dating, which seemed to be the case, they didn't seem very happy. Although it was possible that Sloane was just upset that Raymond was moving to Africa. They might even be breaking up over it, and Sloane wasn't pleased.

"It's not like that," Raymond said again, his tone indicating they'd had this discussion before. "You know I owe him."

"Owe who?" I asked, even though it wasn't any of my business. Still, I found myself sucked into the drama of these friends about to go their separate ways.

"It's why we're here," Mace said.

"To find the answers, once and for all," Lynette added.

I was about to ask what answers they were looking for when Sue magically appeared. "Ready to order some food, or do you want to wait?"

Want to keep reading? Grab your copy of **Murder Among Friends** here:

MPWnovels.com/book/murder-among-friends

More *Charlie Kingsley Mysteries:*
A Grave Error (a prequel novella)
Murder Before Christmas (Book 1)
Ice Cold Murder (Book 2)
Murder Among Friends (Book 4)
The Murder of Sleepy Hollow (Book 5)
Red Hot Murder (Book 6)
A Cornucopia of Murder (Book 7)
A Wedding to Murder For (novella)
Loch Ness Murder (novella)

Secrets of Redemption *series:*
It Began With a Lie (Book 1)
This Happened to Jessica (Book 2)
The Evil That Was Done (Book 3)
The Summoning (Book 4)
The Reckoning (Book 5)
The Girl Who Wasn't There (Book 6)
The Room at the Top of the Stairs (Book 7)
The Search (Book 8)
The Secret Diary of Helen Blackstone (free novella)

Standalone books:
Today I'll See Her (free novella)
The Taking
The Third Nanny
Mirror Image
The Stolen Twin

Access your free exclusive bonus scenes from *Murder Next Door* right here:

MPWNovels.com/r/q/murder-next-door-bonus

Acknowledgements

It's a team effort to birth a book, and I'd like to take a moment to thank everyone who helped, especially my wonderful editor, Megan Yakovich, who is always so patient with me, Rea Carr for her expert proofing support, and my husband Paul, for his love and support during this sometimes-painful birthing process.

Any mistakes are mine and mine alone.

About Michele

A USA Today Bestselling, award-winning author, Michele taught herself to read at 3 years old because she wanted to write stories so badly. It took some time (and some detours) but she does spend much of her time writing stories now. Mystery stories, to be exact. They're clean and twisty, and range from psychological thrillers to cozies, with a dash of romance and supernatural thrown into the mix. If that wasn't enough, she posts lots of fun things on her blog, including short stories, puzzles, recipes and more, at MPWNovels.com.

Michele grew up in Wisconsin, (hence why all her books take place there), and still visits regularly, but she herself escaped the cold and now lives in the mountains of Prescott, Arizona with her husband and southern squirrel hunter Cassie.

When she's not writing, she's usually reading, hanging out with her dog, or watching the Food Network and imagining she's an awesome cook. (Spoiler alert, she's not. Luckily for the whole family, Mr. PW is in charge of the cooking.)